CW00868451

HER DUKE OF SECRETS
Brethren of the Lords Series

For more information about the author:
www.christicaldwellauthor.com
christicaldwellauthor@gmail.com
Twitter: @ChristiCaldwell
Or on Facebook at: Christi Caldwell Author

For first glimpse at covers, excerpts, and free bonus material, be sure to sign up for my monthly newsletter!

Printed in the USA.

Cover Design and Interior Format
© The Killion Group Inc.

Her Duke of Secrets

CHRISTI CALDWELL©

Other Titles by Christi Caldwell

THE HEART OF A SCANDAL

In Need of a Knight—Prequel Novella
Schooling the Duke
Heart of a Duke
In Need of a Duke—Prequel Novella
For Love of the Duke
More than a Duke
The Love of a Rogue
Loved by a Duke
To Love a Lord
The Heart of a Scoundrel
To Wed His Christmas Lady
To Trust a Rogue
The Lure of a Rake
To Woo a Widow

LORDS OF HONOR

Seduced by a Lady's Heart
Captivated by a Lady's Charm
Rescued by a Lady's Love
Tempted by a Lady's Smile

SCANDALOUS SEASONS

Forever Betrothed, Never the Bride
Never Courted, Suddenly Wed
Always Proper, Suddenly Scandalous
Always a Rogue, Forever Her Love
A Marquess for Christmas
Once a Wallflower, at Last His Love

SINFUL BRIDES

The Rogue's Wager

The Scoundrel's Honor

THE THEODOSIA SWORD

Only for His Lady

DANBY

A Season of Hope

Winning a Lady's Heart

BRETHREN OF THE LORDS

My Lady of Deception

Memoir: Non-Fiction

Uninterrupted Joy

DEDICATION

For Doug—You are my other half. My best friend. My hero.

CHAPTER 1

Bladon
The Cotswolds, England
1806

RAP-PAUSE-RAP-PAUSE. RAP-RAP.

Heart hammering, Miss Elsie Allenby went motionless in the straw rocker in which she'd been moments away from dozing off.

It was the knock.

With careful, measured movements, she set the book on her lap on the side table.

There hadn't been a late-night caller in five years. Four years and two hundred and sixty-six days, if one wished to be truly precise. There hadn't been a reason for it. Elsie's father, the only reason for a caller, had been gone that many years, and with his death had also come an absence of those *visitors.*

As such, that staccato, timed knock, signaling *their* presence, held her frozen at the hearth.

Then it went silent, ushering in a familiar, safer quiet. The crack and hiss of the hearth, the only sound, amplified in its eeriness, was lent an even more sinister aura by the shadows that flickered and danced on the cracked plaster walls.

Mayhap she'd merely imagined it. Mayhap being shut away from the world, on the edge of civilization, one eventually lost one's sanity and dissolved into a place of past histories and old memories.

Bear, the enormous slumbering dog at her side, pushed to his feet, his nails scraping the floor deafeningly loud in the otherwise still of the rooms.

Her gaze trained on that scarred wood panel built and hung by her late father's hands. Yes, mayhap she'd merely imagined it. A dearth of human contact and the late-night quiet invariably played tricks upon the mind.

Except…

Her gaze flickered to the loyal dog, crouched in a battle-ready position.

Nay, there could be no other accounting for the aging dog's response.

Bracing her palms on the arm of her chair, she slowly pushed herself to her feet.

The straw reeds creaked in damning proof of her presence, and Elsie forced herself upright, hurriedly completing the movement, until she stood.

Bear angled his enormous head up.

She ruffled the coarse fur between his ears, until his eyes grew heavy once more, and he sank back down onto the floor. Collecting her wrapper from the back of her chair, she shrugged into the fraying garment, belting it at the waist.

All the while, she kept her gaze trained on the front door.

Mindful of the loose plank boards, Elsie picked her way across the room, skirting furniture until she reached the shelving built into the wall. She briefly removed her attention from the door and, stretching up on her tiptoes, fished around the top shelf.

Her fingers collided with cold metal, and she drew the weapon from its place, finding some assurance with the weight of the pistol in her grip.

And a memory trickled in.

"I am not going to shoot someone, Papa."

"But you may need to, poppet. If it is your life or theirs, I will always choose your life. And I expect the same of you."

The scissoring of pain ripped her back from the oldest of memories, and she forcibly thrust those distracting thoughts of her father—and the time before—into the furthest chambers of her mind.

"Focus," she mouthed, winding a careful path to the door. Pressing herself tight against the wall, she held her gun aloft in one hand and with the other grasped the rusty handle.

One, two, three…

Elsie pushed the door open a crack, slipped outside and… stopped.

A grayish wryneck paused in midpeck of the chipped wooden window frame. The creature angled its head back and forth, contemplating her with its small, unblinking black eyes.

Some of the tension left her, escaping her lips on a soft, breathless laugh that stirred a faint puff of white in the cool spring night. "You're a peculiar fellow, aren't you?" she murmured, her voice echoing quietly around the gardened landscape. The tall hedges and bushes and sea of flowers long-ago planted allowed the modest ivy-covered cottage to blend in with the Bladon landscape as easily as any shrub or bright splash of greenery. "What are you doing at this hour?" Elsie lowered her arm back to her side, glancing down at Bear, who'd joined her on the slate steps. "We do have a visitor," she explained, motioning to the wryneck. "He is too proud to join the other wrynecks on the ground. Not that there is anything wrong with being different," she rushed to assure the motionless bird.

Different was a state she could well identify with. Both the solitary state and the oddness that set one apart. Kept away from the whole of the world, rarely leaving their small patch of land, she and her father had only ever been met with curious stares and suspicious looks when they were required to go into the village. Feeling a kindred connection to that painfully still bird, she took a step closer.

Bear growled and crouched in a fighting stance once more.

The wryneck took flight, raining down feathers in its haste to flee.

"You scared him," she chided, snapping her fingers once.

Bear whined, nudging his head against her skirts, but then ultimately followed her command. He sank to his haunches, staring up at her with enormous, sad brown eyes.

"It is fine," she pardoned, giving his head another affectionate pat. "You are a loyal pup."

More than ten years old, the creature had been beaten and branded on his belly by bullying village boys before he was rescued by Elsie's father. Eventually, the scarred and scared pup who'd hissed and snapped at everyone had become an affectionate, loving member of the small Allenby family. He'd also been the only company she'd known these nearly five years.

Midnight quiet reigned once more, punctured only by the occasional chitter of a cricket or the sporadic song of the frogs. Elsie did a sweep of the grounds. The full moon's glow bathed the earth in a soft light, illuminating the gardens.

Reflexively, she drew her pistol close, and the gooseflesh rose on her arms. *Do not be silly.* Papa hadn't raised her to cower at shadows. And she'd been alone long enough that the nighttime shouldn't scare her.

But everything dark comes at night… death and dying and—

"Come," she urged, snapping twice, and Bear popped up. "Such loyalty certainly deserves a treat," she murmured, needing to hear her voice in the quiet.

With Bear trotting at her heels, Elsie reentered the cottage. She closed the door and, this time, put the clever locks built along the whole front panel by her late father into their proper places.

No good could come from being careless. No good ever had come from it.

She stumbled over her task and squeezed her eyes briefly closed.

Except, the door to the past had been opened by the faint raps, and when those darkest moments slipped in, they would remain…

"I'll return, Elsie. These men require my help."

The muscles of her throat constricted, and she struggled to swallow past the lump. That long-ago lesson had proved the peril in… helping. It had been an inherent part of who her father was and who he'd always been. And that inherent goodness had seen him dead.

Bear growled.

Elsie opened her eyes. "Hush," she chided gently, struggling with the last, rusted lock. It fell into place with a satisfying click. She turned and made to return to her chair, abandoning all hope of rest this night. "There is nothing to be…" Her words trailed off.

A scream climbed up her throat as a wave of fear surged through her.

Turning back, she lunged for the door. Panic exploded in her chest as she scrabbled with the clever chains.

Trapped. Locked in by her own hand.

"Tell your dog to stand down, Miss Allenby."

Miss Allenby.

Spoken not in the country tones of the village people, but the cultured ones belonging to men of rank and privilege. Men of rank and privilege never had a need for her. They once had a use for her father, but they'd done just that—used him and then abandoned him. And despite his many sacrifices, he'd paid with his life, left defenseless by noble gentlemen.

A sob tore from her as she wrenched at the handle.

Terror buzzed loudly in her ears, squeezing out logical thought, and tunneling the voices of those strangers and Bear's barking.

"I said, tell your dog to stand down." The quiet command cut across the din in Elsie's ears.

They destroyed your father. Do not cower before them. That reminder of the wrongs done by these men and her hatred for them and all they represented replaced the fear, and she fed the anger. Found courage in it.

She whipped around and alternated the barrel of her pistol on first one of the darkly clad strangers and then the other. "Or what?" she rasped, hating the faintly breathy quality of those two words. "You'll kill me?" She directed that at the taller of the gentlemen. "My dog?" Elsie tossed at the other. She'd expect anything from these ruthless sorts. They were capable of anything.

The two men exchanged looks. One was tall and dark, the other several inches shorter and fair-haired. They might as well have been Lucifer and the Lord himself teamed up to wreak havoc on her already uncertain existence.

And despite her earlier resolve, dread scraped along her spine and made a mockery of her attempts at bravery. Her gun shook in her hands, and she steadied her hold on it.

Crouched low, all the hair on his back standing upright, Bear barked all the harder. The remarkably stoic composure of the men who'd invaded her household revealed not even a crack at the vicious fangs bared on them. Neither brandished weapons.

And yet…

She swallowed hard. The men were in possession of two very different frames—one stocky, the other taller. Both, however, were muscularly defined and exuded strength. They could end her, or

Bear, with a skill that wouldn't leave a mark and would see them both forgotten, until Mrs. Dalright brought Elsie's next delivery of wildflowers.

Elsie snapped her fingers twice, and Bear instantly sat beside her.

He continued growling. The menacing rumble left both gentlemen unfazed.

"What do you want?" she asked quietly, keeping her pistol trained between the men, where she could easily get a shot off at the first who made a rush for her.

"If you would?" the taller stranger drawled, waving a lazy hand at her weapon. "I hardly find that the best way to begin a discussion is at gunpoint."

"And I hardly consider one's home being invaded in the dead of night conducive either. Therefore, I should say we are even on *that* score," she snapped.

Did she imagine the ghost of a smile that hovered on the other gentleman's lips? Elsie fixed her gun at the center of his chest. "Do you find this amusing?"

"On the contrary."

He shot a hand out, relieving her of her pistol before she could even draw breath into her lungs. So quick, so silent. The usually alert Bear registered nothing but the faint whoosh of air.

"There," he said crisply. "Now, why don't we sit?"

She'd be a fool to believe his was anything but a command, a directive issued in her own household by men who'd slipped inside and laid claim to this entire midnight exchange.

She jutted her chin up. "If you feel so inclined, then you may sit, but I am—"

Creeeeak. The stocky stranger dragged a chair over and thrust it at her. "Sit." His flinty-eyed stare bore through her, hard, unforgiving… and impatient.

Bear picked his head up.

Over the years, Elsie had overseen the care of animals brought to her by her father or local villagers for healing. Usually injured by snares, or abandoned by negligent providers, those creatures had all found a place in the Allenby household. Betrayal and suffering had forever scarred the souls of those animals, wounds that went far deeper than the physical ones she'd tended. Those who were impatient around them, made quick steps, or let fear drive them, invariably found themselves bitten or backed into a corner by the wounded creature.

Elsie hesitated, staking some claim of control of the situation, and then she sat.

With matched movements better suited to men in the King's army, they collected the matching sack-back Windsor chairs from the hearth and set them close on either side of her.

Palms dampening, Elsie gripped the arms of her chair.

"Do not," the scarred gentleman warned as she made to stand.

"I'd be a fool to believe you don't intend to prevent me from moving," she spat. The unpredicted element of this meeting erased a necessary element of fear.

"We've no intention of harming you," the dark gentleman said in cool tones that conveyed a pragmatism and no attempt at easing her anxiety. "Dismiss your dog."

"If you don't intend to harm me, then it should hardly matter whether or not he sits and takes part in our discussion."

The gentleman sat back and contemplated her.

As the moments ticked by on the mantel clock, she struggled to remain absolutely still, to not be the next to speak or capitulate any more than she already had.

The members of the Home Office who'd visited this cottage sensed weakness and used it to their advantage. As long as one served them, no questions asked, they were content to leave one be.

Her heart twisted. Or that had been the case. That was what she'd believed, until they'd repaid her father's efforts on their behalf, with… nothing.

"My name is Lord Edward Helling. This"—he gestured to the gentleman at his side—"is Mr. Cedric Bennett."

"What do you want?" she snapped, hatred making her voice emerge sharper. Their names mattered naught.

"You know who we are, then," the dark-haired gentleman remarked, curiosity layered into that statement.

"I do." Her gaze went to the gold signet upon the angry-eyed gentleman's littlest finger. As soon as the admission left her mouth, she silently cursed that impulsivity. She darted her stare about, seeking escape. For one did not reveal one knew… anything about the organization these two strangers belonged to. It was a secret to all, and those who discovered, or revealed anything about it, invariably found themselves felled for their carelessness.

The stocky stranger spoke. "Your *father* spoke of us, then?" Did she imagine the faint disdain attached to that word?

"The Brethren?" Her taunting rebuttal sucked the energy out of the all-purpose room. It sent tension whipping through the pair who had her effectively cornered. "The ancient group of distinguished gentlemen who serve the king, preserving Crown and country? I'm well aware of who you are." She peered down the length of her nose. "Of what you are," she corrected. Bitterness soured her tongue. Yes, the members of the Brethren were emotionally deadened men who'd step over the dead body of anyone who'd faithfully served their ranks, without a glance back for the services once given.

An answering silence met her brave—nay, foolish—retort. And both gentlemen watched her with equally dark, piercing gazes.

Her stomach muscles clenched, squeezing at her insides, like the adder she'd once stumbled upon with a mole caught in its twisted grip. And yet, when one no longer had anything to lose, one was fearless… or careless. Or mayhap both.

"If they come, poppet? Leave. Do not trust them. Do not do their bidding. Slip out the back, hide, and, when they are at last gone, run."

That desperate advice, the last words given by her father before he'd perished, whispered forward—too late.

Too late. She was always too late.

A log shifted in the hearth, and Elsie jumped, and the fear pounding away at her breast made a mockery of her earlier bravado.

In the end, it was the bulkier of the two gentlemen who spoke again. "That is disappointing," he murmured, and she'd be a fool to believe those casual tones were anything conversational in nature. He peeled off his gloves, revealing the matching signet on his finger. "Though unsurprising, I might add, that your father should reveal privileged information."

She glowered. "What did you expect?" Fear of her fate forgotten, she'd be damned ten times to Sunday before she allowed this man to mock her late father. "I lived in the same household when your"—she curled her lip in a derisive sneer—"honorable members came here to have their wounds tended, cared for by my father. Did you think I should not have learned who you men are?"

Mr. Bennett flashed a cold smile, a go-to-hell expression that said he didn't care if she were the daughter of His Lord and Savior himself, that he'd sized up the man who'd given her life and reared her alone… and found him wanting. And nothing she said would ever alter his opinion. "You know a good deal less than you think, Miss Allenby. For our numbers are not exclusively comprised of gentlemen. We've been known to enlist the services of… worthy females."

Something in that word indicated he'd assessed her *worth* by her name alone… and found her wanting. Elsie crushed the fabric of her skirts in her hands, hating that this man's opinion of her and her family should matter.

"Enough," Lord Edward warned, casting a long look at his truculent partner.

Mr. Bennett set his thin lips into a hard line, but instead of attempting to further bait Elsie, he smoothed his features into an unreadable mask.

The other gentleman turned back, refocusing his attentions on Elsie. "Now, Miss Allenby," he began, "I'll not waste any more of our time."

Oh, God. That serpent of dread slithered around inside, spreading its venom.

Elsie jumped up.

Except, she stood entangled by the deliberately arranged circle of chairs, with Bear on the outside.

The younger of the gentleman reached inside his jacket, and Elsie closed her eyes, hunched her shoulders. Would it be a knife to the throat like…

Her breath rasped loudly. And then…

A crunching sound.

Befuddled by the absence of a blade or bullet to her flesh, Elsie opened her eyes and settled on—

Bear munched contentedly on a bone balanced between his paws.

Traitor.

As soon as the word slipped in, she winced. "What do you want?" she repeated for a third time.

"We've come to enlist your services."

She cocked her head. "What?" Surely she'd misheard him. Or perhaps all these years spent alone with only her nightmares for company had left her mad.

"Will you please sit?" Lord Edward murmured.

This time, it was not fear but surprise that compelled her to retake her seat.

"We have an assignment suited for one with your talents."

Her talents. "I care for animals," she said flatly. "Unless you have a horse or some other beloved pet who's been injured, you've wasted your time. For there is no help I'd give you"—Elsie glanced over at his partner—"or any of your kind."

"It is a member of the Brethren," Lord Edward went on, as though she hadn't spoken.

"And you'd enlist my services?" Everything about their presence here—the request, the exchange itself—smelled of a snare. "You must be mad."

The gentleman's jaw flexed. "You've not even heard the assignment."

"I don't need to," Elsie said automatically.

"Not even to restore the honor of your family?" Cedric Bennett whispered.

Her family's honor. Nay, her father's honor. Elsie didn't give a jot what the world said of her. But her father... She wavered for the fraction of a heartbeat.

You are the one who is mad. That you'd consider offering them... anything? After what they did. "Get out," she said.

Lord Edward snapped his gloves together and made a show of stuffing them in his front jacket pocket. Making himself comfortable. Settling in for a debate. Making her aware that he had no intention of letting her end their meeting. "I'd not be here... unless I had no other choice."

"We always have a choice," she tossed back, the same fateful statement delivered to her father by some unknown member of the Brethren when danger had been closing in and Elsie and her father had been just a breath away from destruction.

"You worked extensively with your father," he continued, not missing a beat.

Warning bells went off. They'd only ever had one use for the late Francis Allenby—heal their badly wounded, scarred members and send them back to Polite Society, living and intact.

"I work with animals," she said carefully.

"But then, isn't that what we all are?" Mr. Bennett put forward in a steely whisper. "Animals?"

She pushed back her chair and slipped from their circle. "I've come to appreciate that the four-legged sorts are estimably more loyal, capable, and honorable than the two-legged sorts. Now, if you will."

"It is vital to the organization that we secure your help," Lord Edward called over, briefly staying her.

"Vital to the organization," she repeated. For two such distinguished operatives to come, they did so not for one of a like rank, but rather… "He must be someone important," she speculated.

They met her statement with stony silence.

And then it dawned on Elsie. Shock pulled at her. "It is one of your leaders." The mysterious figures had never been referenced by name among the men who'd been cared for at these very lodgings, but they'd been spoken of in shadowed and veiled terms. "It is the Sovereign?" she whispered.

Mr. Bennett exploded forward, and she gasped, stumbling away, but he was faster. He caught her hard about the shoulders and propelled her back. Elsie stiffened, braced for the strike—that did not come. For the unrelenting grip he had upon her, there was a restraint to Mr. Bennett's hold, and the evidence of that brought her eyes open. "What do you know of the Sovereign?" he asked.

Bear growled, abandoning the bone with which they'd bribed him.

"Have your dog stand down," he whispered. Or…

It was a challenge she'd not make. Not when doing so put the beloved dog at any risk.

Her heart pounding, Elsie snapped her fingers twice.

The dog sank back onto the floor, retraining his energies on his bone.

"Release her," Lord Edward ordered from over the gentleman's shoulder.

Mr. Bennett hesitated and then set her free.

Elsie hurried to put space between them, sidestepping his burly figure, until she had her back to a seemingly safer Lord Edward.

"He is my brother," Lord Edward said quietly.

His brother. That was why this member of the Brethren had come.

Elsie stared vacantly at the nicks upon the door, marked with her father's whittling knife to signify the inches she'd attained through girlhood.

It did not matter. None of these single-minded men or their fates or futures were a concern to her. Not after their betrayal. Not after how they'd used and then failed her father.

And yet…

An image flashed forward in her mind, vibrant and stunning for the realness of it.

"It is what we do, poppet. We help," Papa murmured, accepting a wet cloth from Elsie's fingers.

"Only the good ones," she supplanted.

Her father paused in his task, glancing over. "We all have traces of good within us. Some just lose their way. To not care for them would make us worse."

Her throat worked as the memory dissolved.

With his magnanimity, her father, however, had always been better than she… in soul, spirit, and heart. In every way.

"Your brother isn't my business," she said in deadened tones.

"Oh, but we are making him… your business," Mr. Bennett warned.

She stiffened, and her nape prickled as she braced for them to finish her for what she knew and what she refused to do for them.

A barely audible murmur passed from Lord Edward to the other gentleman.

"I do not believe you feel that way," Lord Edward directed at Elsie. "I believe you're very much your father's daughter." He paused. "In every way."

"You are wrong," she said automatically. Elsie faced the pair. "Neither of you know anything about me." Nothing outside her connection to one of the greatest healers in England. Nay, one of the greatest *former* healers. "And you knew even less about my father."

"Ah, but that is where you are wrong." Mr. Bennett sat back in his chair. "On both scores. Your father? We've already established he was a traitor to the Crown." All her muscles went taut. "Shall we focus on what we know about you?" He didn't await an answer.

"A thirty-year old spinster, you've never wed. You've lived on the outskirts of the Cotswolds with your only visitor an old village woman who sells you herbs. Herbs which you already grow, which leads one to believe yours is merely a gesture of charity."

Her cheeks fired hot. These men saw everything. And with his every word, Elsie was reminded of the folly in having any dealings with them.

"Shall I continue?" Mr. Bennett asked. "You once visited the village weekly, every Saturday, with your"—he glanced down at Bear—"dog in tow. Neither of you were greeted with kindness."

Nay, she'd been shunned as a girl who spoke to birds and animals and would have likely been burned a witch in another unfortunate time. Elsie clenched and unclenched her fists.

"And you worked alongside your father, treating the thirty-five patients carried into this household."

A chill went through her, and she involuntarily wrapped her arms about her middle. "Who are you?" she whispered.

He flashed another hard smile. "Who I am is irrelevant. Who you are? Now, *that* matters."

"My brother suffered an injury," Lord Edward said quietly. "Nearly a year ago."

Despite the urge to send him to the devil, to tell him she didn't care, she felt the part of her that was very much her father's daughter awaken at that revelation. "What happened to him?"

"It does not matter. He is a changed man. What matters is that you help restore him to his former state."

"It very much matters." Elsie's feet moved of their own volition, carrying her back to her chair. Standing behind that seat, she kept it as a barrier between them. "The person who will help… heal him"—a person who would not be her—"will not be able to divorce his past from what brought him to his present."

"They'll have to," Mr. Bennett said at her side. "His past belongs to no one."

She frowned, ignoring the presumptuous gentleman. Everyone thought they knew what another person needed. If they did, however, they'd not be here, even now.

"His injuries… are they physical or emotional in nature?"

Lord Edward's face spasmed, a crack that displayed him as… human. "They are both. He was injured in a carriage accident and suffered a head wound that saw him unconscious for nearly two months."

Two months.

"He speaks to few and no longer accepts polite company."

By the pain reflected in Lord Edward's gaze, that extended to the gentleman's family.

"Can you help?" Mr. Bennett asked impatiently. "If you can…" he dangled, "it would be an opportunity for you to restore honor to your family's name."

Rage simmered in her breast, and she ignored the insult he'd offered her. When she trusted herself to not hurl invectives at him, she forced herself to look at Mr. Bennett. His impatience was stamped on his features. "There's no need for restoration. I know precisely the manner of man my father was." With his love and need to help all, Francis Allenby had proven greater than the two who now sat before her. "He was one who cared about people."

Mr. Bennett flicked an imagined speck from his sleeve. "Enough that he betrayed the Crown."

She recoiled. "Get—"

"Please," Lord Edward said quietly, his faint entreaty slashing across the immediate urge to throw both men out of her modest cottage. "My brother… his name is William. William Helling, the Duke of Aubrey."

She sat back. "A duke," she repeated dumbly. They wished her, an oddity without her father's skill who lived on the fringe of the world, to care for a duke? "You believe me a traitor," she offered Mr. Bennett before looking back to the taller, darker gentleman. "You must be desperate to come to me."

Lord Edward glanced at his partner. The gentleman lifted his head slightly and, without a word, took his leave.

"We require someone unconventional," Lord Edward said as soon as the door had closed behind Mr. Bennett. "Someone versed in healing like your father… and you are rumored to be capable of both."

She shook her head. "Let me say this aloud to see if I understand. You men, who abandoned my father"—and in that, Elsie herself—"after all the work he provided for you and your organization"—her fingers curled into tight fists—"nay, not organization. *Men.*" She enunciated that single syllable. "My father cared for gentlemen connected to your organization. Now, all these years later, after everything you did to my father, you would come here and ask me to help one of your family members?"

"Yes," he said simply.

Elsie wrapped her fingers around the top of her chair, digging half-moons into the soft wood with her jagged fingernails. "Then you are mad. Even if I had my father' skill and willingness to help you people, I would not do it." She stalked to the door. "Now, if you would? Get out."

He stood, but otherwise made no move to heed her orders. "My brother is broken," he said, and the haunting quality of the admission sent the gooseflesh climbing up her arms. "You've tended animals whose spirits and minds have been affected. My brother..." He stretched a hand out in entreaty, the gesture leaving her wholly unmoved.

It was his words.

Damn him.

And damn you for being so weak.

"He is not right, in any way," Lord Edward went on. "He's suffered greatly, and I know you know something of suffering."

She knew too much of it. That kind of horror and heartbreak robbed a person of sleep and then riddled one's life with haunting remembrances of times past.

The gentleman drifted over, so that only a pace separated them. He cast a glance beyond her shoulder to the doorway, and she followed his stare. When he returned his focus to Elsie, his meaning was clear: Mr. Bennett listened in.

"I will speak candidly," he said in hushed tones. "There are those... outside of my family, whose only concern is who my brother is and his role." Within the Brethren.

"And what is his 'role' exactly?"

He shook his head once. "That is irrelevant. What matters is William. William needs saving." He drew in a slow breath. "My brother will ultimately die." Something there said that the duke's wounds moved beyond the physical sort, the kind that ran far deeper and ultimately felled a person.

Elsie took several steps around him, needing space, needing to think. Battling with herself.

Was this simply another test? To determine, as Mr. Bennett had suggested, the level of her loyalty? And if she did not do their bidding…? She shivered. Her fingers curled with the memory of when blood had stained her palms, crimson, sticky, and hot. Elsie focused again on breathing to keep from dissolving into the jumbled mess she'd been those years ago. Focused instead on what Lord Edward asked of her. For the Allenbys ultimately always failed where the Brethren were concerned.

"I do not have experience working with human patients."

"By your own admission, you worked alongside your father," he returned, without inflection.

"But never alone, and that was five years ago." She searched his face for some indication of deserved guilt for the role he and his fellow members of the Brethren had played. And found none. "I cannot do this. I wish your brother all the best with his recovery, but I cannot be the one to help him."

"I see." Lord Edward removed his gloves from his pocket and pulled them on with precise movements, until that hated signet disappeared inside the brown leather article. "I will leave you to your important work." He took a step to go and then stopped alongside Bear.

Elsie stiffened, but the gentleman merely sank to a knee.

He tugged off one glove and held out his palm, the hand without the signet upon it. An unspoken signal.

He came to her not as a member of the Brethren, but as a brother, as a man whose family was more important to him, and that bond was one, God help her, she could understand.

As if the universe sensed her weakening and sought to break her down even more, Bear flipped onto his back and presented his belly for the stranger.

The show of supplication from a dog who trusted… none spoke more than any of the cherished medical journals that filled her father's long-quiet office.

Lord Edward stood. "I bid you good night, Miss Allenby."

Elsie squeezed her eyes shut once more. "Lord Edward? I will meet him." Hope flared in his eyes. "But I cannot promise I can save him." The one person whose life had mattered more than any others, she'd ultimately been unable to heal or help.

Lord Edward held her gaze. "That is all I ask." He bowed his head in silent thanks. "You will be richly compensated—"

"I'm not doing this for money," she cut him off.

"Of course." He hastily pulled on his other glove. "I will allow you some time to gather your things." He turned to go.

Elsie's mind raced.

Gather her…?

She took a hurried step after him. "Where are we going?"

He paused, glancing back. "Why, to London, of course."

To London. "I don't leave Bladon." She'd gone but once. Long ago, with her father. Pain assaulted her senses.

Lord Edward gave her a knowing look full of pity. "No, I know that. But this time… you have no choice."

And with that, he left.

CHAPTER 2

London, England
Early morn

SINCE HIS WIFE HAD BEEN cut down on the muddied cobblestones of Mayfair three hundred and fifty days earlier, there was not much William Helling, the Duke of Aubrey, had to be grateful for.

On the days that his head was not throbbing from the injury sustained in that crash, the memories of Adeline's sightless eyes staring up, untrained on anything but the sky above, ravaged his mind.

Quiet.

That was the one, small, remaining gift left to him in an otherwise desolate world.

And even that should be taken from him on this day.

The rap on his chamber doors might as well have been a thundering pounding, for the break in stillness that had become such a part of this household, one previously so full of life and laughter and—

He dragged a pillow over his head, trying to will the sound gone. The reflexive movement inadvertently sent pain shooting to his temples.

Rolling onto his side, he covered his head with his hands, a groan tearing from him, muffled by his pillow and lost to the sputtering snores of the two women at his sides.

Moments later, the door opened, and William shoved the pillow aside enough to see who'd entered his chambers.

Reeve Stone stepped inside. "You've a visitor, Your Grace," he announced in his gravelly voice. His heavily scarred face gave no outward notice of the barely clad whores in the throes of sleep, or the gentleman he served who writhed in his bed like a wounded beast. Not a once-great leader. But then, Stone had long ago earned a reputation as the most ruthless member to ever serve in the ranks of the Brethren.

And now he played at the role of caregiver.

A bloody waste of his efforts, and a mark of the obstinacy of all those bastards.

William's brother stepped into the room, the most obstinate of all the bastards. A different groan, one born of frustration and not agony, pulled from him. Lying on his back, he slapped his palms over his face.

The well-sated crimson-haired beauty emitted a bleating snort, but remained sleeping.

Edward frowned. With an ease better suited to the role of Sovereign than William himself commanded, his younger brother clapped his hands loudly. "That will be all," he called out.

Shrieking, both women popped up. Eyes heavy with sleep and red from the bottles of spirits the three of them had consumed hours ago, they searched the room.

"You are looking better than you usually do," Edward greeted William as he picked his way around the room, fishing the scandalous gowns from the floor.

"Get out," William mumbled.

Ignoring him, Edward tossed the garments to William's latest bed partners. "It is time to leave, ladies," he drawled.

"The evening's only begun," the more voluptuous beauty slurred.

"It is afternoon, and you are done here," Edward said crisply.

They pouted, glancing briefly to William, and when no words of protest were forthcoming, they climbed from the mattress and quickly dressed.

"Need a visit tomorrow, Your Grace?" the shorter, plumper, blonde beauty offered, flashing him an enticing, yellow-toothed smile.

Need a visit? From them? William needed nothing. Those fleeting moments of mindless bliss provided by the string of actresses and whores were mere distractions. "Tomorrow," William agreed.

Edward watched the exchange with disapproval in his hard eyes. Returning to the doorway, he held the oak panel, ushering the women into the hall.

William scoffed. How easy it was for one to be disapproving of how he now lived his life. His brother's once-turbulent marriage was now a blissful one. He had a son and a babe on the way. All gifts that William would now never know.

His heart clenched, and he angled his head away from the sight of his brother.

"Use the servants' stairs," Edward called out to the women as they stepped into the hall. When they'd gone, Edward shut the door behind them.

Without hesitation, his brother moved deeper into the room, and as casually as pulling up a chair at White's, he dragged the leather armchair closer to where William lay and sat there—in silence.

The quiet was a telling statement of control from a man who had no intention of leaving.

There was a time when Edward would have obeyed, at all costs, an order to get out. There was a time when he would have dropped a bow and beat a hasty retreat, regardless of their fraternal relationship.

But that had been before, when William had been the respected, all-powerful Sovereign and leader of the Brethren. When people had answered to him and found themselves among the ranks of the Brethren, or dead—whatever command had dripped from his lips on a given day.

Back when I was a living, breathing man… and not… this.

He laid his arms out and stared up through his greasy hair at the nauseatingly cheerful mural overhead. And then promptly closed his eyes. But it was too late. The pale pinks, blues, and purples of chubby cherubs flitted past, ushering in the past. Ushering in a singsong voice filled with a purity and enthusiasm reserved only for children.

There are angels, William. They are so very beautiful. I should like them painted upon my own ceiling, so I feel closer to you—

"I've come with news."

William blinked, cursing the interruption, railing in his mind at Edward for stealing the sound of a voice that had become increasingly distorted in its clarity.

I've come with news. Something else familiar in a world that had been flipped upside down, with no meaning or order to it.

That phrase had once been shared by agents revealing the status of their assignments. Long ago, a thrill had accompanied that revelation, excitement that had come only from his work with the most secret branch of the Home Office, answering only to the king.

In the end, an unwillingness to abandon that thrill and be grateful for what would be fleeting happiness with a woman he'd never deserved had cost him everything.

Guilt stabbed at his chest, a thousand dull blades that, with the mere remembrance of her name, unfailingly found their mark.

Edward hooked a knee across his opposite ankle. "There was a time that statement would have had you demanding every last detail," his brother finally said.

William stared grimly overhead, refusing to answer.

After all, what was there to say?

He'd been forever changed. Broken, shattered, and destroyed, a fate he'd exacted on other men.

Mayhap this had been his punishment, then.

Only, she had paid the ultimate price.

"I've found someone to help you."

That pierced the fog.

William angled his head sideways, peering at his brother through the slick, disheveled strands covering his eyes.

"I see I have your attention."

How the roles had been reversed between them. Two years younger, Edward had looked up to William, come to him for guidance when they'd been boys. When he'd been admitted into the Brethren, with William as his superior, the role of elder sibling in possession of knowledge and experiences that his brother wasn't had shifted a fraction, morphing into a relationship that was similar and yet different in every way.

"I don't want help."

Edward shifted in his chair, rolling his shoulders. "It does not escape my attention that you do not deny *needing* help."

"I don't need help," he said belatedly, the words coming out thick. His tongue struggled to form words that were slightly garbled from another evening of drinking and his aching jaw.

"I'm your younger brother, William," his sibling said gently. "Your inferior in rank, skill, and place within the Brethren. I'm not, however, a simpleton."

His inferior in rank? If that were indeed true, it would be Edward's life that had been upended. His wife lost. His head broken. His mouth unable to form coherent words.

And it was another dark mark upon his worthless soul that, for a fraction of a moment, he wished it had been Edward. That his own life had been left intact, his wife spared.

He felt Edward's gaze on him.

"Your initial rejection of help spoke more clearly than your useless denial."

William remained fixed on the hated mural. What would it be to paint over it? To make the jubilant smiles and overjoyed expressions go away. But then, that would require people to enter this place, to steal this room that was a sanctuary of sorts.

Nay, a prison. He'd made it into the cell he deserved.

"Are you listening to me?" Edward asked impatiently.

"No," he said in a deadened tone.

"You've a family that cares about you. A family that needs you." Edward paused. "*Leo* needs you."

That arrow found its mark. Leopold, his nephew and godson, a far-too-clever-for-his-own-good lad, had been born with a perpetual air of sadness upon the passing of William's sister.

So many people failed. *My wife. My sister, who I let marry a black-hearted devil. Leo.*

His tongue grew heavy, the craving for a drink hitting like a physical blow to his senses.

"You are not even curious about the person I've brought to help you?" his brother was saying. "You have no questions? A well-planned interrogation? You always do."

Correction, William always *had*. But that had been before. What Edward, Bennett, Stone, and all the ranking members of the Brethren failed to realize was that one had to care to put questions forward. There was nothing for which William cared enough to rouse himself from his room. "Get out," he repeated for a second time.

Edward chuckled, the first laugh he'd heard from his brother—or anyone—in a year. It grated. And what scraped his nerves raw more was the damned need to know what had his younger sibling so amused. And God help him, he hated him all the more for being able to laugh when William had forever lost the ability.

"You want to ask me," Edward correctly surmised. "You wish to know what I could possibly have found humor in that I'd freely laugh before you, that I could manage it."

William scrubbed a hand over tired eyes. Damn Edward for knowing him far more than he'd ever credited. Just another area of his miserable existence in which he'd pompously overestimated his own skills.

The leather groaned, indicating his brother had shifted in his chair. "Because you are my brother, I will take pity on you one more time—"

"I don't want your pity," he rasped, and pain exploded at his temples from the echo of his own voice in his ears.

"—and tell you what has me so amused," Edward went on as if William hadn't strung together the most words he had in a year for his benefit. "It is what you said."

William had once been perceptive and quick to make sense of dialogue.

His brother's smile faded. "You don't recall what we were speaking of," he said quietly, with a dawning understanding in his like eyes.

William angled his head away from Edward, training it on the rumpled sheets of his four-poster bed, which took up a large portion of the center of his rooms. He'd picked out hidden meanings conveyed by adversaries, expressed in nothing more than a look and a grunt. As such, the last vestige of a pride he'd already thought shattered snapped in that instant over his inability to follow what his brother was talking about and what he'd previously said.

A failure. You are a bloody, blasted, pathetic excuse of a man.

And they wished him to resume his roles and responsibilities with the Brethren. They were as mad as he'd become.

"You told me to get out," Edward reminded him. "Those are the same words tossed at me by the one person I believe can help you."

Because Edward still had not given up on the foolish hope that William could be somehow fixed.

"And you brought him anyway," he said emotionlessly. As dulled as his reflexes and ability to think had become, he was still astute enough to know his brother wouldn't have failed to bring forth anyone if he so wished it.

Edward chuckled again. "You presume much." Shoving to his feet, he stepped over the tangle of Williams' garments and made a path to the armoire. Without asking or awaiting permission, he opened the rose-inlaid doors and fished around the dark articles that hung there.

More than a year out of fashion, the garments stood frozen in time, a reminder of what life had been when he'd donned the finely tailored pieces. Happy. A man wholly content with the world and his place in it.

He'd been so blinded by a belief in his own infallibility. Until it had been too late.

"Here," Edward murmured, withdrawing a jacket, trousers, and shirt. Returning with his arms full, he stopped so that he hovered above William. "You stink like sweat and whores."

"Because I spent the early morn hours bedding two whores," he said flatly. He'd shrived them until he'd passed out in blessed oblivion, and they'd drunk themselves into a like stupor.

His brother grunted. "You'll need to bathe." Shifting the garments to his left arm, Edward fished out the familial watch fob given to every Helling male and consulted the timepiece. "Eventually," he amended as he let the chain fall between his fingers. "You do not have time."

Ironically, all that William had left in this world was time. Too much of it. Each day stretched on, eternal, both a purgatory and a hell combined, a waiting room of sorts until he would find himself burning alongside Satan for all the wrongs he'd done on this earth.

"William?" Edward urged.

"I've no intention of meeting anyone whom you believe will"—he peeled his lip in a sneer—"help me."

Edward tossed the swiftly wrinkling garments onto the chair he'd vacated moments ago. They landed with a solid thump.

For a moment, William believed his younger brother would go

and, this time, finally leave him be. He hoped for it, wanting him gone, so he could…

What? Lie here and wait for an end that will not come?

Alas, he still apparently had not yet learned the folly in *hope*.

Edward dropped to a knee. "You cannot go on like this."

He spoke as though William had a choice. As though everything that had come before could be set aside and forgotten, all the suffering and pain undone because, for the world, time enough had passed. But this was William's life. And what had come before could not be untangled from who he'd become.

"You were happy before Adeline," Edward went on.

Wrong. William had been a carefree rogue, seducing widows and unhappy wives, all the while believing himself happy. He hadn't been.

"If you cannot move on from the loss of A—"

William skewered him with a single look, silencing the remainder of the name he didn't want to hear spoken aloud.

"From the loss," his brother substituted, "then do so for the Brethren. You've not been severed from your position."

"Because the king is as mad as the world proclaims him to be," he muttered.

"You are needed. For the good of king and—"

"To hell with king and country," he rasped, struggling up onto his elbows. William pushed himself upright and swung his legs, weak under him, over the side of the bed. "King and country can rot." And he'd not feel an ounce of emotion over the loss, because he was incapable of feeling anything. They'd taken it all from him. Because he'd allowed it. He'd cared about the Brethren and his role within that noble organization more than anyone or anything else and hadn't realized until it had all been taken away that the Brethren and his role within it was nothing but rubbish. All of it.

Grief knifed at him, rolling together with guilt and lancing at wounds that would never heal.

"You don't mean that," Edward said somberly.

He did. He'd not, however, debate the point with his brother, whose life within the Brethren and with his wife was still whole. As such, he couldn't understand.

One didn't… until it was too late.

William stood on unsteady feet, and Edward rose alongside him.

"Tell him to find another."

"The order of succession is clear. The only way for you to be severed from the role is through a direct appeal to the king or by a lack-of-confidence petition made by at least three members of the Brethren."

He chuckled, the sound rusty and sharp. "I'm sure you can find a good deal more."

"No one will betray you, William. Therefore, you are the only one who can end your service to the Brethren, by petitioning the king yourself." Edward gave him a pointed look. "And I believe the fact that you haven't indicates that, for all your protestations, you have not given up on the work you do."

A mirthless laugh, bleak, black, and empty, rattled William's chest. "Is that what you believe? That I *want* this title? You are a bloody fool." But then, why shouldn't Edward believe that? William had displayed a single-minded devotion to his role and the organization.

Edward didn't so much as flinch at the invective tossed at him. "Very well, then the Brethren can go hang," he said in hushed tones. Damning words that, if overheard, would see him absolved of his role. "The others, the members, they are concerned about the implications for the Brethren." He took a step toward William. "I care about what happens to you. You were fortunate enough to survive. I don't want to see you like this anymore."

Like what? Battered by headaches, eerily empty, incapable of feeling… of being around anyone.

Edward settled a hand on his shoulder. "You must at least want justice."

"Justice," he repeated, the echo dripping with condescension. "Justice is the rubbish of books and ancient legends." What good would justice do? It would change nothing. The woman whose safety and happiness had fallen to him had been failed. Whoever his enemy was, and the number of suspects was undoubtedly vast, he—or she—had won. The only end that would see him nameless foe ultimately triumph was William's death, and that was a fate he'd prayed for daily over the past year.

"I'll not bother you any further…"

"Good. Do not."

"I'll ask you but one more time to think of your godson."

Leo. His bookish nephew's somber visage flashed in his mind's eye.

Had his brother always been this damned tenacious? William ground his teeth, and as soon as he did, agony bolted along his jawline. He swallowed back a gasp, refusing to give in to the pain. William struggled for control of it.

Edward held William's gaze, his eyes tortured. "This is not who you are."

"You are wrong," he said flatly. Pinpricks of pain dotted his vision. "And furthermore…" He sank back into the mattress. "No one can help me."

In the days following the attack, when William had hovered between life and death, the king's best, most-skilled doctors had tended him. Not a single one had managed to rouse him. And when William had at last opened his eyes to a blurred world and a buzzing in his ears, they hadn't helped then either. Instead, he'd drawn forth only fragmented memories that, when put together, did not make a whole story. Those gaps remained still, with only Adeline's terrified screams cementing the experience.

His temples pulsed, and a sharp ache radiated along his jaw.

"But if someone could…" Edward dangled. "A life free of pain. One where you don't spend your days bedding whores and losing yourself in drunken oblivion."

William fixed on the former part of that enticement. Those five words hung there, a temptation.

A life free of pain.

What his brother spoke of was not an emotional healing that could never come, but rather, the healing of a physical wound that had turned William into a prisoner in his own household. It was a gift he didn't deserve, but he'd always been selfish. He proved as much now.

Wordlessly, William nodded slowly. The movement and the extensive talking he'd done this day sent agony lancing through him.

Edward opened and closed his mouth several times. "I… I… I will return shortly." And as if he feared William would change his mind and toss him and the supposed savior out on their arses, his brother rushed off.

As soon as the door clicked shut behind Edward, William

hunched over and gave in to the pain that the exchange had cost him. Curling into a ball, he moaned.

Edward insisted that he was fortunate to be alive. When, in truth, his nameless enemy had notched the ultimate victory, for William had survived when death would have been easier… and preferable.

CHAPTER 3

ELSIE HAD NOT SLEPT IN more than thirty-three hours.

It was not the first time she'd gone without sleep, and thirty-three hours was certainly not the longest amount of time that sleep had eluded her. Sleeplessness was an all-too-familiar state for her since her father's death.

One's body eventually passed a point far beyond exhaustion and entered a realm where sheer rote living drove one.

For Elsie, after agreeing to accompany her two nighttime visitors to London, it had become terror that prevented her from any real rest.

Instead, she and Bear had traveled at the edge of gold velvet squabs more comfortable than the mattress Elsie lay upon each night, braced for the moment of her murder.

Just like Papa.

Just like Papa.

Just like…

"Nervous, are you, Miss Allenby?" Mr. Bennett called over. His voice echoed from the rafters of the palatial foyer ceiling.

On the carved mahogany hall bench, Elsie stiffened. Bear sat up at her side.

She stole a glance out of the corner of her eye. Bennett lounged against the black double doors. With his back resting against those heavy panels, his arms at his chest, and the heel of his right boot propped up, he'd set himself up as a sentry. His message rang clearer than his taunt: She was caught.

Her heart thumped an off-beat rhythm. Why had she agreed to come to this place? Because she'd had a momentary lapse in sanity. "I wouldn't be here if I were afraid."

"Ah, but I did not say afraid," he pointed out. "I said nervous. They're two entirely different sentiments," he explained, speaking in the way he might to a young child slow to process a detailed lesson, and that only ratcheted her annoyance up a notch. "One is a primal instinct by one who knows they've been bested. The other?" He sneered. "Is possessed by one who knows she is guilty of wrongdoing."

He is trying to get a rise out of you.

From the moment Mr. Bennett had invaded her cottage and then handed her down from the carriage nearly thirty minutes ago, he'd been attempting to do so. And she'd be damned if she gave him, or any other of those within his distinguished organization, that satisfaction.

Elsie reclined against the wall in a display of feigned indifference, even as outrage snapped through her. "Given the lack of loyalty shown by the members of your organization, you'd be far more accurate substituting 'he' for 'she.'"

Mr. Bennett let his foot fall to the floor. "I don't trust you," he stated flatly.

Elsie tipped her chin up. "That is shocking."

He frowned. "What?" he asked, suspicion rich in his nearly obsidian gaze.

"We concur on something." She peered down the tip of her nose at him. "I don't trust you either. Nor do I like you."

Mr. Bennett smiled coldly. "Ah, and *that* is where we differ. For I don't care whether anyone likes me or does not. And certainly not you. A traitor's daughter."

There it was, stated baldly in plain terms. No more dancing around what had otherwise been an insinuation from the gentleman. It had been inevitable. She'd been expecting it.

Still, the allegation sucked the air from her lungs, and a tense energy exploded in the room.

Elsie seethed. "How dare you?" Using the arm of the bench, she pushed herself to standing. The length of their carriage ride had drained the energy from her limbs, and they trembled faintly.

A harsh amusement glinted in his eyes.

"You can go to hell." Her dog growled his support. "You and—"

"Miss Allenby, my apologies for keeping you."

Elsie turned so quickly, she stumbled and hurried to right herself.

Lord Edward Helling stalked forward.

But for the faintest growth upon his cheeks, he didn't have the appearance of one who'd ridden for hours to Bladon and then back to London a mere hour after he'd arrived at her cottage. His garments were unwrinkled, without a speck of dust. Even his cravat was an artful display that Beau Brummell himself would have striven to emulate.

"This is not going to work," she blurted when he neared her.

That brought him up short. He completed his steps, closing the remaining distance between them. "I beg your pardon?" he asked coolly.

Her gaze slid to Mr. Bennett, and the taller gentleman, who'd somehow managed to convince her against her better judgment to accompany him, followed her stare.

Lord Edward gave the man a look. "I'd have a moment with Miss Allenby."

The other man dropped his head in a mocking bow. "Miss Allenby."

As soon as he'd gone, Elsie dropped her hands on her hips. "You'd both expect me to help one of yours, while my father and our name should be disparaged by you?"

His mouth tightened. "I've no time for offended sensibilities. What your father was or was not no longer matters." Because he was dead. Elsie flinched at the unspoken reminder. "My brother, however, is alive and in need of your assistance." Narrowing his eyes, Lord Edward lowered his head, shrinking the more than one foot of distance between them. "And for any belief you had that this might have been a decision within your control? Let me assure you, it was not. The ultimate result was your coming and helping my brother. Now"—he swept an arm forward, motioning down the same intersecting hall from which he'd arrived moments ago—"if you'll follow me."

A shiver racked her frame, and she moved closer to her dog.

Her father had made faulty missteps where the Brethren were

concerned, and in her letting momentary pity overshadow everything she knew about these people and joining them anyway, she'd also made a perilous mistake. If one danced with the devil, one ultimately found oneself burned by that dark demon's flames.

And it was a certainty they'd make her regret leaving. She read it in this man's cold, unyielding eyes. Motioning for Bear to stay behind, she swept ahead.

Lord Edward immediately fell into step beside her, his long-legged stride erasing her lead.

"If you're expecting to find a proper duke awaiting you, you are wrong."

She glanced up.

Lord Edward's attention remained on the path ahead.

"I have no expectations, Lord Edward." Elsie's dealings with wounded, scarred animals over the years had proven that it was better to not have expectations that compromised one's ability to avoid forming preconceived ideas about a treatment plan.

"You'll find him—"

"I do not need you to tell me how I will find him. I'll see for myself," she interjected. "And then I shall evaluate my ability to help… or not help him."

Lord Edward brought them to a stop before a heavy oak door. He reached for the handle, but she intercepted him.

He stared at her with a question in his eyes.

"He is aware I'm coming?"

The gentleman gave a curt nod.

"Then there is no need for formal introductions. I will meet him alone."

"Impossible," he said flatly. "I'm his brother, I'll be there, and someone will be there with you at all times."

The arrogance of these gentlemen. Of course, the guardians of the kingdom and its people would have an inflated sense of self and their role in… everything. "Lord Edward," she said calmly, "every encounter and experience I've ever had with wounded animals have been conducted in private, with only myself and the creature. His Grace will be no different."

He thinned his eyes into narrow slits. "My brother is no animal."

Elsie offered a gentle smile. "Lord Edward… we are all animals."

The obstinate gentleman opened his mouth to object, and she

lifted a finger. "You insisted I come here, and I've done so. Now I'd ask that you allow me the freedom to see to the task with which I am charged." She paused. "Or… I can just leave?"

Even as she said it, she knew the lie in that suggestion. The Brethren would not simply allow her to return to her Bladon cottage and become the invisible figure she'd made herself into these nearly five years. Or, the figure she'd thought she'd made herself into. They'd known all along about her. They'd just been waiting until they'd had need of her. Because they always exacted some form of repayment.

Even so, she saw the war that waged in the tall stranger. *He needs me more than he doesn't trust me.* It was why she knew many long moments before he spoke that Lord Edward Helling would ultimately capitulate. "Very well," he said gruffly, retreating a step.

That concurrence, however, had also come too easily.

Lord Edward, and the world, might protest any similarities made between people and animals, and yet, both shared a like wariness that made them equally predictable.

Therefore, his *agreement* wasn't enough. "Nor do I wish you to wait outside the rooms, listening in on our meeting."

No sooner had that order left her mouth than Lord Edward sharpened his gaze on her. "You expect I should trust you."

"You think I'd harm him?" she shot back. His silence stood as his answer. Appalled, Elsie shook her head. What manner of beasts were these men? "And yet, you brought me here anyway."

"Because I am desperate," he gritted out.

Elsie took a step toward him, so the tips of their shoes brushed. "Then let me do my work here," she whispered, angling her head back to meet his hostile gaze.

They remained locked in battle.

He was the first to look away, his gaze wandering to the heavy paneled door. Lord Edward cursed quietly. "Very well," he mouthed. "But if he is harmed in any way, either deliberately or through your… treatments, you will pay, Miss Allenby. You will pay dearly."

A sad smile tipped her lips up. They still did not realize. "You've already taken everything from me," she said in hushed tones. "There is nothing more you can do and no greater harm you can inflict."

"That is what you think." Ice frosted his eyes. "And that is where you are wrong."

With that ominous pronouncement, Lord Edward retreated, backing slowly down the hall, keeping his ruthless gaze trained on her until he disappeared into the next corridor.

Long after he'd gone, Elsie remained rooted to the spot, her body faintly trembling from the chill he'd left behind, his hardened, unspoken promise more dangerous than the words he'd hurled.

Do not give a single one of them the satisfaction of your fear…

Elsie drew a slow, calming breath in through her nose. And she concentrated on the slight whistled inhalation and counted as she exhaled.

However, as she opened her eyes, the calming technique she'd used with so many of her father's patients failed.

My brother…He is not right, in any way…He's suffered greatly…

The hollow warning flitted ominously around her mind, stirring the unease that sat like a stone in her belly.

He is just a man.

A man who was also the leader of the organization that ultimately saw her father killed. The Duke of Aubrey gave orders as to who would live and who would die with the same ease he might select a bottle of spirits from a servant at White's or Brooks's.

Elsie faltered, briefly contemplating the path she'd traveled, considering her escape.

There was no escaping, though. Not truly. These men would find a person wherever they hid. Neither she nor her father had been born to their world, and therefore, she was no match for their ruthlessness. It was why she and Papa had failed so mightily when evil had arrived at their doorstep.

Elsie's fingers curled reflexively around the door handle, the cold metal biting into her palm as thoughts intruded of that summer night that left her shattered and forever marred.

No. no. no. Please, do not leave me…

Elsie's breath hitched noisily, and she clamped her hands over her ears, blotting out the melded screams of suffering that had belonged to them both, but now lived on only with her.

Enough. Enough. En—

Elsie forced her arms back to her sides. "You are better than this," she whispered to her distorted reflection in the glimmering gold door handle. And before the ugliness of her past staked its claim once again and her courage deserted her, Elsie grabbed the handle and let herself into the chamber.

It took a moment for her eyes to adjust to the more dimly lit room. Had the layered white-gold and seafoam-green curtains been tightly drawn, the room would have been cast as more of a caricature from a Gothic novel, the ones where all the darkest, most-scarred figures remained locked away, denying themselves even basic sunlight. But the fringed curtains with their gold pelmets had been cleverly drawn back just a smidgeon to let in the afternoon sun. Soft rays penetrated the crack in the fabric, illuminating a path along the floor.

Elsie cocked her head, forgetting the figure who lurked somewhere close. Instead, she fixed on the peculiar but telling detail that revealed that the man who dwelled in this space, the one Lord Edward Helling believed lost to civilization, in fact craved the light and the world outside his crystal windowpanes. For the first time since she'd agreed to Lord Edward's request—nay, demands—her being here had nothing to do with threats or orders and everything to do with the inherent need that had driven both her and Papa. As such, she lingered there, deliberately letting the moments stretch on. Measured. Careful. Never move too quickly, but neither move too slow.

Turning, Elsie closed the door behind her and then faced forward once more. She did not take a step, choosing instead to recognize that this space belonged to another, and she was an interloper here. "Hullo," she said softly, another test.

Her greeting pinged around the cavernous chambers.

When that call was met with only an answering silence, she stepped deeper into the duke's rooms.

"Not another step."

The command brought her to an abrupt stop in the center of the chambers, the timing in no way coincidental. She'd been lured there by one exerting his influence, sizing her up.

Not making any sudden moves, Elsie did a slow sweep with her gaze, searching for the duke…

And finding him.

Elsie stilled.

Neither of them spoke. It was a primitive match she'd wager

existed from the basest beast to the lords of London's finest drawing rooms. The fight for supremacy.

Once upon a lifetime ago, back when she'd discovered an innate ability to deal with the injured animals around Bladon, she'd come upon a dog on a return walk from the village. His mangy fur matted to his frame, the woeful creature had planted himself before her. And with his white teeth flashing, he'd held her immobile.

How very much this tall, wiry figure was akin to that feral dog.

This was the duke?

He was clad in dark trousers and a jacket, the only mark of color the crisp, white lawn shirt carelessly stuffed into the waistband of his trousers. The garments were finer than anything she'd donned in her whole life, and yet, that hint of material wealth was where all hint of gentlemanliness ended. He was not, however, the physically incapacitated figure she'd made him out to be in her mind. Of course, it was the other scars that invariably ran deeper.

His black hair hung in a greasy tangle about his stubbled face. Dark circles lined bloodshot eyes.

She wrinkled her nose.

And he stunk to high heaven.

"Have I offended you?" he whispered, and the harsh amusement revealed one who reveled in her shock.

"I assure you, not at all." The sight and smell of such a man would have sent most women fleeing. Elsie, however, had encountered all manner of men who'd required her father's care.

His Grace sharpened his gaze on her face.

Not for the first time, she wondered what suffering had brought this man, a slip away from royalty and a vaunted member of the Brethren, to the state he now found himself.

By the icy deadness in his eyes, those were secrets the Duke of Aubrey intended to hold tight to. Her family having been privy to information from the Brethren before, Elsie had learned long ago that no good could come from knowing their secrets.

CHAPTER 4

THIS WAS RICH.

They'd sent all manner of doctors to see him.

Old ones, who tended the king himself. Younger ones, newly out of university, renowned for their skill, and exclusive agents of the Home Office.

This was the first time that they'd sent… a woman.

And why not?

"Get on with it," William said sharply. He rolled his shoulders, his muscles chafing at the burden of the jacket his brother had insisted he don. With a growl, he shrugged out of it and hurled it at a nearby armchair. It landed with a *whoosh* along the back. "Well?" he demanded, stalking out of the shadows so he could better see the latest person sent to help him.

The woman cocked her head, like Prinny's lazy terrier on a hunt.

"Isn't that why you're here?" he pressed impatiently. "At my brother's request?" And the Brethren's, of course. His entire existence had only ever been about that noble organization. He sneered. "Here to ease my pain and restore me to my former greatness?"

"Behest."

She smiled, dimpling her olive-hued cheeks. That soft expression turned her bow-shaped lips up at the corners, knocking him slightly off his axis. The reaction came from too much drink and too little sleep the night prior. Nonetheless, hers was a face accustomed to sun, one that had gone without the benefit of a bonnet.

"What?"

"A behest," she said, enunciating each of the three syllables. There was a lilting, almost singsong quality to her voice. *Light. Airy. Pure.* The tones, better belonging to a mythical fairy than a mortal woman, wrapped around him, enthralling. "An authoritative order. A command." She took a step toward him and stopped. There was a calculated measure to her movements and speech, and she wielded both like a skilled swordsman. "The act or an instance of asking for something. Something that is *asked* for. *That*," she said with deliberate emphasis, "is the distinction… Your Grace." She tacked on that last part, his title.

William stared unblinkingly at the insolent baggage.

Mayhap he'd gone mad after all. By God, was the chit truly giving him a tutor's lecture on the damned word *behest*? He narrowed his eyes. The only other possibility was that the woman was… mocking him. Either, even with his reduced faculties and power, proved an unfamiliar state for him. Men did not challenge or question him. Had he said, as a duke, that it was sunny in the midst of a rainstorm, all of Polite Society would have nodded their heads like eager chicks pecking at the ground. And anyone who'd dared challenge him, the Sovereign, would have been removed from power.

"Who are you?" he barked.

"Miss Allenby." She gave him a long look.

She expected something from him.

But then, everyone always expected something. The only one who hadn't had been wholly deserving of everything, and in the end, he'd given her… nothing. Pain radiated up his jaw, striking his temples and forehead.

"Your name means nothing to me," he said flatly, stalking over to the Chinese red lacquer cabinet. Making quick work of the intricate metal locks that protected the stock, he fished out a bottle.

"I did not expect it should."

Something in that quiet retort gave him pause.

He glanced over his shoulder, but the woman stood there, revealing nothing in her delicate features, her face a perfect mask that any member of the Brethren would have a struggle emulating. "On with it, then," he snapped, whipping his decanter about. The liquid sloshed noisily within the crystal bottle. "Work whatever magic you possess that resulted in my brother bringing you here."

"I have no magic," she said quietly. "I rather suspect it was desperation on Lord Edward's part that resulted in his visiting me."

And she proved an excellent read of character. He dropped his hip atop the liquor cabinet. "I've been seen by more than six and twenty doctors or healers. What makes you believe you can help?" He yanked the stopper out with his teeth and spit it to the floor.

He'd give credit where credit was due. The lady gave no outward reaction at the uncouth display.

"I never said I can help," she pointed out.

No, she hadn't. His brother, however, had insisted as much. William tipped the bottle back and downed a long, slow swallow of the brew. It had long since lost its burn.

He felt the woman's eyes on him, studying him.

William wiped the back of his shirtsleeve over his mouth. "Then get out."

The tenacious wench remained. "I never said I could not help." She lifted her palms slightly. "Nor will I know until I try."

"Greater men than you have tried," he said, taking another pull from his bottle.

"With all due respect, they can't really be greater than I, if they are no longer here, and I am." The woman's eyes sparkled, eyes that were neither wholly green, nor brown, but rather, a perfect blending of both those colors.

As such, it took a moment for her words to register.

William set the decanter down behind him with a noiseless click and strolled forward. He stalked a circle around Miss Allenby. Nearly half a foot shorter than he, her frame painfully slender, she had a physique that could be confused for a child's. If one did not look too closely… and appreciate the generous flare of her hips and bounteous breasts. He stopped behind the lady, tracing his gaze down the expanse of her back and lower, to the curve of her buttocks. Her body stiffened. "Are you being deliberately insolent?" he whispered.

"Only if one considers honesty insolence, as has been my experience with Polite Society."

He pounced. "You have experience with Polite Society, then."

Her voice grew shuttered. "I had enough."

Another clue about the mysterious chit. She spoke in the past tense.

"Furthermore," she demurred, "I never promised your brother that I would take on your care."

Take on his care. As though he were a bothersome child a lord or lady wished to rid themselves of. "I'm not looking for a damned nursemaid," he hissed.

"I merely promised that I would meet with you and determine whether I thought I might help," she said over his words.

No one could help. And yet…

Through the hurt humiliation, his curiosity stirred. When was the last time anyone had told him, the Duke of Aubrey, no?

When every other man who'd entered his rooms had either averted their gazes in deference to his title, made his head dizzy with the amount of bows they'd bestowed, or tripped over their words from fear of the man he'd become, this slip of a woman remained composed.

Almost… bored.

"What medical skills do you possess?" he tossed, and for the condescension that crept into that query, an inherent part of his speech this past year, a genuine hungering to know evoked the question.

There was an element of unexpected intrigue to the fresh-faced girl.

"Few," she conceded.

"My, my. You are either modest, or failingly honest."

"I believe you mean 'unfailingly,'" she corrected him once again. "Either way, I'm one who speaks only the truth."

No one, not even his wife, had challenged him. Unlike this chit, who did so at every score.

William lowered his head and placed his lips close to the shell of her ear. "I do not misspeak, Miss Allenby. I said what I meant. Honesty," he whispered, so close he detected the little shudder that went through her slender frame, "is a failing. It will destroy you every time." Such had been the lesson he'd instructed the men who served under him.

She shook her head once. "You are wrong."

He stiffened.

This marked the first time in the whole of his thirty-three years that he'd been told he was incorrect—about anything. No one challenged him. No one questioned him. He'd been born in the right, and it was a state that had only been strengthened through his appointment as the Sovereign.

Until now.

Until her.

William folded his arms at his chest. "Well, then, Miss Allenby, enlighten me as to your distinguished schooling and patients."

"I never made any assertions about my skills. I am not schooled in medicine," she said quietly. "Nor do I have patients." She hesitated a hair of a moment. "That is... the... hum... sor..."

His ears pricked up. Either his hearing was a good deal more improved than he'd credited since he'd been thrown from a shattered carriage, or he was hearing things. "Speak up, Miss Allenby." William resumed his path around the young woman, and this time, he stopped so that they faced each other. "What was that?" he asked, cupping a hand about his right ear. "It sounded as though you said you do not have patients of the *human sort*."

She gave a toss of her dark curls, and the disheveled knot at her nape freed several more auburn-tinged strands. In any other woman, that gesture would have only ever been construed as flirtatious. In this spitfire, it was another mark of her defiance.

"I am a horse doctor."

His mouth moved, but no words were forthcoming. His brother had brought him a...?

"I've cared for dogs, cats, and birds, as well," she added. "Badgers."

"Badgers?" he mouthed.

She nodded. "Indeed."

He started, unaware he'd spoken aloud.

The young woman continued her never-ending enumeration. "Grey wagtails. Tree creepers." By God, at this point, the minx could be making up beasts and he'd have no idea if she were funning at his expense. "Goldfinches." Miss Allenby scrunched up a slightly too-small nose in an endearing wrinkle, and she lingered her stare pointedly on him. "I've cared for *all* animals, really. They are not so very different from humans."

He blinked. By God, surely she wasn't implying... Surely she didn't mean that he himself... "I should throw you out on your arse," he whispered.

Her cheeks exploded with color in the first crack in her otherwise remarkable composure. And at a bloody curse word.

"Where in hell did my brother find you?"

"The Cotswolds."

His had been a rhetorical question more than anything. She'd answered anyway. William pressed his index fingers and middle fingers against his temples.

"That won't help, you know."

His already muddled mind struggled to make sense of that.

The young woman matched his movements, placing callused fingers to her own head. "Your headaches."

He gnashed his teeth and then immediately regretted the reflexive movement. William swallowed back a groan. "I trust my brother"—the disloyal cur who must have designs on driving William into complete madness—"illuminated you as to my—"

"Impairments?" she asked, so casually that he could not stop himself from wincing. "No," she explained. "Lord Edward was not forthcoming. I gathered as much from… this…" Miss Allenby dragged a fingernail down her own jawline. Strong enough that it was borderline masculine in its lines, and yet, it lent an exotic quality to the peculiar chit. "And this…" She ran her fingers over her lips, drawing his gaze to the plump, bow-shaped flesh. "Your mouth," she murmured. "It barely moves as you speak." This time, it was the minx who took a step closer, scrutinizing him through long, black lashes. "As if… it pains you."

It did. It was a searing agony that had held him prisoner since he'd been tossed from a carriage and landed face-down upon the pavement.

Of its own volition, his gaze worked a path over her sun-kissed cheeks.

He'd tupped two whores last evening, transforming this very room into a den of carnality. Those wicked, wanton women had been no different than so many others whom he'd spent mindless hours this past year burying himself within. But this spitfire had an air of innocence and strength rolled together, a merger of sentiments he'd believed could not exist within one person.

A wave of lust gripped him, and he fought to rein in that yearning, instead focusing on her unerringly accurate assessment of his injury.

"Am I correct?" she ventured, her hesitancy pulling him back. "Is it your jaw?" Miss Allenby hovered on the balls of her feet in anticipation of his answer.

He'd belonged to the Brethren enough to know not to ever concede a personal fact about oneself or one's family. Everything she'd gleaned could have come as easily from the scandal sheets that had written of the Duke and Duchess of Aubrey's tragic accident and his subsequent *recovery*.

"Well?" he taunted. "Doctor of animals. Can you help?"

ELSIE IGNORED THE TAUNTING AND focused on his question.

Could she help?

The better question to be asked was… did he wish to be helped? After all, he'd pointedly ignored the query she'd put to him regarding his jawbone.

As such, her immediate answer would be no.

Some creatures were content to remain in a corner and lick their wounds until they drew their last labored breath.

And there could be no disputing the truth: His Grace, the Duke of Aubrey, was as much a wounded beast as any of the ones she'd cared for over the years.

Snarling. Lashing out. And, in his case, drinking too much spirits. The Duke of Aubrey as he stood before her was certainly not what she'd expected of the gentleman.

When Lord Edward had sought her out, Elsie had assumed the gentleman had spoken of physical wounds that his brother had suffered. Given the work he did for the Home Office, and the injured agents her father had tended from that organization, she'd expected there would be marks just as the one he wore upon his jaw.

But this man before her? Elsie did a sweep of him. He was vastly more complex than that.

If one looked too closely, one would miss the details she herself had seen. And yet, though there were no outward scars revealing a physical suffering, that did not mean none existed.

No, but that being true, the most visible, the most tangible marks of this man's misery were subtle. His sunken cheeks, covered with several days' worth of growth. The tangle of greasy black curls that hung over his face. And the most telling of all… the ease with which he downed spirits that would have seen any other man ape-drunk.

The Duke of Aubrey was very much broken.

"Well?" he prodded. "Do you believe you can help?"

Tell him no. An angry, unforgiving figure such as he would never question the reasons for that answer. He'd want to lick away at his wounded pride and, therefore, would be as content with her leaving as she herself would be.

"I'll ask you again. *Where* did my brother find you?"

"Bladon," she clarified. "It's a small village in the Cotsw—"

"Are you being deliberately obtuse?" he shot back.

"He came knowing my father, Francis Allenby, was more skilled than any doctor to have set foot in this household," she said with the Allenby pride her father once predicted would be the ruin of her. As soon as the admission left her mouth, she recoiled. She'd said too much.

And yet…

Elsie searched for a hint that her revelation meant… something to this man. That it meant *anything.*

His face remained coldly blank. "So, your reputation has been earned because of who your father was?"

A haze of red descended over her eyes as the implications of that question slammed into her with a force, knocking the air from her chest.

Why… why… He truly did not know of the work her father had done. He neither recognized her name, nor the service Francis Allenby had provided for the country.

But then, what should she expect of an organization who'd use a man as they had her father and let him perish in the cruelest way possible at the hands of an enemy?

"Miss Allenby?" His Grace demanded impatiently.

"I suppose it is no different than one earning one's reputation from a title one was born with," she shot back. Elsie rocked back on her heels as all the hatred, pain, and horror this man and his organization had caused consumed her. It eradicated the inherent need to help, the curiosity to meet the once-great leader of the Brethren. All the suffering he knew was deserved. "You are correct. I cannot help you." Elsie turned to leave. She'd done all that she'd promised she would. She'd met with the gentleman and evaluated him. She owed neither him, nor his brother, nor the Brethren, another blasted thing.

Elsie made it no farther than three steps.

The duke slid himself before her, blocking her path to the door.

Run, poppet… Run…

The warning bells screamed as the past merged with the present, jumbling it all in her mind, melding the Duke of Aubrey's face with that of another.

Crying out, Elsie let her fist fly.

The duke instantly caught it.

The unexpected human touch, firm yet hot, seared her skin and snapped her from the reverie. Shivers radiated from her hand, tingling up her arm. This hold, also as unrelenting as another's had been, was yet so very different. There was a gentleness to the grip at odds with the one that haunted her still five years later.

Elsie blinked wildly.

I am safe. I am safe. I am safe.

She let the mantra envelop her in a steadying calm.

She was safe.

Or as safe as one could be in this man's presence.

The Duke of Aubrey released her.

Elsie brought her shoulders back and braced for an interrogation or chastisement.

After all, one did not lift a finger to a duke, and certainly not the Sovereign.

His Grace spoke. "I have not dismissed you."

Yet.

That single, unspoken syllable hung there.

And still, the innate understanding she'd always possessed of battle-worn creatures hinted at one who wouldn't dismiss her. He'd keep her here… regardless of what she wished or didn't wish.

"You worked alongside your father," he murmured. And a half-mad laugh gurgled in her throat. Any other nobleman would have railed at her for having dared to lift a hand with even the threat of violence. This gentleman carried on like they merely resumed a pleasant discourse over tea. "Was he a man of some skill?"

Skill enough that he'd been entrusted with the most wounded, broken men in the Brethren. "He was," she said, her voice thick.

The capacity in which her father had served, however, was a detail she kept close. By his own valuable reminder of moments ago, one should be careful with what information one dispensed. Or mayhap he merely toyed with her. Mayhap this was as much a test as the one they'd put to her late papa, and the Duke of Aubrey well knew who her father was and of what he'd been accused.

Elsie peered at him, searching his breathtakingly chiseled features.

And finding… nothing. No guilt. No understanding. No larger game he played.

And that absolute lack of knowing was somehow worse. It left her bereft and aching. Her father had given of his services, tending men within the Brethren, and this man, their great, fearless, vaunted leader had no recollection.

"And some of those skills have transferred to you, the daughter."

Elsie didn't wish to remain here, caring for a dissolute lord who'd lost himself in drink and sorrow. She weighed her response. "That is what your brother presumes." And pain. He'd lost himself in pain.

Never turn your back on those who are suffering, poppet.

The reminder, given to her by her father with the arrival of each midnight patient, pinged around her mind, sending guilt through her.

"What about you?" His Grace pressed. "What is your assessment of your own abilities?" There was a faint thread underlying his words. One tinged with… hope that the gentleman himself likely couldn't hear and didn't know. And she despised with every fiber of her being the heightened attunement her father had called a gift, but now proved very much to be a curse.

Elsie contemplated the doorway, yearning to put the heavy oak panel between her… and this world of treachery and darkness she'd vowed to never again be part of. She briefly closed her eyes, damning the lessons ingrained into her by her father. She opened her eyes and looked up at the towering gentleman. "There is no proper reply I can give to that question." At his questioning look, Elsie lifted her shoulders in a little shrug. "To proclaim myself my father's equal in skill"—which would be false in every way—"would mark me conceited, and that level of conceit would diminish any capabilities I might otherwise possess. But to insist none of his talents transferred would suggest I was inadequate."

He pierced her with his obsidian gaze, that probing stare capable of stealing secrets that he had no right to but would command at a whim if he so wished.

"You are correct," he said at last, the admission unexpected. "It's my jaw. I broke it a year ago."

Elsie waited for him to say more on it, but he shared nothing else. "I… see." And yet, she didn't. Questions remained about how he'd sustained the wound, details she'd wager he'd tell her to go to hell if she dared ask about. "I venture your…" *Pain.* She called the word back. All animals took umbrage with the world witnessing or knowing of their suffering. "…mouth and head are also afflicted by the previous injury."

A muscle ticked at the corner of his right eye. He gave a tight, infinitesimal nod. "You have three weeks," he said flatly, striding past her and stopping at the door. "Let us hope you are as skilled as they say, Miss Allenby," he murmured as he drew the door open.

Gooseflesh climbed along her arms, and as Elsie took her leave, she could not dispel the sense that she'd just made the same deal with the Devil her father had all those years ago.

CHAPTER 5

LATER THAT NIGHT, THE HOUSE long abed and sleep still his enemy, William sprawled on the too-small-for-his-frame leather button sofa in his office.

This marked the one space that had proven safe this past year, for it was the one place she'd never stepped foot within. He'd given the command, in gentle tones, that she not visit him when he was overseeing matters of business, and she'd simply accepted that directive. Because that was who his late wife had been. She'd been demure and obedient, relegating herself to the cheerful sunlit parlors, where she tended her needlepoint and entertained Society's leading hostesses.

No, Adeline had been nothing like the spitfire who'd invaded William's chambers that morning. A woman who couldn't be bothered with a polite form of address or a curtsy and, had his understanding of her intentions been correct, had wanted nothing to do with overseeing his "care," as she'd humiliatingly put it.

For the first time in a year, it was not guilt or the memory of a wife whose face was losing its clarity in his mind that occupied his thoughts… but rather, Miss Allenby.

Miss Allenby, whose first name he still did not know.

It felt like a betrayal of sorts, comparing the two and finding the woman he'd loved and promised to care for second in any regard. Because his wife had not possessed the skills most needed to survive. She'd been delicate. A refined lady in every way, such that she'd been horrified on the rare occasions that silverware was slightly askew before a household of guests.

She'd been all golden perfection, and he'd been completely entranced by her beauty. And then he'd courted her, against his own best judgment as the Sovereign. Delicately blushing and given to discourse about mundane matters on which the security of the Crown and its subjects weren't dependent, she'd been so unlike any other in his world that he'd been bewitched from their first meeting.

That moment and the subsequent ones to follow with Adeline had been so very much like the first time he, as an eight-year-old boy, had stepped inside The Pot and Pineapple. As a ducal heir whose father was friend to the king, the world had been laid out before him. One morning, a private appointment had been granted whereby William, accompanied by his nursemaid, had received a personal showing and tasting of the exotic wet sweetmeats, ices, and custards. Foreign. Unique. He'd been confused and entranced, at the same time, by each dessert presented.

The selfishness on his part, the taste he'd had and enjoyed of her innocence, had left Adeline vulnerable.

He'd allowed her to live in a fictitious world as though she and William were any other proper lord and lady, when in truth they'd never been that. It had been a secret she'd not been privy to, and she'd not pressed him on details about business or life outside of social events and house décor.

"I believe you mean 'unfailingly.' Either way, I'm one who speaks only the truth."

The lilting, singsong quality of Miss Allenby's voice had not erased the layer of steel and strength to it, and William had been shockingly enticed by it—and haunted ever since. She'd displayed a mix of authority and womanly softness, a seeming contradiction that had emerged more as an erotic melding.

A knock sounded at the door. *Rap-rap-rap.*

That one-two-three quick signal of Home Office business.

All enticing thoughts of Miss Allenby faded.

Bloody, bloody hell.

William scrubbed a hand over eyes that were dry from days of sleeplessness.

They would not leave him be. But then, that was what happened when one sold one's life and soul to the devil. In this case, the devil had proven to be the king himself, and William had traded all in service to that great liege.

What had once filled him with honor and excitement was met with a now familiar annoyance.

The four o'clock hour had long been the hour of the Brethren. It was the time at which members of Polite Society abandoned their inane revelries and sought out their elegant townhouses. Those who did not—the rogues, rakes, and rapscallions—could be found at their clubs, or wandering the streets drunken and unknowing that their very safety and security was owed them by lords who were alert and always working.

Rap-rap-rap.

They'd enter anyway. Oh, they'd put on a display, honoring time-old respect shown a *duke*. But William's rank of Sovereign superseded even that.

After one more of those staccato announcements, Stone let himself inside and bowed. "You've company, Your Grace."

Wordlessly, Cedric Bennett, the Delegator of the Brethren, entered. Second only to William in position and power within the organization, Bennett was responsible for evaluating missions and handing assignments out to men best suited. "Your Grace," he greeted as the other man took his leave and closed the door behind him. A familiar folder in hand, Bennett rooted himself at the door, waiting for the command.

Because that was what their world was based on: rank and orders.

William shoved himself upright, his muscles screaming in protest of the abrupt shift after hours of a prone state.

He strode across the room, taking up a seat at his desk. His desk, once tidy, had over the year become overrun with papers that no servant could touch and that William didn't care one way or the other about.

Using his action as an invitation, Bennett strode forward, his black cloak whipping angrily about his ankles. He stopped before William's desk. His gaze crept along first the cluttered space and then the thick growth covering William's cheeks. The other man's distaste for both untidy states was reflected in his sneer. "I require your seal," he finally said, settling himself onto the leather winged chair across from William.

That was one thing William still appreciated about those who served in the Brethren. They did not bother with formalities or pleasantries. All that compelled them in any matter was their business on behalf of the Crown. Even the attempts to find one who'd help rid William of his debilitating pain was driven by the need for William to assume the responsibilities for which he'd taken an oath. His own brother was included in those ranks.

Wordlessly, William tugged open the center desk drawer. His fingers found the clever latch inside in an act made rote for the decade of service he'd served in this role, and it gave way with a quiet *click*. Fishing out the ink and seal, he set them atop a stack of ledgers.

William continued through the motions. He leaned over, and with the taper held between his thumb and forefinger, he held it above the lamp stand precariously situated at the edge of his desk. He held the wax above the candle, so it barely touched the point of the flame. When it was soft on all sides, he drew his arm back too quickly, and crimson droplets splashed several of his leather folios.

He felt Bennett's stare taking in every movement. "You've no questions about the assignment you've just put your seal to?"

"I don't give a damn." William turned through the pages written in Bennett's hand, finding the next place requiring the Brethren seal. He set the page aside where it might cool and continued on to the next.

"You have to give a damn. It is your role."

"It's a role I don't want," he gritted out.

Bennett abandoned his negligent pose. Uncrossing his knee, the broader man sat forward. "Regardless, the terms are clear. Only death or madness can sever your role."

Madness.

He let that word roll around his brain.

He'd witnessed all number of men and women reduced to that very state. Miserable souls locked away in Bedlam, destroyed by a disease of their mind.

He was not vastly different from those pitiable bastards, incapable of feeling, caring. Ruled by pain and the reminders of his own failings.

"You are not mad," Bennett said coolly, correctly following the path William's thoughts had traversed. With his flinty stare and life-hardened eyes, Bennett would never, ever be mistaken for offering any kind of assurance meant to calm. It was given as a matter-of-fact, from one fixed not on William's well-being but on his status within the organization. "As such, your role and service… continue."

A vise clenched, tightened, and squeezed, over and over. This was to be his hell. A prison he could not be free of. A role he could not separate himself from. Instead, he'd be forced to serve at the mercy of a king who honored the time-old history of the Brethren.

Returning to his task, William grabbed the puce and sprinkled the powder upon his marks, lightly blowing on them. "Now get out," he ordered in gravelly tones when he'd finished.

RUN, POPPET, RUN

Gasping for breath, Elsie sprang up. Her chest moving fast and hard, she struggled with the sheets tangled about her. She did a frantic sweep of the darkened chambers, searching out the one who'd hunted her.

She blinked, struggling to make sense of the surroundings.

A quiet whine cut through her panic. "Bear," she whispered, solely to hear the sound of her own voice as reality came trickling in. It wasn't her father's assailants after her, but rather, a different threat. No less dangerous territory she'd willingly stepped foot into.

Bear rested his enormous head on the edge of her mattress and lapped at her fingers. She immediately stroked the place between his ears until a low rumble of appreciation met her efforts. "What time is it?" she asked her faithful, aging companion.

He nuzzled his wet nose into her palm.

"That's hardly a response," she chided. Squinting, she attempted to bring the silver and colorful enamel clock atop the mantel into focus. She blinked several times. "Surely not."

Not even eighteen minutes had passed since she'd closed her eyes and at last managed to sleep.

Elsie collapsed back into the folds of the feather mattress and stared at the mural overhead, the clouds, trellises, and pink roses vivid enough one might actually believe oneself tucked away in a far-flung, forgotten corner of the English countryside.

The sleeplessness that had plagued her these past five years reared its head once more, robbing her of desperately needed rest and leaving her only nightmares and horror-laden memories for company. And when they came, nothing could shake them free.

But here, there were no animals awaiting her care whom she could visit and see to in the dead of night. Nor herb gardens to tend, with the moon illuminating her works and allowing an illusory vision of daylight.

No, there was no hint of English countryside or calming ease to be found in this household.

The Duke of Aubrey's visage flashed forward.

Elsie shivered, and huddling deeper into the blankets, she allowed herself to think of her patient.

He'd not been as she'd expected.

The man his brother had made him out to be was one bedbound and physically incapacitated.

The Duke of Aubrey, despite the tangible pain caused by wounds he'd not speak of, possessed an aura of strength. A power that made it too easy for one seeing to his care to fix on. But who was he? This duke who served the secretive division within the Home Office? Those peers, by the very nature of their titles, didn't see to anything beyond their own comforts and pleasures, and yet, not only had he joined the Brethren, but he served as a leader.

He was a man with secrets, and though he'd insisted she remain and oversee his recovery, Elsie could not manage such a feat unless she knew more about him. And his past and everything that had brought him to this point.

And then she would be free of this place and, God willing, these people and their all-powerful organization.

Her vision now adjusted to the dark, Elsie stole another, clearer glance at the clock.

Four o'clock is when the world sleeps and the sheep cease bleating.

It is the time that birds fall silent and the earth gives way to quiet.

The hour of…

"Peace." She whispered the nighttime poem her father had murmured to her as a small girl when dark dreams had awakened her. Back when those darkest dreams had been made up only of pretend monsters and imagined demons. Before life had invariably shown her what real nightmares were made of.

Elsie pushed herself upright. Mindful of Bear at her feet, she swung her legs over the side and climbed down from the half-tester bed. The plush, ornate Aubusson carpet muted her steps as she crossed to the Venetian carved mirror. Plucking her cotton wrapper from the gilded bird along the top, Elsie shrugged into the article and, as she belted it at the waist, made her way to the door.

Panting with excitement, Bear trotted over.

"Aww, pup," she said gently. Elsie sank to a knee and rubbed the tip of his silken ear between her fingers. "You know the rules."

He whined in canine protest and nosed at her skirts.

"I venture first and determine if it is safe for the both of us." It was a rule she'd put into effect after the night their lives had been upended. The then-younger dog had kept pace with her as she'd bolted through dense brush and forests, until he'd been felled by a bullet meant for her. Elsie's fingers automatically found the scar along his left side. He'd merely been grazed, but the blood loss had nearly killed him. Caring for him had sustained her in those immediate days. She swallowed past a ball of emotion in her throat. "What would I do without you?" she asked hoarsely. Because, when he was gone, then she would be well and truly… alone. Alone in ways she hadn't been even when her father had perished.

Bear wiggled his massive body and plopped himself down. Leveling his large, dark eyes on her face, he dropped his head between his paws and stared accusatorily up.

Giving her head a shake, she dispelled the useless lamentations. Hadn't her own father's murder proven that no one person had the promise of any one day?

"It is for your own good," she promised and sprang to her feet. With an uncharacteristic obstinacy, Bear planted himself between her and the door. "Oh, fine, you troublesome fellow." She softened the rebuke with another stroke of his ears. With Bear at her side, Elsie collected the candlestick and set off to explore the duke's residence.

Holding the delicate, hand-painted porcelain chamber stick close, Elsie wound her way through the hallways. She took in every detail of the duke's household. Everything, from the pale pink hall carpets, to the matching pink hyacinth silk wallpaper, to the white alabaster statues of The Three Graces, bore an air of femininity that did not fit with the masculine figure who dwelled here.

Knock. Knock. Knock.

She jumped, losing her grip on the chamber stick. It clattered to the floor, splashing wax over the immaculate carpet.

Cursing quietly, she dropped to her knees and patted out the faint flickering of flame. A damning black burn mark met her efforts. At another time, mayhap in the light of a new day, she'd be filled with proper horror and remorse at sullying a duke's lavish residence. On unsteady feet, she rose, her gaze trained in the direction of the odd pounding.

Knock. Knock. Knock.

There it was again.

Elsie closed her eyes.

Run, poppet… Run…

Bear pushed his nose into her side, and its damp touch penetrated her thin skirts.

She wetted her lips. *Return to your rooms. Better yet… leave this home altogether.*

Knock. Knock. Knock. Knock. Knock.

Drawn toward the errant, untimed beat, Elsie drifted silently down the hall and then stopped.

A door hung partially opened, jammed by a branch.

"A branch," she mouthed. Her earlier terror lifted, and compelled this time by a far safer intrigue, Elsie walked the remaining steps to that door.

Bear, who'd followed at her side, promptly sank onto his heels beside her.

Pushing the panel open, she peeked outside.

Her breath caught.

Bear sat upright with a like appreciation, his entire body poised to rush forward, and yet, he restrained himself.

"Gardens," she whispered. A tangled, overgrown space of untended trees and flowers and weeds. At first glance, one might even believe oneself upon an uninhabited swatch of land in the wilds of Bladon. Everything from these grounds to belongings scattered throughout the household bore the touch of a woman. Yet there was no duchess? Or had each piece and detail been selected within part of some larger plot at confusing the outside world about the activities that went on in this place?

Bear emitted a small whine.

"What is it?" she whispered, reluctantly drawing the door closed.

His hackles up, his ears raised, Bear stared down the left hall, his gaze fixed.

She shivered, and for the first time since she'd begun her exploration, an uneasiness rooted around her belly. "Come," she urged. "We'll return tomorrow, I promise."

Except, Bear remained fixed not on the outside grounds that had pulled him moments ago, but on something… or someone in the opposite direction.

"Bear," she urged once more.

He lunged to his feet and took off running.

Bloody hell.

Elsie grabbed her skirts and chased after her dog.

This was the last place one wished to be caught snooping. As she raced down the corridor, her breath came hard not from exertions but from panic. Nor did the unease have anything to do with the fact that a duke resided here, but rather, a member of that ruthless organization. "Bear," she entreated.

Suddenly, he stopped. The dog nudged his head at the door.

"No," she mouthed.

He nudged his head again and let out a keening whine.

Oh, blast and damn. Raising a finger to her lips, she pressed her ear to the panel and strained for a hint of sound within the rooms. Only the muted ring of silence met her.

"There is no one in there," she assured him.

Or I've been heard.

As that ominous possibility crept in, another wave of cold racked her, and she drew her robe more tightly about her person. *I've done nothing wrong. I've merely explored this residence they'd make me call home for the next three weeks.*

Wetting her lips, Elsie raised her palm. She hovered her fist inches from the panel.

Rap-pause-rap-pause. Rap-rap.

She waited, breath held, for… something.

When no greeting was called out, she glanced down. His head tilted back, Bear's wide brown eyes met her gaze. "I told you," she mouthed. "Now, let us go."

Except… Bear lifted a paw.

"I knocked," she insisted in hushed tones.

He gave her one of his familiar accusatory, wide-eyed stares.

"Fine." Gritting her teeth, Elsie tried the handle.

It gave with a surprising ease, and the door swung wide on well-oiled hinges.

She paused. Had the room been of any importance, its master would have surely seen the door locked…

"See? There is no one here. Nothing here. Now let us—" Bear surged ahead, entering the rooms.

Cursing one of the more inventive words introduced to her by one of her father's long-ago patients, Elsie hurried into the room and closed the door behind her.

This was all she needed. To be caught snooping about His Grace's…

She glanced around the well-lit space and cursed again.

His offices. She'd invaded his offices. "It is time to go," she repeated, this time more firmly, doing a search for her dog.

And finding him.

Her heart sank.

From where he lounged on the leather button sofa, the Duke of Aubrey rested a large, menacing palm upon Bear's head. A dangerous grin iced hard, unyielding lips. "Miss Allenby," he said frostily. "How very *unexpected* to see you here."

Bloody hell. "Your Grace," she returned in measured tones. How was she so calm?

"Now," he went on, swinging his legs over the side of the sofa. "Why don't you begin first by telling me how you know 'that' and then explaining what the hell you're doing here."

CHAPTER 6

ELSIE ALLENBY KNEW THE KNOCK.

It had been a perfectly mastered *rap-pause-rap-pause, rap-rap* used only by members of the Brethren.

He didn't believe for a moment that it was any mere coincidence.

And the mysterious chit traveled with an ugly mutt that was more bear than dog. He flicked his gaze on the bored-looking creature, assessed him, and then shifted his attention over to the more threatening figure.

William stood slowly, and the young woman took one step backward, enough so she needn't crane her head to look at him, but no more than would indicate she sought to flee.

At her silence, William arched an eyebrow. "How did you know that?" he demanded again when she still said nothing.

"Know what?"

"Your rapping, Miss Allenby." He drifted closer, stealing the space she'd sought to build between them.

"You heard me." His early-morn visitor folded her arms at a mutinous set. "Why didn't you answer if you heard knocking?"

God, she was feisty. It lent an enchanting color to her olive-hued cheeks. "Because I did not want to be bothered," he drawled.

She didn't blink for several moments. "Oh. Uh… fair enough."

That absolute lack of artifice threw into question his immediate opinion of moments ago that she was some recent addition to the ranks of the Brethren. That would have, of course, explained her presence here, why Edward had trusted her and brought her here. But her inability to dissemble made a mockery of his earlier assumption. And yet… how to explain her knowledge of that rapping? He frowned, leveling a hard gaze on her face. "Do you truly expect me to believe the manner in which you announced your arrival was in any way… a coincidence?"

She darted her tongue out, trailing the enticing tip of pink flesh around the seam of her lips. He'd known the woman less than a day and gathered that telltale gesture of her nervousness. It had been essential that he hone such an assessment of a person over his career with the Home Office.

This, however, this pulled at him, sucked him under whatever siren's spell the damned imp possessed. Small, dark-haired, she bore no hint of the statuesque beauty of his late wife, and subsequent lovers.

It was her spirit. There was no other accounting for the maddening rush of desire that flooded him at her every challenge.

"Hmm?" he urged.

"I did not know there was a question there."

William collected her forearm, ringing a soft gasp from the lady.

The dog, previously relegated to the forgotten, pricked its ears up between them. "Do not play games with me, Miss Allenby," he warned, placing his lips close to her ear. Some citrusy scent that was neither lemon nor orange, but a melding of both, wafted about him, and he resisted its pull. "No one," he whispered. "I'll repeat just once, no one ever enters these rooms."

The long, graceful column of her throat bobbed. "Your office," she said, her voice threadbare.

She'd known as much when she'd set foot inside, then. He abruptly released her, and she drew that limb close to her side, away from his reach.

"Tell me, what business could you have here, in this room, at this hour?"

"I was unable to sleep," she said softly. The swiftness of that somber admission foretold truth. This stranger his brother had brought into William's household had demons she fought, too.

"You are not allowed in here."

"I'm here to see to your care." She stared at him as if she'd somehow ended the matter with that single pronouncement.

"And, Miss Allenby?" he snapped.

"I cannot properly do so without having access to the areas and aspects of life important to you."

"Rubbish."

"If you think it is rubbish, then you won't trust in my methods, and I therefore cannot help you."

Which brought him back to the question about who in blazes Miss No-First-Name Allenby in fact was.

"What is your name?"

"My name?" Her eyes flared ever so slightly. "Allenby." Again, she stared at him with that expectant little expression that suggested he should know who she was.

He searched his mind.

For, no doubt, he should know her through some connection with the Brethren. That would account for her familiarity with the knock and her borderline-mad degree of brashness. He'd pull those secrets from her. "What is your Christian name, madam?" The ease at distracting an adversary fell effortlessly into place, as if he had not spent nearly a year shut away from the world and his work. And how very good it felt. He felt… alive. It had been so very long, and it was surely a betrayal of his late wife.

So why were his thoughts not on Adeline but on the mysterious creature before him?

The young woman's eyes darkened. "I do not see how my Christian name is relevant."

"Isn't it?" he retorted. "Come, Miss Allenby, you cannot have it both ways, needing access to my personal rooms and artifacts and life… while keeping up barriers yourself."

"Ah, yes. But I neither require nor sought intervention."

"Don't you?" He'd wager his duchy and everything unentailed that went with it that she needed help as much as he did. Mayhap more. Her secrets were reflected in a troubled gaze better suited to the most seasoned agents who served the Home Office.

Miss Allenby blanched and fluttered a hand about her chest.

"I at the very least see the struggles I contend with and own them." He winced. This day, between the minx who tested him at every turn and two meetings with the Brethren, he'd already spoken more than he had in the whole of the damned year. His jaw, mouth, and head throbbed in protest. Feeling the young woman's too-clever stare on his mouth and recalling her earlier insight into his body's slightest movements, he forcibly repressed the need to move under that scrutiny.

Another person would have grown indignant and no doubt challenged his presumption, regardless of the level of truth to it. "My name is Elsie," she said softly.

It was an allowance she'd made out of pity, a hateful, hated, and increasingly familiar sentiment he'd received from all those in his damned life. As such, he wanted to tell her to go to hell with it.

And yet, her lyrical tones continued to work their hypnotic pull.

"Elsie." He wrapped that word around his tongue and mind.

She lifted her chin. "Elspeth, but I've only ever been Elsie."

She'd taken his lack of response as judgment. Rather, the shorter variant suited her. Far more than that more formal, more common one from which it was derived. Diminutive, delicate, and even with her name, the spirited stranger refused to be constrained by the formality the world would insist upon. No, Elsie Allenby would resist all rules and conventions. "Very well. Elsie, then." He motioned to the chair occupied earlier by Bennett.

Elsie followed the gesture and hesitated for the span of a heartbeat before crossing the room and settling her slender frame into the oversized chair.

How easily she went where he now led. It challenged the idea that she was linked to the Brethren and stirred all the more questions about her.

William sat and, bracing his steepled fingers under his chin, met her direct stare. "I am William."

"Does it help you?" she asked.

He puzzled his brow.

"Bracing it as you speak." Elsie mimicked his positioning and stared at him with that damned inquisitive gaze.

His neck went hot.

"Most would not notice," she quickly reassured. "I only did—"

"Because you treat horses and badgers and magpies," he gritted out through compressed lips, forcing the string of words out past the agony throbbing along his jawline.

"Interestingly, I've never cared for a magpie."

"I was being sarcastic, Miss Allenby," he said coolly.

"I believe we settled on first names, William." A pleased smile graced her lips and then was promptly gone.

The truth slammed into William with the same force of the carriage he'd been hurled from a year earlier. "Why, why… That is what you wanted all along, isn't it?"

She inclined her head. "It is always better for the patient to believe he… or she is in control," she said with raw honesty.

William snapped his eyebrows into a single line. By God… "Did you just liken me to your equine patients?" Now, a second time.

Elsie lifted her narrow shoulders in a little shrug. "I indicated they were the only patients I have personally attended without assistance."

Why, this whole time, the clever chit was the one in control of this discussion, which was not really a discussion. He'd even venture she herself would have wanted them to be in possession of each other's first names. He narrowed his eyes. "How pleased you must be with yourself." Outwitted by a… What was she exactly? Who was she? His intrigue grew.

Elsie folded her hands upon her lap in a false display of demureness. "I'd be far more pleased if it was three weeks from now and I was making my return, while you were suffering less from your pain," she confessed.

He sat back in his chair, and this time, the exertions of the dialogue won out. William cradled his jaw, rubbing it in a useless bid to rid himself of the agony.

All the while, his head swam at the young woman's directness. He was confused by it. Nay, by *her*. The spitfire was a rarity, an oddity he didn't know what to do with. By the very nature of his work and title, those he'd kept company with through the years, his own wife included, treated any discourse with him as though it were a chessboard. Lords and ladies, the men and women he dealt with in the Home Office, did not say what they truly wished, or what they were thinking.

Elsie Allenby, however, did—and did so with an impressive bluntness.

The pulsing in his jaw said he should send her on her way. Only… he was unwilling to end his exchange with the spirited minx. "You do not wish to be here, and yet, my brother compelled you to come anyway."

"No one compels me to do anything," she said with a resolute steel in the retort. "I came of my own choice."

"Is that self-choice what also had you wandering my halls and invading my office?"

She blinked, and he reveled in at last knocking her from the perch of control over this discourse. "I already told you…"

"Yes, you were unable to sleep." William dropped his elbows atop his knees and leaned forward. "What gives a young lady such as yourself nightmares?"

Her cheeks drained of color. "I never said anything about nightmares."

"What else would keep a person from peaceful sleep?" he persisted, arching an eyebrow.

She glanced down at her hands, and given his height advantage over her, he was afforded an unrestricted view of his nighttime visitor. Elsie clenched her hands together so tightly that her knuckles went as white as her modest wrapper and nightshift.

He waited, allowing her the time. It was a small concession that put her back in a place of power so that she might continue.

The young woman drew in a noisy breath through her teeth and nodded once, as if seeking to assure herself. She picked her head up. "I will tell you," she said quietly, her once-lyrical tones now haunting and eerie for their emptiness. A chill scraped through his insides. He leaned forward. "If you are willing to also share yours," she added.

She wanted… She thought… He scoffed. "You expect me to freely reveal my circumstances to you, a stranger?"

"No," she corrected. "That is what *you* expect, William. I expect we should come to know one another first, without any expectations or demands placed." Elsie pushed back her chair. "I'll not be interrogated. I'm not a criminal. I'm not a member of your ranks." He stiffened. She knew of the Brethren. "I know enough," she confirmed, unerringly following his musings. "I'm not a young woman. I'm not a spy. I'm nearly thirty-one years old. A healer of animals who joined your brother to see if I can provide a like assistance to you. Now, instead of playing these… games, where you seek to outmaneuver me, I suggest you choose honesty and trust."

With that, the young woman swept from the room, her dog at her side, and left William staring at the door long after she'd gone.

CHAPTER 7

"I PROMISED WE'D COME BACK, and we have."

The following afternoon, Elsie availed herself of the duke's grounds and cared for his long-neglected gardens.

Bear whimpered.

"That isn't what this is about, then," she muttered.

He barked once, the deep rumble sending several finches scattering from their various perches throughout the gardens.

Elsie got to the heart of the matter with her canine companion. "Last evening," she went on, "was peculiar."

Bear whined.

"Oh, hush," Elsie chided, snipping back an overgrown mint bush. "Surely you knew we'd eventually talk about it. The situation was peculiar." A breeze gusted through the grounds, stirring errant leaves that had not been tended in too long. She paused in her task and gave Bear a pointed look. "You do not take to anyone like that."

The dog wiggled back and forth on his belly and bowed his head between his front paws as he shuffled toward her across the threadbare grass.

"I'm not looking for apologies," she clarified. She was looking to understand. Bear's loyalty was, and always had been, first and foremost to Elsie. Since he'd been a pup, the dog had never ignored her, and he'd certainly never rushed headlong into possible peril, with her chasing after.

She sat back on her haunches. "You knew I was safe," she murmured, her gaze on the ivy climbing along the aged brick at the back wall. He'd sensed she wouldn't be harmed. Or mayhap, more… He'd sensed William needed him more in that instant. Her nape tingled, and she straightened. Someone watched her even now. Undoubtedly, there was any number of people it could be in this particular residence, but an innate knowing said that stare belonged to him. From under the wide brim of the straw hat that had once belonged to her mother, Elsie stole a peek at William's townhouse.

Since Lord Edward had entered her cottage with talks of his brother, Elsie had been gripped by wonderings about the gentleman. What had previously been a detached interest had shifted the moment she'd entered his chambers. His lean frame revealed evidence of a physical struggle, but the haunted glint in his eyes, a glimmer she suspected the gentleman himself did not know he possessed, had pierced her, ushering forth questions. About him. His past. And the demons that kept him from leaving his townhouse or resuming whatever role he served with the organization Elsie so hated.

Only, where her father's patients had eyed her presence at their bedside with skepticism, and insisted upon only Francis Allenby's care, the duke hadn't even flinched at the prospect of her overseeing his healing.

A wry grin played at her lips. Rather, he'd chafed at the idea of needing anyone—her included.

Elsie's smile slipped. For even with that, in the end, he'd still insisted she remain. He'd turned his care over to her.

Bear's hackles went up.

Tugging free her hat, Elsie wiped the back of her arm over her damp brow.

She had company.

From behind her, the faint crunch of gravel hinted at his approach, the footfall too heavy to belong to a child or woman and assured enough to hint at his power.

Elsie's fingers tightened about her rusted pruning shears. There had been other men with heavy footfalls. Ones who had charged after her as she'd bolted through Bladon. Angry shouts had dogged her steps, from a pair determined to silence her.

"What are you doing, Miss Allenby?"

Lord Edward's terse greeting was not one born of anger but proved safer. For it… he was real, and there was nothing he nor anyone could take from her.

"I think it should be fairly obvious, Lord Edward." Elsie clipped back the lilac tree, and the soft purple flowers rained to the ground. One of the buds hit Bear on the tail, and he snapped his head up. "I am seeing to your brother's gardens." She'd originally set out to assess and avail herself of the herbs present, but the neglect of this space had called for more.

Lord Edward yanked his hat off, slapping it against his leg as he went. "I've not brought you here to garden," he said tightly, stopping so close that Bear ambled onto all fours and inserted himself between Elsie and the irate gentleman.

"It is fine," she promised, snapping her fingers three times.

Bear trotted past Lord Edward and found a spot on a softer patch of earth. All the while, his large ears remained perked, on alert. As soon as he'd settled, Elsie returned her attentions to the overgrown bush. She cut the front portion of the flowering shrub, the rusty clip of her scissors inordinately loud.

The moment one relinquished all control to these men, the moment they pounced… and won.

"I believe I was clear in what role you'd serve here," William's brother snapped. "And this, madam?" He slashed his black top hat around the grounds. "Was not among your responsibilities."

Elsie made a show of cleaning the pruning shears along the front of her apron and then set them back in the small basket next to her. She stood and finally faced Lord Edward.

His frown deepened. "Do you have nothing to say?"

"You have your men spying on me," she noted with false casualness. She'd been naïve before. She was not so much a fool that she wasn't aware precisely the company she now kept.

Lord Edward drew back, aghast.

"Was that not what you expected me to say, Lord Edward?" she drawled, dusting her muddied palms together.

His cheeks turned a mottled red. "No, it is not."

"Ah." She stretched that single syllable out. "Very well, then." Elsie rested her hands upon her stained apron.

Lord Edward frowned. "What are you on about?"

"Well, it is just that… the same way you've determined where I should spend my time here, perhaps you'd care to instead tell me what you also expect me to say in this instance."

His flush deepened. "I'm not amused by you, Miss Allenby."

"I didn't seek to amuse you."

The gentleman continued speaking over her. "I expected you to give me a full reporting on my brother's condition and a determination of what treatment you might provide and his prognosis of recovering."

In less than a day's time? A soft laugh escaped her.

Lord Edward's eyebrows snapped together. "Have I said something to amuse you?"

She'd be a fool to bait anyone who managed that lethal whisper. And yet, she didn't seek to get a rise out of him.

"You've unreal expectations for me… and of me. I've been here just a day. In that time, I've met your brother but once."

"It should have been more."

Elsie folded her arms at her chest. "And do you trust the duke would have allowed me unfettered access to both him and his time? Furthermore," she continued before he could speak. "If that is the erroneous judgment you have of His Grace, then I suggest you leave the handling of his care in its entirety"—she touched a hand to her chest—"to me."

His eyelid ticked. "I expect a report on his condition by tomorrow evening, Miss Allenby."

With that, he jammed his hat atop his head and stalked off.

Elsie stared after him, carefully following his retreating form with her eyes until he'd gone. At another time, she might have become indignant at Lord Edward's presumptions. As a younger woman helping her father care for countless number of wounded villagers and men with the Home Office, she'd bristled on his and her own behalf at such audacity. That, however, had been before. After her father's death, she'd learned what desperation was and the many layers of that bleak sentiment.

As such, she saw it in both men: the hurt, angry duke and his brother, determined to see him rid of pain.

That familial bond made her patient real in ways she didn't want him to be. It was far safer and easier to see him as the icy, indifferent member of the Brethren, who didn't give a jot about anything or anyone outside their ranks.

Her nape tingled once more.

Elsie glanced up, casting a hand over her eyes to blot out the glaring afternoon sun. This time, she stared boldly up at the duke's chambers, searching for a glimpse of him, knowing a man in his role would be skilled enough to hide himself in plain sight, if he so wished.

Bear licked her fingers.

She glanced down at her dog and favored him with a loving stroke. "Well, that went a good deal better than I'd expected," she said dryly. "Now, shall we continue our work?"

Dropping to her knees, she fetched her pruning shears once more and carried on with her earlier work.

NO ONE HAD SET FOOT in the gardens since his wife died.

Nor had there been any attempt from his servants to do so. Those in his household understood those grounds had belonged to Adeline. When William had awakened in these very chambers after two months of unconsciousness and learned all over again of his wife's murder, he'd found those once-cherished gardens in disarray.

Mayhap it had been unspoken agreement… or perhaps it had been an order.

Either way, no one entered that sacrosanct space.

Until now.

Now, there had been two.

William studied the door his brother had made an angry exit through and dismissed it… and him and instead fixed on the figure who'd commanded his attention that morning and afternoon.

Elsie, her attention trained on a wild lilac bush, reached for one of the aged tools laid out. But first, her fingers found that ugly mutt, stroking his head with a loving affection. Then she brought her arms up to snip back the branches that had grown so long they'd formed an arch overhanging the stone walkway.

Where was the rage at this stranger, this interloper, being in that most sacred of places?

Because you are intrigued by the minx. You don't know what to make of this person who slipped into your household like one who had a right to it. A woman who also thinks nothing of sullying her hands.

His late wife… she had never herself sat upon the earth and overtaken the care of that place. She'd hired masterful gardeners, whom she'd cheerfully greeted each morning, asking after their plans, discussing her own ideas for the gardens.

On the occasion the urns had required fresh flowers, she'd snipped them and placed them into a basket held by a waiting servant.

Not for the first time, Elsie paused to cast some words over at the slumbering dog beside her. He rubbed a palm contemplatively over his mouth, tapping his finger against his bearded cheek.

Mayhap she was mad. That would certainly explain all her eccentricities. It was after all so very easy for one to confuse stupidity with courage, and she'd been nothing if not inordinately brave since she'd entered his rooms.

He furrowed his brow. What point had the minx been debating with his brother? By Edward's flushed cheeks and angry gait, William would wager she'd come out the victor.

Direct. Undaunted. Fearless. She embodied everything ladies of the peerage were not. Including Adeline. He'd fallen in love with her for the air of gentility to her. It had been a breath of fresh air for one whose very nature of work required him to immerse himself in darkness. And this… admiring Elsie Allenby, finding himself spellbound, felt like a betrayal to his late wife's memory.

William squeezed his eyes shut. He was a bastard. There was no other accounting for this fascination with the woman who'd first invaded his home and now Adeline's gardens.

He opened his eyes and froze.

Elsie had moved to tend another bush, this one an explosion of wildly overgrown pale pink roses.

A curse ripped from his chest, and with a thundering shout of fury, William stormed from the rooms in his stockinged feet.

The handful of Brethren guards, acting now as servants, widened their eyes as he sprinted past them, sans jacket, his tangled black hair whipping like a lion's mane about his scruffy cheeks.

They think me mad…

Good, then perhaps the king would at least free William of his responsibilities. Enlivened with every angry step that brought him closer to the damned interloper, William lengthened his stride.

At last, he was filled with a suitable outrage for this woman his brother had thrust into William's household.

How dare she?

He panted, his chest heaving from the exertion of storming through his own household, hating himself for that weakness. Hating Elsie Allenby for forcing him to see just how weak he'd become.

William stumbled to a stop, catching himself hard against the doorjamb of the outdoor gardens. Yanking the door open, he recoiled.

Sunlight blared bright into the dimly lit halls, momentarily blinding him. He brought his arms protectively about his face, shielding himself from the offense.

Pinpricks of tiny spherical light danced behind his eyes, and he jammed his palms into the sockets. The dots continued to dance and float there.

Panic set in, holding him in its cruel snare, a vulnerability that came from his weakened state and the knowledge of what fate awaited those whose guard came down.

"It is better if you relax." Elsie's soothing, singsong tone ripped across his tumult.

William forced his arms back down to his sides and fought to adjust to the sunlight.

Squinting, he did a sweep and found her precisely where he'd last spied her… snipping at that pink rosebush.

Clip.

"Your eyes, that is," Elsie clarified. "If you attain relaxation, the need for squinting will lessen. If you continue to squint, it will only strain your eyes."

He rocked back. *Attain relaxation.* What in blazes did that even mean?

She paused in her pruning and brushed the back of her forearm across her perspiring brow. "You'll have to find out what that means for you," she murmured, following with an unerring accuracy his very thoughts.

Further entranced by the lyrical pull of her voice, William squinted and then immediately tried to calm those muscles. "How does a woman come to be skilled in matters pertaining to vision?" he barked. With every meeting, the questions about this woman surpassed any answers he received about her.

Under the brim of a heinous bonnet, her eyes sparkled. "I trust the same way any man does. Through observation of one's eyesight on sunlit days."

He frowned.

Elsie matched that with an answering smile, that dimpled her sun-kissed cheeks in an expression of such pure warmth it tore up his earlier anger and reason for being here. "I would recommend you gradually become accustomed to the sunlight by being outdoors more than you have been." With that pronouncement, she angled her body dismissively and clipped another branch.

Pink rose petals rained down about her like teardrops.

William... I c-cannot... I l-love...

He squeezed his eyes shut as guilt battered at him. Adeline had rasped those disjointed, gurgling words while he lay there beside her, able to move only his head, before it had all faded to black—that day, her life, his existence.

"Are you all right, William?" The sound of his name on the spitfire's lips pierced the horrors, her query somber and concerned, when it was safer for him if she were her challenging, vexing self.

He forced his eyes open. "Release yours scissors, madam," he thundered, gnashing his teeth before he realized what he'd done. Agony shot up William's temples, and he gasped.

The young woman paused, then clipped the branch caught in her long fingers. A branch of soft pink roses fluttered to the ground at her booted feet.

That ugly, enormous dog that was more bear than pup lurched up and ambled over to William.

And that was another thing.

"I don't want your damned dog in my house."

The dog whined and ducked his head.

Elsie drew back like William had physically struck her. "That is dreadful." She stalked over toward him. "He's been nothing but pleasant to you, when he likes no one. He sought to meet you last evening."

He backed away as she continued her aggressive approach. "Meet me," he mouthed.

"Yes, *meet you*. To verify that you are fine."

"I am fine," he bit out.

"Yes, so fine that you can no longer bear sunlight. And if you believe..."

As she launched into a rather impressive diatribe, William continued moving back. *What in blazes?* He didn't know if he should be furious with the chit for announcing his weakness for all the world to hear, or himself for possessing that fragility—and retreating from a slender slip of a woman who was smaller than most boys. But her size was where all similarities to a boy or child ended. He stopped abruptly. Of its own volition, William's gaze went to the generous curve of her hips, accentuated by a heinous gray gown. Lust bolted through him. In a move that both tormented and taunted, Elsie settled her hands on those wide hips. "Furthermore, if you were upset by Bear's presence, I expect you would have said as much at your first meeting earlier this morn."

"You would expect, madam?" he asked on a silken whisper.

Her lips trembled, but she gave a jerky little nod. "Indeed."

By God, there was no limit to this woman's brazenness. He didn't know if he wanted to toss her out on her rounded buttocks or kiss that crimson, bow-shaped flesh.

In your wife's gardens...

His conscience decried him for the blackguard he was, but still did not effectively crush his hungering. Alas, the body cared not for betrayal.

Still squinting from the struggle to see in the bright spring day, William lowered his mouth close to hers. "I was more concerned about *your* unwanted presence."

She tipped her head back and squarely met his gaze. "Was it really unwanted, though?" Her whisper sent her breath tangling with his lips. So close, all he needed to do was angle his head just so, and their mouths would meet. His throat worked painfully.

"Is that an invitation?" he asked hoarsely. *Please, let it be an invitation.*

Elsie did not blink for several moments, and then her black eyebrows shot to her hairline. She squeaked and, swatting at his hand, danced out of William's reach. "You're trying to shock me," she chided. However, there was a faint tremble to her voice, a breathless quality that hinted at desire for him. A hungering that was shared. "It will take a good deal more than a rogue's whisper and naughty words to shock me, William."

He'd give credit where credit was due. Any other young lady would have tossed his title back as a barrier of flimsy defenses. This spitfire required no false shows.

Indignation and the hot afternoon sun had lent a rose-colored hue to her cheeks. "Bear is not leaving. If you wish to turn him out, then I leave with him."

"Fitting damned name," he muttered.

Elsie beamed. "Thank you. I have had him since he was a pup and knew the moment I saw his paws—"

"It wasn't a bloody compliment," he said brusquely.

She pulled her bonnet off and gave a little toss of her dark curls. "Well, either way, I shall take it as such, as a compliment is vastly preferable to an insult. Now, if that is all, I've work to oversee here." With that ridiculous fraying bonnet that belonged to the century prior, the minx pointed at the door. His door.

And then promptly lifted her scissors.

He stiffened, lurching back.

Elsie cast him an arch glance. "You've insisted I remain and assess your injury, and yet, you believe I'd bury my pruning shears in your chest?"

His neck went hot.

With a shake of her head, Elsie snipped branch after branch, raining down the once-cherished wild blooms.

He stared on, disbelief sweeping through him.

Why… she was dismissing him.

Snip.

Snip-snip.

And doing so—

Snip-snip-snip.

—while she destroyed that bush.

"Enough," he whispered.

Snip.

"I said, enough."

Elsie paused.

Snip-snip-snip.

William caught her wrist, and she gasped.

At last, the obstinate beauty looked back with something she'd not shown until now—fear. It was that familiar sentiment possessed by every doctor or healer who'd entered his presence, and he clung to the unease that at last built a wall between them.

"I said, enough," he whispered.

Elsie swallowed loudly. "This is why you've emerged from inside after a year? To stop me from cutting this rosebush?" she asked haltingly, layers of questions threaded through her tone.

Why had he come?

And then he recalled: the rosebush, her affront, the reason he'd at last left his townhouse during the day.

She saw too much.

William abruptly released her, his stomach roiling. "Do not touch this bush, madam." He turned to leave.

"William?" she called after him.

He stilled, but made no move to glance back.

"Do you know what I believe?"

William balled his hands tight. "I trust you intend to tell me, regardless of my answer," he taunted.

"I don't believe you came outside to gripe about my tending your rosebush, or to have Bear removed from your household." Dry soil and gravel crunched under her boots, indicating she'd moved. "I don't even believe you came out here to shout at me."

He stared sightlessly at the door that beckoned strongly, urging him to flee the undaunted and too-clever woman's flowing words. "And why do you think I am here?" he asked flatly. Was that question for her or for himself? His mind balked, shying away from the truth of the answer.

"Because you wanted to be. You wanted to feel the sun and smell the air and not hide away in your rooms, and you've locked yourself away indoors, letting the world believe you forever changed. And so… the only way you can justify being out here to yourself and the world is by bullying me for some imagined transgression."

His body jolted, and he whipped around to face her. "It was my wife's," he said quietly.

His own shock at that revelation was reflected back in her pretty eyes. Her mouth moved, and for the first time, the magpie was shockingly and effectively silenced. "Oh." Just that, a single, breathless sound.

"So do not go near it again, Miss Allenby."

And with that, he stormed off.

CHAPTER 8

HE'D BEEN MARRIED.

It was a detail about the gentleman that his brother, nor Mr. Bennett, had thought to share with her, but one so very vital to understanding who he was… and what he'd become.

And his pain.

For it had been there, in ravaged eyes that had known loss. She knew it for she'd seen it staring back in the bevel mirror of her small Bladon cottage.

Seated on her bed, with only Bear and the flickering shadows cast by the hearth for company, Elsie abandoned all hope of attending the aging leather volume in her hands. She placed it gently atop the other precious journals that had belonged to her father.

The feminine touches throughout the residence bore the mark of the late duchess. The pale pink upholsteries, the walled-in garden, the delicate porcelain articles throughout were all marks of the departed woman's influence here.

Dragging her knees to her chest, Elsie dropped her chin atop and rubbed back and forth, staring at the stacked logs ablaze within the hearth. "What happened to her?" she whispered into the quiet. How did William's physical injuries connect to his wife's death? And who had he been before that loss?

His visage flickered before her, as he'd been earlier that afternoon. With his bearded cheeks and wiry frame stalking toward her, he'd been all primal strength. And for one dizzying instance, she'd believed he intended to kiss her.

Is that an invitation?

She slapped her hands against her cheeks and did a horrified sweep of her temporary chambers.

Bear's accusatory gaze met hers. "It is impossible," she whispered. Of course she hadn't wished for his kiss. She was here to determine if she could help him.

In that instant, you did want it. You believed he would dip his head and claim your mouth...

When no man ever had. And no man ever would.

She cringed at the humiliating truth of that.

And because she was no more a liar than her father had been, Elsie admitted to herself that she'd wanted to know his kiss. Had wanted a taste of the desire she'd seen in his gaze.

"Desire," she muttered, grabbing up a journal. "Of course he does not desire you."

To believe he did in any way was preposterous. William Helling, the Duke of Aubrey, had been surly and snappish since they met. Why, he'd given no hint that he even liked her a smidge.

She flipped through the pages of her father's journal, fanning them and stirring a gentle breeze.

What manner of husband would he have been?

Had he always been the angry, icy figure who'd have shouted down the gardens? After all, a member of the Home Office, serving in the role he did, one would have to be without a single shred of humanity to one's soul. That was what she'd come to believe after they'd cut her devoted father loose and left him and Elsie, because of her connection as Francis Allenby's daughter, to their fates.

Something in her told her that there was far more there. That as angry in life as the duke was, he must have loved very much the woman who'd passed.

A muffled cackle echoed from outside her rooms.

Elsie jumped, and the book slipped from her fingers and toppled over the edge of the bed.

The previously dozing Bear hopped up with the same speed he'd possessed as a pup and growled at the door.

She stilled, braced for another hint of that grating, eerie laugh. All the while, her every nerve on alert, Elsie stared with an unblinking gaze at the door. The clock ticked six seconds.

Another half-mad-sounding laugh rumbled around the midnight quiet. This time more distant, muffled.

A mournful whine escaping the now thoroughly awake dog, he paced back and forth.

Leave this place… It is haunted…

"Do not be silly," she whispered. There was no such thing as ghosts or hauntings.

But that was what her father had believed. He'd believed those who died wandered among the living long after they'd departed. As a child whose mother had perished delivering her into the world, Elsie had found great solace in the promise that the woman who'd given her life would always be there in some way.

But there was no solace now. Not in this foreign home with an angry duke mourning a wife.

Another cackle came, this one strident and high-pitched and slightly different than the one that had preceded it. Closer than before.

She shivered and hugged her arms tight to her middle.

Bear's pacing took on a frantic rhythm. Periodically, he looked back over at her. For assurance? Or as a warning?

"Or to point out how very pathetic you are for your needless worrying," she muttered. She gave her head a disgusted shake. She'd not only lived on her own all these years, but she had also faced men with souls blacker than Satan. Those men who'd tried to kill her had also proven that nothing and no one could surpass the living when it came to evil.

Forcing aside her disquiet, Elsie swung her legs over the side of the mattress and jumped down. She quickly grabbed the cotton wrapper thrown haphazardly at the foot of her bed. "Easy," she said softly, for both herself and Bear. "It could have been anything." And it surely was.

Nonetheless, she carefully picked her way to the front of the room, keeping her path to the soft Aubusson carpet to mute the sounds of her footfalls.

Touching a finger to her lips, Elsie clasped the handle. She waited, counting the passing seconds until at last the chiming clock struck up its announcement of the changing hour.

Taking advantage of that concealment, she let herself out. Bear slipped into the hall, joining her.

Not breaking stride, she pointed her finger down at the carpet just a pace behind her.

With that command, Bear moved along at the quick pace Elsie set.

Ears trained for a hint of that haunting laughter, she drifted in the direction from which it had come. It wasn't her place to know to whom those cold expressions of mirth had belonged. It was undoubtedly safer that she not know. Safer to return to her rooms, turn the lock, climb atop her bed with covers drawn, and forget everything she'd heard.

The devil's business was conducted here, only done so in the name of the Brethren.

And she'd learned firsthand the peril of burying her head from the danger her father had unwittingly drawn them into. Running away from it had seen her father killed, with no one at his side while she huddled like a pathetic creature under dense brush.

Elsie stopped and held a palm up behind her, staying Bear.

She peered down each intersecting hall, straining her ears.

There it was.

Gathering her wrapper, she shrugged into it and rushed onward toward the odd, eerie cackling. The sounds grew increasingly close. Not one. Not two. But three variations of that cold, empty laughter.

She turned the next hall quickly and then skidded to a stop, so quickly that Bear crashed into her legs.

Elsie stared past the scarred butler eyeing her impatiently. "Return to your rooms." He clipped out the icy command, and his regal tones revealed plainly that he was no mere servant, but rather, a member of the ranks.

She pointedly ignored the order. She'd come here at the behest of Lord Edward and was charged with William's care. She'd not be directed about like an underfoot child. "What is the meaning of this?" Elsie demanded, tipping her chin at the trio of scandalously clad beauties. Arms interlocked, they stared back at Elsie with a like annoyance.

With rouged lips and plunging bodices in silk gowns of crimson and black, there could be no doubting the manner of women they in fact were.

Why… why…

There were no ghosts here. They were *mistresses.*

She wrinkled her brow. Was it possible for one man to have *three* mistresses? Surely that was in bad form for a gentleman.

"Listen to the servant, lovey, and step out of the way," a blonde-haired woman near in height to Elsie called over in thinly concealed Cockney. "We've a meeting with His Grace."

A meeting. She snorted. "You do?" She glanced among them. "*All* of you?"

They laughed uproariously, as if she'd delivered the most hilarious of jests.

Elsie's cheeks burned with embarrassment.

The towering, burly gentleman stepped between them. "Don't bother yourself with His Grace," he said to Elsie. "Step out of the way. He has company."

The group took a collective step forward.

Elsie promptly planted her hands on her hips and blocked their path. Bear lined himself up next to her. "Do not bother myself with His Grace?" she asked incredulously. "I, sir, have been tasked with his care."

"You?" One of the whores giggled. "Don't seem His Grace's usual type, but you can join us."

Join them? Elsie choked on her swallow, strangled by it. Surely they were not suggesting… A sea of wicked conjuring entered her mind. Surely not.

"Do not knock it until you try it, lovey." The leader at the center of the group winked. She angled her head in unspoken urging.

Elsie brought her hands up defensively. "Absolutely not." She looked to the butler, who'd avoided her gaze since she arrived "These women are not allowed to see His Grace."

Several moments passed, and then a series of cries and shouts went up.

The determined trio charged forward.

Bear sprang into action, planting himself between his mistress and the group, growling and barking until they'd backed up a handful of steps.

"Enough," the servant thundered. "His Grace does not answer to you."

Elsie lowered her eyebrows and met his fury with an equanimous calm. "As long as I'm living here, he most certainly does."

She might as well have shouted the statement for the charged silence she ushered in.

Good, the sooner that this man, the duke and… and… the duke's company understood her role and her place in this household, the better off they would all be. But there was one certainty… William's days of drinking, whoring, and shutting himself away were at an end.

The tallest of the women stepped forward, her lips pursed tight from her annoyance. "Do ya think ya are going to stop us from seeing His Grace, lovey? Do ya think you are enough to satisfy him?"

"Satisfy him?" she echoed, and then the implication hit her. Elsie widened her eyes. "Why, you believe… you think…?"

Laughter exploded from her lungs, echoing around the halls. Elsie doubled over. They believed her actions were driven by jealousy? That she coveted the role of duke's mistress? "You think…" She dissolved into another fit, unable to squeeze out the remainder of those words. The trio of beautiful women looked at her as though she had lost her mind and was in desperate need of a cart to Bedlam. "I assure you, madam," she managed to rasp out through her hilarity. Elsie dusted tears of amusement from her eyes. "The last thing I desire is a place in His Grace's bed."

"Splendid." The low, melodious baritone sounded from over her shoulder. "Now that we've clarified that important detail, will someone tell me what the hell is going on here?"

All hint of mirth fled, and Elsie froze.

She turned about slowly.

William stood, sans jacket, in nothing but a lawn shirt, breeches, and stockinged feet.

Oh, blast.

CHAPTER 9

WILLIAM GLANCED AROUND THE ODD gathering of people—his agent Stone, the two actresses who'd been invited back by himself only last evening, along with a *friend*… and Elsie Allenby, the primly attired, petite spitfire who'd stopped all four of that *seemingly* more threatening group.

Elsie edged her chin up in a daring challenge, a breathtaking one that put her on display as a far more magnificent beauty for that spirit. A woman, who by her own admission moments ago, desired nothing less than a place in his bed.

For the first time in nearly a year, a smile tugged at his lips, straining the tense muscles and no doubt forming more grimace than grin.

The trio of women still clinging to one another's arms tripped over themselves in their haste to back away from him.

Stone was the first to break the tense silence.

"Forgive me, Your Grace." The agent who'd slipped into the unenviable role of butler glowered at Elsie. "This one has yet to learn her place."

Any other man, woman, or child would have been properly quelled by the viciousness in that life-hardened gaze. Elsie narrowed her eyes. "I do not need to learn my place. I already know it."

Stone took a jerky step toward her, and the minx matched his steps.

"Enough," William said quietly, and the pair stopped. Still glowering at each other, neither paid him a glance. "You are dismissed."

The trio of Covent Garden actresses smirked.

"Stone, if you would show my guests for the evening to the front door."

"But…" started Joanna. The blonde actress had boldly come round back the servants' entrance some months ago, seeking a place in his bed. Her words trailed off. She tightened her mouth, the tension transforming her sharp features into an unpleasant mask. "Come," she snapped, patting her elegant coiffure. Whirling around, she marched off with Lucy and Diana close behind.

Stone lingered. "Your Grace?" He shot a questioning glance in William's direction.

The meaning of the query was clear: Did William want to be free of the insolent Elsie Allenby?

For some unexplainable reason, when that had been the case with the company of all—his own family included—he didn't want to turn the stoic beauty away. Nor did the need to keep her close have anything to do with lust, the one mindless emotion he'd allowed himself to succumb to this past year. *Which is why you should send her away.*

He hesitated, and glancing over the top of her dark, plaited hair, he gave a slight shake of his head.

Without hesitation, Stone stalked off.

Not a word was said, nor look exchanged, until the soft, nearly imperceptible tread of the other man's footfalls had faded.

"You take exception with my company, Elsie."

An endearing blush blazed across her cheeks. "I *took* exception with what you'd intended with your company. Had you sought proper companionship of those who wished to read or walk outside or… or play the pianoforte…"

"All suitably approved activities?"

"Undoubtedly." Elsie folded her hands primly before her. "This is not the manner of residence I agreed to live within, and you are not…" She clamped her lips together, her words trailing off.

Nonetheless, he latched on to the unspoken remainder. "What?" he asked, resting a shoulder against the wall. "The manner of man you expected to find here?" He lifted an eyebrow. "Did you expect to find a broken, scarred man confined to his bed, like your injured animals?"

She smiled sadly at him. "You are no different than the figures you speak of."

He jerked his head back reflexively. The abruptness of the movement strained the muscles of his neck and sent a familiar pain radiating up his jaw. "How dare you?"

"Isn't it the truth, William?" she asked quietly, her matter-of-fact calm more infuriating than any insult she'd levy. "A man is not scarred or broken because he does not have full, functioning use of his body." Elsie took a step toward him. "But rather, it is because of what exists and what has been done to this." She touched her fingertips to her chest, to the place where her heart beat.

His mouth went dry, and the need to hurl invectives at her, and flee, ran strong within him.

The delicate beauty drifted closer, white skirts dancing about her trim ankles, casting a haunting aura about her, and holding him frozen, while everything within him said to run. She stopped so only a handful of steps divided them. "You are not confined to your bed, but this?" She stretched her arms wide. "This magnificent townhouse you refuse to leave? It is still a prison. And if you are well enough to—"

William kissed her, and there was an immediate rush of heat and energy that blazed to life within him. There was the familiar pain in using his jaw—but also, something *more*. Something that reminded him he was very much alive, when he'd merely existed this past year.

Elsie's slender body went taut, and then she leaned into him and met his kiss, first with a tentativeness that bespoke of innocence, her hesitancy fleeting as it was replaced with the boldness she demonstrated at every turn.

Desire sucked him within its enticing hold, this woman ensnaring him with an allure that could only prove dangerous, that needed to be resisted.

Later.

Moments. Hours. Days. Just *later*.

Now, he wanted only her. So much that he'd take her mouth and welcome the agony because of the pleasure that eclipsed all pain.

And she met his hungering unapologetically. She gripped his shirtfront and dragged herself closer as they danced with their mouths in an age-old rhythm.

This embrace was no different than the countless others he'd known after his wife's passing. Those, however, had been mindless unions. This? With her breath coming in rapid little spurts between each joining and then break and rejoining of their lips, this awakened some dormant part within him that he'd believed dead.

And it sucked him deeper and deeper into the bliss of *feeling*.

William parted her lips and slipped his tongue inside.

Elsie touched hers first tentatively to his, and he stroked her. Tasted her. Learned the hypnotic taste of her that was honey and mint and purity. And his body throbbed with the need to reclaim a hint of those sentiments, even as he did not deserve that gift.

But he'd always been a bastard.

With a groan, William filled his palms with her buttocks, cupping her. The modest wrapper and nightshift served as a flimsy barrier, and that only heightened his desire. He worked one hand between them and slipped loose the belt at her waist.

The fabric gaped slightly, exposing her flushed neckline to the cooler night air. Elsie moaned, the reverberations of her desire thrumming within his mouth.

His shaft throbbed against the soft swell of her belly. Everything about this woman, from her courage, to her strength, to her innocence, called to him. Through the fabric of her nightshift, he took her breast in his right hand, tweaking the pebbled flesh.

She moaned, undulating her hips.

Panting, William continued to stroke her, weighing her right breast. How perfectly she fit in his hand. She was unlike the voluptuous actresses and whores who'd come, enticed by his title and all the wealth it afforded him, and asked first the size of the purse that would await them.

Elsie pressed herself closer. Their kiss took on a frantic, primal ardor. There was nothing practiced or false or greedy, just whimpering moans that spilled from her throat.

God help him, she was all unrestrained emotion and feeling. All sentiments he'd sworn never to allow himself to feel again. His existence was to be mindless, with hedonistic pursuits all that drove him. Because that lack of feeling was what would keep him safe.

But this?

He devoured her mouth, and their tongues rasped against each other, two people who battled at every turn continuing that challenge here, now.

He slanted his lips over hers again and again, learning their texture, memorizing the taste of her. Wanting to lose himself in her.

The earth shifted, knocking him off-balance.

Or rather, a dog had.

Breaking the kiss, William cursed and quickly caught himself and righted Elsie.

Her eyes flew open, their green depths glazed with passion and confusion. She blinked and glanced about… as reality intruded—for the both of them. A slow, dawning horror lit her eyes.

The ugly mutt nudged William behind the knees with his enormous head for a second time, and this time, William anticipated the angry dog's response. "You should have kept to your rooms." His heart thundered in his chest as he fought to get himself back to a place of ordered logic.

With a gasp, Ellie scrambled out of his reach, and he railed at that separation, cursing her damned dog to perdition. "I-I sh-should have," she stammered, her always assured speech faltering for the first time, and not because he'd challenged her. Not because he'd snarled or snapped, but because he'd kissed her.

And I want to continue that embrace. He wanted to forget that they'd been dragged away from that too-brief interlude. And instead lose himself once more in feeling something other than anger or guilt or misery.

"S-stayed in my chambers," she clarified, directing that at the tie about her wrapper that she struggled to collect. "I will, however, point out—"

"I was talking to your damned dog," he muttered.

She paused midtask and stared up with impossibly rounded eyes. "Indeed? You talk to dogs?"

William's neck went hot. "It is apparently a habit I've developed over the past two days."

There was a softening in her eyes, some seismic shift. He blanched. That was too much.

"Here," he said gruffly. Snatching the fraying strips from her hands, he set to work belting the tie at her trim waist with equally unsteady fingers.

"Y-you do not need to do that," she squeaked.

Ignoring her protest, he tied the article.

Did she recognize the inherent silliness in that flimsy barrier? She hugged her arms tight to her middle. "I should not be here."

"Yes, you've said as much." And for the first time since he'd descended into a hedonistic state, he felt… shame. Shame that this woman, an innocent, had witnessed the depravity he'd surrendered to after his wife's passing. "I'd advise you not to wander the halls, as you never know who you might encounter," William said curtly. With that, he stalked off.

He made it no farther than three steps.

"You misunderstand me," she called behind him, halting William in his tracks. "I did not refer to your corridors, but rather, your household."

That brought him quickly back around to face her. He frowned. "What are you on about?"

Even as he knew. She was an innocent, a woman who by her speech and demeanor revealed herself to be respectable. She'd not tolerate life in a debauched household. She deserved more.

Her blush deepened, and she glanced back to where the three actresses had recently stood. "If you are well enough to… to…" Elsie shifted back and forth on her bare feet, her dainty toes peeking out from under the hem of her skirts, oddly enthralling.

He shot her an impatient look. "Miss Allenby?"

She immediately ceased her distracted movements and stood proud, shoulders back, chin up. "Do that, then you are capable enough to reenter the land of the living."

She spoke of his leaving this household and again facing the world. Horrifying prospects that robbed him of sleep and riddled him with nausea. And yet, he could fix on only the former part of the spitfire's words.

"*That*, Elsie?" he purred. "I'm afraid you'll need to be more… clear."

She scoffed. "Save your wicked rogue's tone for the whores who'll be waiting when I leave." With that, she made to step around him.

After she left? His heart thundering with an unexplainable panic, William slid into her path. He'd known her but a day, and it was rubbish and nonsense and illogical in every way. But he was bereft at the thought of her gone. "You could always stay on in… other capacities," he suggested, husking his voice. "Not as my nurse."

"I'm not your nurse," she replied automatically. "I was never here as your doctor. I was merely brought to assess your state."

The coolly impersonal words spoke of a woman who did not want to be here with him, but had been forced into the task. As a duke who'd had women of all stations and levels of respectability clamoring for his attention, it was an unfamiliar state. "You do not simply get to leave, madam."

"Don't I?" Elsie flicked a cool stare up and down his frame, lingering on his bearded cheeks, and when she met his gaze, it was clear more than had she'd uttered the words aloud that she'd found him wanting. "That is, unless you intend to keep me as your prisoner?" This time, a flash of fear lit her eyes.

Who knew the sentiment shame could also be a physical feeling? It sat low in one's belly like a stone and churned the gut. *And how many men and women in your work for the Brethren did you make to feel this same way?* "I would never force you here against your will," he said with a gentleness he'd believed himself incapable of anymore. For at one time, he would have commanded her or any person if it had benefited him or the Brethren.

Some of the tension lifted from Elsie's delicate shoulders. "Very good." She nodded slowly. "Then please step aside so I might pass." With an air of finality, she clapped her hands once.

Bear shot him a disappointed look before trotting over to join his mistress.

The pair continued down the corridor.

William fisted his hands. She was leaving. Good, let her go. In fact, she should. He'd crossed a line. And he'd done so quite deliberately, too. All with the intention of shocking, but also… testing. He closed his eyes a moment and then turned about quick. "No mistresses," he called out.

Elsie stopped. With all the regal grace of a queen facing a lesser subject, she turned toward him. "Go on," she said, her face as impressively blank as her tone.

"I'll concede to… whatever treatment you advise."

"And your drinking?" she shot back, glossing over the humbling concession he'd just given.

He stared quizzically at her. "You want me to give up spirits, madam?"

"I do."

So she'd gauged that quickly the frequency with which he drank. He'd mastered his ability to handle spirits, and yet, she knew anyway.

"You had the smell of them upon you at our first meeting and… earlier, in the gardens," she explained, again showing an eerie synchronicity with his very thoughts.

William stiffened. That was the first reference made to the volatile exchange in which he'd revealed anything to this woman about his late wife.

"I'll not give up brandy," he said tightly, his jaw beginning to throb. "I do not need it." Since he'd awakened ten months ago, riddled with agony in facial muscles he hadn't known a person possessed, William had taken care to say little. He'd used few words and moved his mouth sparingly. What was it about Elsie Allenby that made him forget that? At Elsie's pointed silence, he snapped, "What?"

"Don't you? Need liquor?" she clarified.

"I don't," he reiterated. *You owe her nothing more than that. Save your words and mouth movements.* "I enjoy it. Just as I enjoy an evening spent with women," he added matter-of-factly. "Wanting something and needing something? They are vastly different beasts, Elsie."

Her cheeks pinkened, but he'd hand it to the minx, she revealed no other hint of chagrin to that scandalous admission.

"When Bear was just a pup, he wandered away. I found him with his left paw stuck in a trap that had been set by one of the villagers."

At the abrupt shift, William cocked his head.

Elsie sank to her knees alongside the mutt and stroked her hand down the creature's front left leg. "My father believed we needed to take the leg," she said softly, her distant tones belonging to one who'd forgotten William's presence and saw only the memory in her mind.

Memory of another dog flickered forward. Smaller. His fur black and white spotted, but silky where Elsie's dog's fur was coarse. "He did not advise you put him down, though," he murmured. God, he'd not thought of that dog in… a lifetime.

Elsie paused midstroke and looked up at him with stricken eyes. "And why should he have? He was merely injured, William. Not dead." Elsie hugged her arms about Bear's neck and whispered something into the creature's ear.

William stared blankly at the pair at his feet as a memory trickled in of another dog at another point in his life.

When he'd been a boy, his dog Honor had come up lame, and there had been no opinions sought beyond the lead stable master. His father had stood at William's side while the bullet had been put through the dog's head.

Injured creatures, not unlike injured people, serve no purpose, William. It is essential you learn that now, and let that guide you to what you are meant to be.

The Sovereign.

His stomach muscles clenched. He'd of course not known what his father had spoken of at the time. The lesson had come to make sense only later, when he'd ceded his rank within the Brethren to his son. "Most are not of a like opinion on injured animals." *Or people.* "They are disposable," he repeated flatly, in rote remembrance. *Always remember that…*

I did nothing when my father insisted Honor be put down. I simply… accepted it.

And who could imagine that act from long ago could cause new shame all these years later?

Elsie pierced him with a gaze. "Do *you* believe that?"

Something in him said that whatever answer he gave to her in this instant mattered more than anything. His response would ultimately determine whether she stayed… or left.

He opened his mouth to offer the obvious, expected answer. The one ingrained in him at the Home Office and by his own father. "I don't know," he conceded gruffly, a damningly weak admission, the first of its kind that he'd allowed himself. He tapped a hand against his leg, drumming a beat there until he caught Elsie's stare on him.

William abruptly stopped the distracted movement. Why were they even now talking about this? She wished to leave, and he revealed nothing to anyone. Not even his own wife had been privy to those moments of his childhood. He contemplated the path over her shoulder that led to his chambers, but her gaze called to him, pulled him back.

Elsie motioned to the place beside her and Bear.

William hesitated, glancing up and down the hall, before sinking to a knee beside her. "The clamp caught Bear's forefoot. Here," she murmured, taking William's hand in her own.

His fingers curled around hers, seeking the warmth of that touch. Craving—

She placed his palm upon Bear's left paw, showing him the place of the old wound.

William forced his attention from the one who truly held him transfixed and attended the large paw in his grip.

"It severed his dew claw and ripped off two nails." Bear whined, and Elsie made some nonsensical soothing noises that had a calming effect on her dog, and William understood it, for warmth suffused his chest, sweeping through him when he'd been cold for so long.

"What happened to him?" he asked. There were layers to that question that he didn't himself want the answer to.

She held a palm up, which the dog lapped at with a large, pink tongue, and then Elsie went on. "There was so much blood. At first glance, his paw was mangled. He had it curled up close to his chest and bled everywhere. Had the snare caught him here at his ankle?" She covered William's fingers with her own, and his mouth went dry as she guided him over the coarse fur and then stopped, leaving their hands joined upon that portion of Bear's leg. The touch was innocent, and yet, with every fleeting brush, it drew him deeper and deeper into whatever spell she'd woven over him. "Bear would have lost it. Most would have, as you'd said, put him down. At the very least, they would have taken the leg." Elsie smiled wistfully up at him. "My father was a healer. He did not end lives…" Her throat worked. "He *saved* them. And that generosity extended to animals." Pain and heartache twined in her singsong voice.

He'd become jaded to those two sentiments in his work long, long ago, only to find himself not immune now. His heart twisted, and even as he warred with himself to keep barriers between himself and this woman chipping away at them, he spoke, the need to distract her from her pain greater than his need for self-preservation.

"And he recovered completely under your and your father's care," he ventured, trusting that had been the original intention. To disprove the point he had made.

"Not at all," she countered.

Of course not. He could read everyone to near perfection… except this woman and her intentions.

William stroked a hand down the dog's back, and Bear leaned into his touch.

When William registered the silence in the room, he glanced over and found Elsie's gaze trained on his palm as he petted her ancient dog.

Clearing her throat, Elsie went on with her telling. "Long after it mended, Bear was still not wholly recovered. He was able to walk and run."

"Isn't that healed?" he asked, briefly halting his caress, until Bear nudged him back into action.

"To some," she explained. "Your father. You. And most others would equate wellness with the recovery of a physical injury." She looped her arms around the dog's neck, giving him another hug and knocking William's hand loose.

He'd never believed it possible, but William found himself envying a damned dog. He gave his head a slight, imperceptible shake.

"There were certain times we would journey to the village," Elsie explained, her cheek still rested upon Bear's matted fur, "where he'd be stubborn, barking at everything, and when we returned home, he'd simply sit in the corner, licking where the wound had once been until the paw was raw and bloodied. It took four times before I realized it…"

He sat forward. "What?"

"We were journeying by the place where he'd been hurt," she said gently. "Each time we passed it, he remembered what happened to him. That spot of his remembered pain held him prisoner."

Understanding dawned, and bitterness wadded in his throat as her meaning rang clear. "And you believe that simply avoiding that… place is enough to make one forget." Somewhere along the way, he'd stopped pretending as though they spoke of Bear. He'd never forget his wife, or everything he'd cost her.

"No." Elsie looked at William squarely, holding his eyes. "That memory will always be there. It does not go away, but if one forces oneself to live and see only that darkest moment over and over, one will eventually go mad."

I am already there. He'd descended into that state the day of the attack.

Hadn't he?

Before Elsie had arrived, the answer to that would have been instantaneous and far more certain.

Elsie stiffened and made to draw her hand back. "It is late." She pushed to her feet, and William rushed to stand.

She was leaving. The intent was there still in the set of her mouth.

"I'll give up spirits," he conceded gruffly. As long as she was here. He kept that particular detail to himself.

She narrowed her eyes and peered up at him through a too-clever-for-his-good gaze. "And then when I leave? What then?"

God, she was tenacious. With her ability to ferret out promises a man didn't want to give, she'd have been better suited to the ranks of the Brethren. "Do you truly expect me to give up spirits forever?" It was unnatural in the order of his universe. Gents drank.

"No," she said, shaking her head. "But I do expect you to give up liquor until you learn proper restraint over it… and yourself."

Had anyone told him a slip of a woman nearly a foot and a half smaller than he would be here doling out requirements and expectations and questioning his, William Helling, the Duke of Aubrey's restraint, he'd have laughed his arse off.

"Fine," he conceded grudgingly. He silently cursed. "What else?"

"You allow me to evaluate you and work with you. We begin tomorrow. Each morning, at six o'clock, we shall meet."

"You rise at six o'clock?" he asked, unable to keep the surprise from his voice. His own wife had risen well after the afternoon sun had climbed into the sky. As had his mother.

"Hardly. If that were the case, I'd be meeting with you in my nightshift," she said dryly, and he shifted his gaze to the very garments she'd referenced.

Desire stirred once more. "Which would hardly be surprising," he forced himself to say, "given that you've been here just two days and it is now the second time I've seen you in such a state of undress."

She drew the already closed folds of her night wrapper closer to her person.

And he proved very much the rogue she'd accused him to be, for he yearned to tug at that neat bow he'd belted at her waist and slide the garment from her shoulders, continuing his earlier exploration.

"Six o'clock," she repeated.

William released a sigh. "Very well. Six o'clock. Shall we meet in the schoolroom?" he asked, his expression deadpan.

Elsie puzzled her brow. "Of course n—" She stopped, her cheeks pinkening. "Oh, you are funning me."

Funning her? He'd not made light of... any topic or discourse in so long, he'd believed himself incapable of it. "I... I suppose I was," he conceded, tugging at the collar of his shirt, and he accepted the truth... She'd been correct. He had become a beast, unable to interact as he once had with the world around him.

A smile curled her lips up into a gentle expression of happiness. "That is good. We will meet in the breakfast room, and then again thereafter for"—he was already shaking his head—"the midday meal and supper—"

"All three?" he choked out. She not only expected him to leave his rooms in the middle of the day, but she intended to sit opposite him and watch him suffer through the simplest task that was eating? "No."

"I've never been particularly fond of the midday meal either, but the more opportunities I have to observe you using your jaw, the greater the likelihood I might be able to help you."

William searched her face. "You believe you can help me." His was a statement.

She hesitated. "I do not know. Nor will I offer you false hope," she said on a rush. "I'll not be able to determine as much until I observe you more and discuss the pain you are dealing with." She spoke of the agony that had resulted in Edward seeking her out. "Until tomorrow, William." Then, dismissing him outright, she patted a hand against her leg.

"Wait," he called.

She stopped abruptly and looked to him with a question in her gaze.

"If I might... Your dog... I..." he said tersely.

Elsie firmed her lips. "I've already been clear. If I'm to remain, Bear—"

"I want your damned dog to remain." William grimaced. Oh, God, what was becoming of him? Where in blazes had that request come from? Or mayhap the better question was what had become of him?

His surprise was reflected back in the young woman's expression. "You want…" He cringed. "Oh," she said softly.

Just that. A single syllable. His ears burned hot the same way they had when his father had caught him nursing one of the injured barn cats in the stables. His request had simply been inspired by the maudlin memory of his own blasted dog from long ago. He scraped his hand through his hair. "Never mind. It was—"

"Of course he can remain, William."

She snapped three times, and Bear bounded over to William's side.

They stood there, man and dog, staring after Elsie as she took her leave, and he remained there long after she'd gone, Bear dutifully at his side.

This time when sleep would not come, it was not because of the nightmares, guilt, and agony at all he'd lost—but because of her.

He was in serious danger of remembering he was a gentleman—what possible good might come of that?

CHAPTER 10

THE FOLLOWING MORNING, ELSIE WOUND her way through the same corridors she'd traveled the night before.

When Elsie had set her terms last evening for William, she'd expected him to flatly reject each one. And after their embrace, she'd wanted him to send her packing because he'd unsettled her in ways she'd never been. She'd been so sure he would.

A scoundrel who drank too much and bedded scandalous women—several at the same time—was not one who'd willingly give up those pursuits. Nor was a duke, and leader within a powerful, secret organization, one to take orders, and from a woman, no less.

Or that was what she'd believed.

With every meeting, and every turn, he unbalanced her, and she was left more and more unsteady within a household where it would be dangerous to let her guard down.

He'd craved Bear's company. When all the noblemen who'd come to her cottage had either sneered or ordered the dog to another room or outside, William had freely stroked the dog's matted back. He would, of course, see asking Bear to stay with him as a humbling request. His flushed cheeks had bespoken the embarrassment he'd felt in asking, and yet… he'd asked.

Never trust a man who doesn't love an animal, her father had warned.

But what level of trust did one have in a man whose business centered around secrets and bringing men—and women—down?

Click-click-click-click.

Heart racing, she searched for the source of the rapidly approaching sound.

Relief went through her as Bear bound over to her.

Elsie immediately dropped to her knees and hugged his familiar body weight. "Did you have a good night?" she murmured against his ear. His rough tongue lapped at her ear.

Last night had marked the first that she and Bear had been apart in the whole of their lives together. He, however, had seemed far more comfortable with the prospect of sleeping with a stranger. A dark stranger who Elsie had kissed.

A shiver prickled down her spine. *You're a fool to be so trusting. You're walking into the same trap your father did.* Elsie's senses went on alert. And here she'd been so awestruck by the fact that William had requested the presence of her dog. Why, either one of them could have been harmed last evening for that carelessness. She quickly pushed to her feet.

She glanced about, touching her gaze on every corner. The hum of silence served as her only company. *At least that you know of.*

Bear, in his customary spot alongside her, eased some of the anxiety that came in being among the men in this organization once again.

Hugging the wall, she resumed walking, increasing her stride as she went.

Yes, she'd be a fool to wholeheartedly trust that they still wouldn't destroy her on a whim. People such as she and her father were expendable. The world took what it needed, and when their perceived use had been met, they were cast out.

It is why you are a fool for being here.

The taunt pinged around her mind. The Brethren had taken years upon years of her father's services and skills and then killed him. And still she'd come for their leader. Because despite their betrayal, Papa had first and foremost insisted that he and Elsie, where able, helped those in need.

She'd come, but she needn't be the same naïve fool she and Papa had been five years ago. The leader of that hated organization had shown some affection for her dog, and she'd let her guard down because of it.

Never again.

She'd come because of the lessons ingrained in her by her father.

And *that* was why she now found herself here with William. A gentleman who asked—nay, demanded—her assistance, but who did not even remember her father. The man who'd given his services, all hours of the evening, bringing men on the brink of death back to the living, and William did not even recognize Elsie as Francis Allenby's daughter.

And why should he recognize you when he did not seem to remember the doctor who'd been so very vital to Crown business?

How many times had she heard that very word uttered by those within the Brethren, as rote as the knock they'd rapped at her family's cottage door?

"Vital," she whispered, her voice catching. They'd repaid that vitality with a dagger to the chest. Those were the pieces she'd be wise to remember about William Helling, the Duke of Aubrey.

Oh, God.

Elsie stumbled to a stop. The familiar hatred, pain, and regret roared to life within her, filling every corner of her being with an icy cold. She called herself a pathetic fool for not having held tight enough to those sentiments since she'd arrived here. *And I kissed him.* A man who'd only existed as the enemy. It's why she'd fought all remembrance of that embrace. Elsie squeezed her eyes shut and laid her back against the wall, taking support from it.

For the truth was, though neither William, nor Lord Edward, nor miserable Bennett had thrust that blade repeatedly into her father's chest until he'd choked on his own blood, they might as well have landed the death blows all the same.

Do not think of it... Do not think of it...

Not here. Not now.

Focus on leaving. Focus on fleeing this place...

A panicky half laugh, half sob stuck in her throat. He'd never let her leave. She was as trapped as her father had been. It was her inevitable fate to fall as Papa had. With his pure heart, he'd inadvertently tied them to the devil, and there could be no severing the connections.

Elsie smacked the back of her head against the wall, over and over.

Do not let the memories in...

Except the dam opened up, as it inevitably did, and sucked her into a past that could never be buried. One that would forever haunt her. Elsie's breath came in frantic, ragged spurts, rasping loud in her ears. It blended with the hideous gurgling as her father had struggled to make words.

Whimpering, she clamped her hands over her ears in a bid to blot out the sounds.

Always remember who we are, p-poppet… We…

"Help," she rasped.

Bear whined forlornly.

"Elsie?"

Elsie's eyes flew open. Elsie? Her name. Spoken by only one another. *Papa.*

Disoriented, she darted her gaze frantically about, searching.

And finding him.

Not her father. Of course. He'd been dead five years now, cut down in the most brutal of ways.

But rather, another man stood before her.

Framed in a doorway five or so paces ahead, William stared back. Even with the space between them, she detected the unexpected flash of concern there.

Reality came rushing back in a noisy whir.

Elsie jumped away from the wall. "William," she greeted in even tones. How was her voice so steady? How, when the memories had come… and William, the Duke of Aubrey and leader within the Brethren, stood opposite her? "Hello," she said quickly, her voice echoing around the wide halls.

William's black eyebrows dipped.

She coughed into her fist. "That is, I'd been calling out hello." She proffered the lie easily and searched for some indication that he sensed the mistruth.

His expression, however, remained a careful, carved mask. "You are late."

She was? Elsie rushed forward, and Bear sprang into step beside her. "Impossible. I'm—" William drew out a gold timepiece, popped the lid open, and dangled it before her. "Late," she breathed. For any appointment she'd had, for any villager who'd summoned her to tend wounded animals, Elsie had been unfailingly punctual. Timing mattered. The loss of crucial minutes had the potential to see a creature forever scarred, or dead. That principle had guided her life.

"I'll not sack you."

Why… why… was he *jesting*?

She craned her head back, searching for some hint of mirth and ultimately finding his face still threateningly blank. Had he seen her lie for the falsehood it was moments ago? The heated intensity of his piercing eyes bespoke a man who would not miss those details.

Nay, he'd be wholly attuned to matters and exchanges directly affecting him.

It is the lives of those around him that don't merit a like focus.

Without verifying whether she followed, without even issuing the command, William entered the breakfast room through the wide doorway.

Elsie stared at the entranceway and let the war within her rage. Could she remain here in the Duke of Aubrey's household? Her resentment, her bitterness would always be there. And where her father had been good and honorable, Elsie did not possess such goodness where she could so easily set aside those sentiments and forget the injustices done to her and Papa.

She chewed at her lower lip. There was, however, one certainty: Whichever decision she came to, she had to commit to that course. One of the many gifts she'd learned under her father's tutelage had been decisiveness. She either had to acknowledge that her resentments ran too deep to ever properly help William. Or, she had to separate those emotions from her logic and evaluate William as she had every patient before him.

Bear butted her hand with the top of his head.

"I can't," she whispered. Whether she proved a disappointment to her father's memory and made a disgrace of the most important lessons he'd passed down, she could not do this.

Bear nudged her again.

Elsie closed her eyes. *No.*

We help, Elsie … We…

"Help," she silently mouthed. When she opened her eyes, she drew in a breath. It was but three weeks. Where she was able, she would help William and then be free of him and the Brethren.

"Very well." She spoke in barely audible tones for Bear's benefit. Smoothing her palms down her skirts, she nodded.

With a spring in his usually now slow step, her dog sprinted into the breakfast room.

She stared after him a moment, trying to puzzle through the inexplicable loyalty he showed at every turn for the man who owned this household. Pulling her shoulders back, she joined Bear… and William.

He remained standing behind a chair placed at the right-hand head of the table. The enormous piece, with no fewer than forty seats, was longer than the length of her entire cottage. With silver candelabras with new wax candles, the table setting was fit for royalty and certainly not for a simple country doctor's daughter.

Elsie forced herself to continue. A servant came forward to pull out her chair. She held up a staying hand. "Thank you. I have it." What manner of world was this in which even the simplest task was carried out for one? She glanced around at the small army of crimson-and-gold-clad servants stationed around the breakfast room. Since she was a small girl, Elsie had conducted work within their modest cottage, cared for the animals in their stables, and assisted her father with any of the medical procedures as he'd required it. This extravagant show was foreign to all she had ever known.

"Do you intend to sit?" William's voice echoed off the walls in a reminder of how very barren this palacelike space was.

Elsie's cheeks warmed at being caught gawking like a country miss. "I'd ask you to dismiss the servants."

Throughout the room, the footmen cast sideways looks at one another.

William frowned. "And why would that be?" The lethal edge there sent shivers up and down her spine.

For the first time, she looked at the servants. Really looked at them. Nearly as tall as, or the same height as the duke, the footmen also possessed muscles that strained the fabric of their uniforms. It was both their form and their gazes. Their eyes were life-hardened. Cold. Unforgiving. She hunched her shoulders protectively. These were no servants. It was an unnecessary reminder of the perilous world she'd allowed herself to be drawn back into. Elsie dropped her voice to a hushed whisper as she spoke. "The sole purpose in my being here is to assist with your injury. I trust that is information you would rather not be shared publicly with your…

servants." She'd have him know that she saw more than he credited her for and was not one to be underestimated.

His black brows dipped a fraction. He'd of course detected the slight emphasis she'd placed on the latter word. Elsie brought her chin up.

After an endless unraveling of time, William gave a slight nod.

The dozen footmen stationed throughout the room instantly fell into a neat line and filed out with an efficiency that Nelson's troops likely couldn't muster.

As soon as the door clicked shut behind the last servant, William reached past her.

She stiffened, but he merely took the back of her chair and dragged the seat out. "I trust there is nothing else you require before you begin your… services?" he asked, coldly mocking.

Elsie searched for a hint of the vulnerable man from last evening who'd sought comfort in Bear's presence… and found none. She might as well have imagined the entire exchange. And this was far easier. Far safer. Seeing William as only a cold, empty-hearted stranger was vastly easier than looking upon him as one who appreciated an old dog like Bear.

Elsie stared pointedly at his hands until he drew them back. She waited, continuing that silent battle. With stiff, reluctant movements, he capitulated first, reclaiming the chair he'd vacated.

After he'd seated himself, Elsie slid into the folds of the throne-like, velvet-upholstered mahogany chair and brought herself closer to the table. "You'd call into question my abilities before you even truly allow me to assess you," she noted, settling into the surprisingly comfortable carved piece. "And yet"—she dropped her arm atop the table and rested her chin in her hand—"you insist I remain. Why is that, William?"

A muscle in his jaw jumped. "The same reason I requested Bear stay with me last evening. Because I am bored."

Not *your dog*. But rather, *Bear*. "I don't believe that," she said without missing a beat.

William matched her body's positioning, framing his jaw with the palm of his hand, stabilizing it as he spoke. "You speak with a good deal of confidence, Miss Allenby."

She was *Miss Allenby* when he sought boundaries. Elsie studied him contemplatively. William Helling was a leader within the

Home Office and yet transparent in so many ways. "If you were bored," she said softly, "you'd not be shut away indoors."

"I have plenty to keep me amused and enthralled *within* doors." He curved his lips up into a wicked grin. "Or I did."

She pushed her chair back and stood. "Do you mean the whores?" His cheeks flushed red. "Or the drinking?"

William yanked at his cravat and eyed the door for a moment. Was he thinking about escape? Looking for help from his servants? Either way, good. The miserable bugger.

Elsie laid her palms on the edge of the table and leaned over him. "If you think to disconcert me with talk of your *previously* scandalous lifestyle, you are destined to be disappointed," she informed him. He tilted his head back, and she braced for the fire in a furious gaze.

Heat spilled from within the fathomless depths of his eyes. Volatile. Alive. And there was certainly not anger there, but some unidentified, but equally dangerous, sentiment.

Elsie drew back quickly and rushed to the buffet. A vast array of breads had been neatly laid out: hot rolls, cold breads, honey cake, morning cake. The generous offering of quality wheat was so vastly different from the half-penny loaf those like her and her late father had eaten. Giving her head a shake, she regained her bearing and filled two plates. Next, she added a small porcelain dish of baked eggs to William's selections. Plates balanced in her hands, she carried them over and set hers down first. She held the other out.

William eyed it in puzzlement.

She waved it under his nose. "You take it," she said gently, without recrimination. Because he'd been born and bred to a position of power, it was hardly his fault that such mundane tasks should escape him.

He swiftly caught the dish and lowered it before him.

Elsie snapped her skirts and settled into her chair. Humming to herself, she made a show of gathering her serviette and laying it upon her lap.

So it began.

CHAPTER 11

HUMMING, CHALLENGING HIM, ELSIE ALLENBY was a master of her emotions.

So much so, that any other person might have easily overlooked the exchange that had taken place moments ago in the corridor.

William studied her bent head as she neatly took apart a cold roll and fed it to the dog seated at her side.

She was haunted.

He'd recognized the dark, vacant glint because it was one that faced him in any mirror he passed. His company had been minimal this past year, and his dialogue even more sparse. But he'd heard the single utterance she'd sought to disguise. *Help.*

And he, who'd cared for nothing beyond his own miseries and losses, found himself wanting to know about this woman's.

"Do you have a queue?" Elsie directed the query to the ugly mutt at her feet. At last, she picked her head up.

"Do I have a…?"

"It is generally a single piece of leather. A velvet ribbon, even?" She shoved back her chair, the legs scraping along the floor noisily, and sent her dog scrambling onto all fours. Elsie stood.

"I know what a—"

She reached behind her and caught the neat plait that hung down the middle of her back, and his annoyance, all rational words, a basic reply, fled his mind as he stared on, transfixed.

Elsie brought the braid over shoulder and tugged free the sapphire velvet piece. "Here," she murmured.

"What are you…?" His words emerged slightly garbled to his own ears, for reasons that for once had nothing to with the pain of moving his jaw and everything to do with his body's heightened awareness of this unconventional woman.

Sticking the frayed ribbon between her teeth, she proceeded to gather the tangled mass of black hair about his face.

William stiffened. He should order her to release him.

He should send her to the devil with curt orders on how to get there for her insolence.

Instead…

His eyes, of their own volition, slid closed. How long had it been since anyone had shown him such tenderness? When was the last time he'd been touched in this way? Had he ever? As a child, there'd never been any shows of affection or warmth. His wife, Adeline, had blushed when he'd taken her hand, but never so much as touched him unsolicited.

After her death, the exchanges William had allowed himself had been mindless meetings driven by that empty emotion of lust. Each one had been nothing more than a primitive joining of like beasts, satiating one another's basest urges. And he'd wanted to be that animal, because his lovers did not know the searing agony of loss and failure and shame.

Is that truly what you've wanted?

He balked. Until Elsie had arrived, he would have answered an unequivocal yes and ordered one of his men to fetch any number of the beauties who'd warmed his bed this year to join him for the day. Lust was safer than… really anything. It was the most primal of the sentiments, where one simply felt sexual gratification that allowed a fleeting release from… everything.

But with Elsie silently stroking his scalp, a different hungering gripped him. One that defied the physical acts of these past months and enshrined warmth and… a host of other sentiments life hadn't given him the experience to identify or name.

While his mind was in tumult, Elsie continued her work. She wound her fingers through the tangle of strands. She drew them delicately between her fingers, like a comb being expertly applied. His scalp tingled under her ministrations. What magic did she possess that she made him remember how life once was and yearn for that existence and not the one he'd laid out for himself?

After working some order into the too-long strands, Elsie drew them back and then, with that aging ribbon that had seen better days, tied them at his nape.

Elsie stepped back and assessed her work. "There," she said, and with a pleased nod, she sat once more, picked up her bread, and popped a bite into her mouth.

That mundanity hit him like a fist to the solar plexus.

His life... had become, at best, a farce.

This slip of a woman had left him sitting here, exposed. Hair that had once been a curtain left his bearded cheeks visible to her intense gaze. *You can always send her away... keep her out, just as you've kept out the members of your family.* Guilt cut through him, an all-too-familiar sentiment. Guilt and something else, something that felt very much like melancholy at the prospect of her leaving.

"I do not see how matters of my personal hygiene are important to you, madam," he said gruffly.

She set her roll down and dusted her palms together. "I cannot fully assess the state of your jaw if you go about hiding your face from me."

"I'm not hiding myself from you," he gritted out, and agony shot down his jawline. Gasping, William dropped his fork and caught his chin in a hand, cradling it, stabilizing it. To no avail.

Through the pain, he registered Bear's nervous whine.

Muscles he'd never known he possessed in his face throbbed, and if he were a weaker man, he'd weep from it. He squeezed his eyes shut. Pinpricks of light danced behind his eyes, and he forced them open...

To find Elsie's intense gaze trained on his, eyes that could look into a man's soul and steal the secrets he desperately sought to cling to. "You are hiding from someone," she said somberly. "Or..." She leaned forward in her chair, closer to him. "Is it something within yourself?"

"How do you...?" William recoiled, halting that damning admission.

There was no triumph in her gaze, which made her discovery all the more intimate, and terrifying for it. Her openness also, for the first time since Adeline's passing, brought the truth freely from his lips. "My wife was killed."

Her lips parted slightly, but she did not seek to follow his statement with empty apologies.

"My enemies are great, and she paid the price. A carriage accident that was no accident at all." His lips twisted in a wry grimace. "And I was the fortunate one to survive."

"But you are… fortunate. And you are squandering that gift of life."

"What rot," he spat. "This," he hissed, slashing his hand in the air, "is some kind of *gift*?" He shoved back his chair with such alacrity that the seat toppled over behind him. "Who the hell do you think you are?" he rasped. "I did not invite you into my household to pry into my past." *You freely offered the details and now you'd rail at her.* William thrust aside logic and fed his frustration.

Pushing her plate aside, Elsie rested her palms primly before her on the table. "Your past is part of your present pain, William."

My God, she was fearless. A slender slip of a woman, and yet, Elsie Allenby was unmatched in courage and strength. And more terrifying, she was dangerously accurate with every supposition she leveled. "You think you are so clever, Elsie."

"I never presumed to be, nor do I seek to impress anyone in any way," she said calmly. "I've confidence enough in who I am and my abilities." That pronouncement couldn't have been more accurately placed and vicious than if she'd slipped the dagger from his boot and shoved it into his belly.

She was, in short, everything he'd once been… and never would be again. William towered over her, willing her to look at him—and unsettled when she did. "I didn't refer to your talents, but rather, your ploys."

Her cheeks colored. "My p-ploys?" For all her remarkable strengths, she was still rot at subterfuge.

Her unevenness restored him. William walked a path about her seat, circling her in the predatory manner he'd perfected under his father's tutelage. "Come," he urged on a silken purr. "Let us cease the games."

"I don't know what games you speak of," she said in a threadbare whisper. "I did not come here to play games. I was forced to come, and you required that I stay."

Fair point. It was an admission he'd not concede.

"Your display, Elsie? Taking meals together so you might… assess me?"

The long column of her throat moved. Her skin paled. And the evidence of her nervousness should have been a victory. Except... William slowed his steps so that he stood behind her chair. Her unease did *not* make him feel any better. Rather, it made him feel like a damned bully, and he hated himself all the more for that weakness. "Hmm?" he prodded when she still said nothing.

"It is t-true." The warble there spoke of a partial lie buried within her words.

William perched his hip on the edge of the table, letting the moments pass, at ease in the silence until she finally, reluctantly lifted her gaze to his. "Is it?" He caught the strands of her braid that had fallen loose since she'd freed them of the ribbon.

She flinched and shot a hand out to try to slap his fingers.

William caught it, anticipating the move. Holding her gaze, he gently lowered her hand back to the table, freeing her, but also reminding her of who was in command of this exchange. "One's past is inextricably linked to one's present." He repeated the words she'd recently spoken. "Every word to leave your lips, every statement you utter, why..." He dipped his head lower, placing his lips alongside her ear, so close that he detected her audible inhalation. "Every uneven breath you take speaks of your feelings... and your intentions." William shifted his mouth closer, filling his lungs with the citrusy scent that clung to her skin. It was intoxicating. She was more potent than the spirits or the laudanum they'd plied him with. And he resisted that pull. "So do not pretend all of this," he whispered, his lips brushing against the shell of her ear, "was driven by a need to evaluate my jaw movement." His pulse throbbed loud in his ears, making a mockery of the illusion of control when his body was so attuned to Elsie's every movement. "You intended to pass our meetings off as medical in nature, when really you sought answers to questions you have." Sneering, William straightened. "About my past." Their gazes locked. "Ask them, but do not play games with me, madam. For you... will never win."

Another would have been cowed by the fury he let spill freely from his eyes. "Would you answer them?" she asked quietly. This woman proved the contrary one in every regard.

"You don't deserve answers."

"I don't," she agreed, pushing her chair back and getting to her feet. "But you deserve to share whatever keeps you imprisoned, because until you do, William, you will not be free."

He caught her hard about the waist, ringing a gasp from her lips.

Through the fabric of her gown, his fingers curled reflexively into the generous curve of her hip. "I have no desire to be free," he whispered, dipping his head so he might better hold her stare. "I have no desire to…"

"Forget," she breathed.

He stared at her full lips, transfixed, sucked further within her spell.

Elsie's long lashes fluttered, and she angled her head back. William battled with himself, wanting to lose himself again in her kiss. He briefly closed his eyes. And yet, if he did, something deep within him said there would be no coming back from the edge of temptation.

William released her.

"I invited you here to do a job, Elsie," he said coolly. "One singular task: to evaluate my jaw and nothing more. Do what you were ordered here to do. Or…" Get the hell out.

Except, he kept those words back.

"Or?" she prodded.

She wants me to throw her out. She'd expressed reservations from the start at being here and had been forced into the role by his brother. And yet, she'd come… and stayed anyway. And would remain here until he issued the declarative.

God help me, I cannot.

With horror sweeping through him, he backed away from her, keeping his eyes on her as he went. The moment he stepped into the hall, William bolted.

"WELL, THAT WAS A SINGULAR disaster," Elsie muttered.

The most essential rule in overseeing anyone or anything—be they human or animal—was to establish a relationship based on trust. That lesson had been one of the first her father had handed over to her as a girl overseeing the care of her first injured animal, a fawn with a broken limb she'd found in the same copse where her father would die years later.

And she'd forgotten it.

Nay, you allowed yourself to forget because you are impatient for answers about William Helling, Duke of Aubrey. Because she wanted to know about him as a man and the losses that had turned him into a surly, angry figure content to live away from the rest of the world.

He'd lost his wife, a woman he'd desperately loved and now punished himself out of some sense of guilt. All these years, she'd taken the nameless stranger who led the Brethren as one incapable of feelings and emotion. Only to find in William one who'd loved so deeply that he'd been reduced to a shadow of a person.

To be so loved. It was a sentiment she'd never allowed herself even a dream of, for she'd been viewed by the world as an oddity more than as a person.

Except for William, the unlikeliest of ones to not turn his nose up at her or her talents. And now, in having resurrected the past, she'd left him hurting.

Bear whined, batting at her skirts with his paw, calling her back from her thoughts. "I know. I know. Go to him," she urged.

The dog immediately sprang into action, rushing from the room with a speed he'd not shown in more years than she could remember.

"What in hell was that about?"

Elsie gasped and whipped her head toward the furious demand.

Lord Edward and his counterpart, Mr. Bennett, stormed into the breakfast room. Their matching black cloaks swirled angrily about their feet. Her heart knocking painfully against her ribcage, she shifted herself behind the high back of the seat William had vacated, sliding her fingers closer to the knife he'd left there. *Do you really think you could use it if need be?* That voice jeered her for the weak woman who'd run while her father had faced down the danger brought by the Brethren. "Lord Edward," she greeted with an equanimous calm that she did not feel. "Mr. Bennett."

"We're not here to exchange morning pleasantries, Miss Allenby," Mr. Bennett said in his brusque, lethal tones. He tugged off immaculate leather gloves and slapped them together. "We're here for a report on your work with His Grace. And by that"—he curled his lip in a derisive sneer—"exchange, you're as useless as everyone to come before you."

As she'd said to William moments ago, she didn't possess an inflated sense of self. She merely sought to help for the sake of helping, not to build a reputation of any sort. As such, Elsie let the insults roll off her person and instead fixed on one detail. She narrowed her eyes on the uglier, angrier of the pair. "You were listening in on our exchange?"

"We were verifying whether you are doing your job," Mr. Bennett shot back.

All her earlier fear dissolved, and the realization proved a restorative fact. They'd been there all along, listening in on her exchange with William… and then Bear. "I'll not be spied on."

"You will as long as you are in our company," he said with a cheerful matter-of-factness far more ominous than any threat he'd previously leveled.

She shivered.

Lord Edward lifted a hand, silencing his partner, and then he turned to Elsie. "Miss Allenby, will you please sit?" he asked, as polite as any gentleman greeting a guest in his parlor.

Elsie hesitated a moment and then took the chair previously occupied by William. She braced for him to tower above her as his brother had and issue veiled threats. Surprise filled her when he sat beside her.

Elsie quickly schooled her features and watched him. His movements were unhurried, deliberate, carried out with the ease of one who didn't wish to jolt a skittish mare. He stacked his gloves neatly alongside her forgotten plate. Then steepling his fingers, he laid them on his flat belly. "I'll speak candidly with you."

Mr. Bennett leveled a sharp glance at the other man that went ignored.

"Oh?" she asked cautiously.

"You gathered my brother's role is of some importance."

"I ventured he is the leader of your organization," she reminded him flatly.

His face remained impressively blank, carved of stone that not even a mason could chisel a hint of emotion or feeling into. "Regardless of what his specific role is or is not, the duke is a man of great importance. Your baiting him does us no good in helping to restore him to his previous state."

She contemplated those words, along with the gentleman before her. "So that is what this is about."

Lord Edward stared back quizzically.

"This..." Elsie waved a hand in front of her. "Me being here isn't about your brother. It is about the Brethren."

"They are one and the same." Both men spoke simultaneously. Of course that would be the answer to them. To these men, that was all anything was ever about. The lives of their victims, or those inadvertently touched by any connection, were disposable. And it would seem, even the leader of the organization itself was useful only for the purpose he served. Or, in this case, did not serve.

A sliver of sadness pierced her heart, settling in there. Was it any wonder William had become the cold, unfeeling figure he had? Not only had he been broken by the event he'd not speak of, but he was viewed more as an entity to serve than a person.

"I would speak with you alone," she said quietly to Lord Edward.

Mr. Bennett growled, "There's nothing you can say about His Grace that you cannot say in front of me."

"Leave us," the other man ordered in cool tones that were a mirror of his brother's.

He waited until Mr. Bennett had taken his leave and then stared at her expectantly.

"You want me to heal your brother," Elsie said without preamble. "You would have me lay hands upon him and take away whatever pain he knows." It was the hope of all the men who'd come before her father, pleading for an escape from their suffering. "Perhaps it is because he is family and you love him?" She hoped that for William's sake, but knew their type enough to know the unlikelihood of that pure emotion driving either of them. "Or perhaps it is because of his role." Elsie lifted her palms, willing him to understand. "But those reasons, and motives, they matter." William's visage flashed to her mind—angry, hurt, desperate—and her heart squeezed all the tighter. "Your brother is hurting, and he needs to find his way, not because of you or the Brethren, but because of him. His pain—" Ran far deeper than the physical effects suffered from a broken jaw.

"What is it?" Lord Edward encouraged.

Elsie looked to the door. Anyone could be standing outside it. Even the very man they spoke of. Discussing him with his brother, or anyone, would only be a betrayal. She weighed her response. "If I help him find freedom from physical pain?" She shook her head sadly. "He'll still not be the man he once was, nor could be, unless he deals with what is broken"—Elsie pressed her hands to her chest—"in here." She searched his face. "I don't expect you to understand that." No one ever truly had. Not the villagers who'd looked upon her as a freak, nor the patients her father had cared for.

"I do, though," he said in somber tones.

Her lips parted.

Lord Edward flashed a small smile. "I've known something of my own pain and what it took to find happiness again."

Which he had. There was a peace that radiated within his eyes. It was a sentiment she'd not seen reflected back in the cracked mirror of her modest chambers in nearly five years.

"What do you require?"

The question took her aback. "Truthfully?"

"I'd rather you not lie," he said dryly, startling a laugh from her. She'd not expected humor from him, or anyone within the Brethren.

"I don't require anything. I just require time and patience. I don't need you visiting daily to see if some unlikely miracle has occurred. Because there are no miracles in life. There is just time that serves as a balm."

"You'll have it," he said so automatically that it threw her off-balance once more.

"And your Mr. Bennett? Will he be of a like opinion?"

Lord Edward snorted. "He's not mine. Cedric Bennett belongs to no one."

She nodded. "Precisely."

All earlier brevity faded. "You'll have what you require. He'll accept the terms as I set them forth." He picked up his gloves and twisted them in his hands a moment, studying his fingers. As if he felt her gaze on his movements, Lord Edward stopped. "I would have you know that Cedric… and others, for them, my brother's *role* is all that matters. But he is suffering, and I'd not see him hurt."

It was the most honest he'd been with her since they'd met. "Thank you," she said softly.

He said nothing for a long while. White lines formed at the corners of his mouth from the tight manner in which he clenched those muscles. "His wife—"

She shook her head, cutting him off. "No." He still did not

understand. But then, the concept was difficult for most to grasp. "You needn't explain." She would learn, as William was ready.

Lord Edward stood. She rushed to her feet beside him. "If you require anything, Miss Allenby…"

"I will certainly notify you," she promised. But she would not need him. Not as long as she was here and not when she left.

Instead of leaving, however, Lord Edward lingered. "I am sorry about the circumstances surrounding your father." She went still at the unexpected statement. "I trust there were reasons—"

"Please do not." The request tore from her throat. "I'm not here to redeem him in your eyes." Their opinions did not matter. Pain and regret stuck in her throat, and she struggled to get words past the emotion. "I know who my father was, and that is enough."

He bowed his head, his silence unaccusing, and a small branch extended.

Lord Edward drew on his gloves and started for the door, but then abruptly stopped. "Miss Allenby?"

She stared back questioningly.

"You insist you are not capable of healing or miracles, and yet, my brother has not broken his fast in this room in a year. He's not had his hair drawn back, and he's certainly never allowed someone to speak as candidly as you did earlier." A smiled ghosted his lips. "Not without having that person tossed out on their ars—ergh." His cheeks flushed, and he coughed into his fist. "You've already done more for William than I'd believed anyone capable of."

Her cheeks warmed under his praise. "You make more of it than there is."

Lord Edward chuckled. "Miss Allenby, I'm a man who deals in facts. I don't make anything out of something that is not there."

And with that, William's brother left.

Elsie stared at the open doorway. He believed she'd reached William, and yet, she could not, and would not, with the approach she'd taken.

They needed to begin again.

Fueled by that, Elsie went in search of her patient.

CHAPTER 12

WILLIAM PACED THE FLOOR OF his chambers.

You deserve to share whatever holds you trapped, because until you do, William, you will not be free...

How dare she? he seethed. How dare she presume what he needed, or what would help him be free? As if he could be free. As if he *deserved* it. He slashed his hand through the air as he walked. Forgiveness, she'd spoken of. Peace. Such sentiments didn't truly exist. Not for him. And not for most. The artificial security possessed by the world was supplied by William and the others who did the work of the Home Office.

William stopped abruptly. Goddamn her. She was right.

He stared blankly at the light that spilled through the crack in his curtains. Elsie had exposed him for the fraud he was. And he was very much a fraud in every way. William caught himself against a table to keep himself standing and clung to it for all he was worth.

His chest heaved as it had when he'd raced Edward through the hills of Kent. Only, this was no boyish game from long-ago times of stolen innocence. This was the reality of now.

"I failed." He forced himself to whisper that truth into existence. His entire body went whipcord straight as the realization slammed into him.

He'd failed. He'd deliberately let himself fail in his role as Sovereign. He'd failed the family that had taken him as the all-powerful duke, not only keeping his own life well-ordered, but the lives of the entire Helling family. He'd failed his godson, a boy with an abusive father, a mere child who'd relied upon William for protection and love. And he'd failed the one woman who'd relied upon him for protection and safety.

As such, he'd been punishing himself ever since.

A faint scratching split the quiet.

William jumped. Bloody hell. What a pathetic bastard he'd become, being caught unaware by servants. It hardly mattered that the servants in his employ were all members vetted and trained by the Home Office. "Go away," he thundered at the door.

Silence met the demand, and as soon as the echo of his voice ceased bouncing around the room, he let his shoulders drop. What was happening to him? His household? The control he'd thought he had?

I never really had it.

He had been exposed for the impostor he was. A man unworthy and undeserving of the great trust that had been placed in his hands. Shame soured his stomach. It had taken nothing more than a diminutive spitfire to make him see the truth of what he was.

Nay, she was not *nothing more.*

Elsie as she'd been a short while ago slipped into his mind, tenaciously clinging to his thoughts. Just as she'd done since she arrived. Two days ago? A lifetime ago? There was a spirit and strength within her, the likes of which he'd never before witnessed in any woman. Not his wife, not any of the women whose services had been enlisted on behalf of the Brethren.

And that is why you stormed off.

Because Elsie scared the hell out of him. God help him, how did he, a man of the clearest logic, rationalize the hold she had over him in this short time?

It's because you do not know what to do with her. He didn't know what to make of her. And what terrified him even more was that she'd proven he was not so immune to feeling emotions he'd rather not feel.

William dragged his hands through his hair, freeing the greasy strands from the neat arrangement she'd made. The faded blue ribbon sailed to the floor at his feet.

He stared blankly at the scrap. It lay there, a faded flash of blue among the brighter shades of his crimson Aubusson carpet. The fabrics stood in a stark juxtaposition of wealth and poverty. Beckoned by the faintest answers contained within that article, William dropped to his haunches. Collecting Elsie's ribbon, he rubbed the fabric between his thumb and forefinger. All the while, he studied the gift she'd conferred.

Who was Elsie Allenby?

Her flawless tones were befitting any refined English lady, while her cheeks, tanned from the sun, spoke of a country miss. One who, by the threadbare quality of her drab gowns and the ribbon he held, had very little. William drew the ribbon close to his nose and slid his eyes closed.

The whisper of lemon and orange that had filled his senses and nearly snapped his control in the breakfast room enticed. But here, in the privacy of his chambers, with the world shut out, he let the innocent fragrances flood him. They threaded through him, wholly understated and yet potently tempting for their subtlety.

Hers was not the sickly sweet perfumes the actresses and mistresses he'd taken this past year had doused themselves in.

The faintest scratch sounded at the door.

The ribbon slipped from William's fingers, and cursing under his breath, he scrambled to collect the fabric. "I said, get the hell out," he bellowed, straightening.

Where his earlier request had been met with a dutiful silence, this time the scratching persisted. A servant's scratch, as he and Edward had so jokingly called the bothersome *raps* at the door by their parents' nauseatingly formal staff. His late father would not, however, have tolerated the insolence of having his orders gainsaid.

But then, he'd proven countless times that he was not his father. Not in the ways that mattered.

Self-loathing brought him to his feet. Slamming down Elsie's ribbon, William stormed over to the door and yanked it open. "Did you not hear what I…" His words faded into nothing as he glanced down at the unlikeliest of intruders.

His large pink tongue lolling out of the side of his mouth, Bear panted heavily.

"Get out," William ordered and made to shut the oak panel. "Last night was a momentary lapse in my sanity." And yet, he stood there, still talking to a dog.

Bear emitted a pathetic little whimper.

His defenses faltered. "Don't you have your mistress to see to?" William pleaded.

Said young woman's dog barked once.

"I don't need company," William protested. As soon as the admission left him, heat spiraled from his neck up to his cheeks. He looked out into the hall and did a frantic search. "Talking to dogs," he muttered under his breath.

Taking that as his proverbial welcome, Bear wedged his enormous frame through the slight gap of the door and trotted inside.

William stared out at the carved-wood settee in the hall and counted to five in his quest for patience. Yes, his life had indeed become a farce. He hesitated a moment and then reentered his rooms.

William pushed the panel closed with the heel of his foot and faced his canine companion.

Seated in the middle of his rooms alongside the mahogany center table, Bear sniffed at the ribbon that lay nearby.

"Spying like your mistress, I see," he muttered, stalking over to the dog. He stopped abruptly several paces away. Talking to a bloody mutt and joining him.

Bear nosed at the fabric.

Speaking to animals would certainly place William firmly in the company of one who'd gone wholly mad. Even with that certainty, he found himself sliding onto the floor alongside Elsie's dog. Drawing his knees to his chest, William stretched a hand out and stroked the top of Bear's neck.

The mutt's back leg reflexively moved in time to that stroking. "So, tell me, why are you really here? Did you also need to escape the chit?"

Bear slid his eyes closed and leaned into William's attention.

Yes, it would seem Elsie Allenby had that effect on both man and beast.

All animals, really... They are not so very different from humans.

What a peculiar woman his brother had thrust into William's household. She had unconventional views of animals and a desire to care for them when Polite Society saw little use for any animals beyond horses for riding and hunting and the hounds whose services they required during those hunts.

William continued to absently stroke the top of Bear's head, until the dog's eyes grew shuttered, and he sank onto his belly.

Moments later, bleating snores escaped from Bear's mouth.

As he petted the dog's coarse coat, he contemplated the graying and white hairs. The creature was old and, by the shadows in his eyes, nearing blindness. Elsie kept him anyway. This large mutt that few would ever want because of his lack of breeding, she insisted on traveling with.

Adeline had cringed at the mere mention of a dog in their household. Not even his explanation of wanting a loyal creature for when his nephew Leopold came 'round had any effect upon that horror.

Dogs were dirty. They tracked paw prints across fine carpets. They were noisy. They were… a whole host of other problems a person did not want in one's household. That had been what she'd said anyway.

An unfaithful thought, a comparison of two women who were nothing alike—one who deserved his loyalty in death, and the other a stranger… who he wished to discover more about. For reasons that had nothing to do with the Brethren. Reasons that defied logic and had only everything to do with Elsie Allenby herself.

Footfalls outside his chambers cut into his musings, and he gave his head a clearing shake, grateful for the intrusion.

The determined steps came to a stop outside his rooms.

Outside his rooms? His servants and staff knew that during the days he was to be left—

A heavy knock reverberated in a sharp echo around the rooms.

Bear's ears pricked up before he dropped his head back between his paws and resumed sleeping.

"You're not much of a damned guard dog," he muttered, pushing himself upright. His jaw throbbed, and swallowing a curse, William caught his chin in his palm.

That will not help…

What the hell did she know? He silently railed at the minx who'd uttered that unhelpful announcement. *And more…what in hell is wrong with me: quarreling with minx and chatting with her damned dog.* Stalking to the door, William drew it open—

And froze.

Her hand poised in the air in midknock, Elsie stared at him with saucer-sized round eyes. "Oh."

At that breathy little exhalation, he sent an eyebrow slashing up. "Expecting another, madam?"

"No," she said quickly. "I was not. I heard you talking to..." Her gaze slid over his shoulder to Bear.

He silently dared her to say anything of it. As Elsie turned back, he stiffened.

She gave him a small smile. "You were teasing again."

Some of the tension went out of him. "I do not tease." He never had. Not even when his wife had been living. Not with his family. And certainly not with those who worked on behalf of the Brethren.

Elsie wrinkled her pert nose. "I trust that is largely true, but given that in our short acquaintance, you've uttered two faintly jesting comments—"

His head ached at her methodical accounting. "Madam," he warned.

"Oh, yes. Forgive me."

"I trust you are looking for him."

They glanced as one over to the slumbering dog, who at that moment flipped onto his back and snored all the louder. "Oh, no. I knew where he was off to. I gave him permission."

She...?

"Gave him permission," she reiterated with a nod. "He was worried about you."

And mayhap the minx was capable of miracles. For the first time in the whole damned year, it was not his jaw, chin, mouth, and every facial muscle that ached, but rather, his blasted head. He jammed his fingertips against his temples and rubbed—to no avail. "Dogs do not worry about people."

She scoffed. "*Of course* they do."

He might as well have stated the sky was in fact green and the grass blue for the effrontery in her tone.

Elsie glowered at him. "I expect one such as you wouldn't know a thing about having an animal and loving him."

"I had a dog, madam. I know something of it."

"You do?" she breathed. "You did?"

"I did, and my father had him put down because of a limp he'd developed after a hunt."

She caught an agonized gasp in her palm. "Oh, William," she said with a wealth of understanding.

William fisted his hands at his sides. My God, where had that admission come from? He'd thought that memory long buried and had never talked of it or shared it with anyone. Not his brother or sister. Not his wife. "It is fine," he said tightly.

Elsie shook her head, challenging him at every turn. "It is not fine," she said with a tenderness that washed through him, a siren's spell she cast over him. "It explains so very much."

"Elsie," he warned impatiently.

Her features softened. "Regardless, I've not come for Bear." Something shifted in his chest.

He should back away from the undefinable emotion in her intense hazel eyes. He should run from whatever these emotions were that she was forcing him to once again feel. Yet, he remained rooted to the spot, inexplicably drawn deeper and deeper into her pull.

"Why are you here?" In this household. In these rooms.

She glanced beyond his shoulder. "May I come in?"

William followed her stare. Into his chambers? Not once in their short marriage had Adeline ever set foot within them. The times they'd been intimate, he'd visited her chambers, and she'd expected him to leave shortly after they'd completed "the act," as she'd referred to it. Since that, whores and actresses had been here, and servants had been here to clean. But this… Elsie entering his chambers would be neither about sex nor a servant's assignments.

His palms went moist, and he curled his hands at his sides to hide the dampness.

Wordlessly, he stepped aside.

Elsie sailed into the room as though this was her rightful place and she was claiming it, no questions asked and no fight expected. She was… breathtaking in that command, fully self-possessed and assured—and unapologetic.

Elsie stopped when she reached Bear and eyed the dog a moment. "I…" Her gaze caught on the ribbon abandoned upon the rose-inlaid table.

He followed her stare. All his muscles strained, urging him forward as he anticipated her actions and yearned to halt her.

Elsie gathered her ribbon and methodically dropped it into the pocket sewn along the front of her dress.

"Is that what you've come for, then?" he drawled, infusing a false boredom into his tones.

"No." She shook her head. "I came to apologize."

William peered at her through the tangle that was his hair, damning it for the hindrance it was for the first time since he'd ceased tending it. "You—"

"I'm sorry," she said simply.

William wandered over, carefully studying her as he walked. "Do tell, Elsie. What exactly are you sorry for?"

For allowing his convincing and far-too-charming brother to cajole her into journeying to William's residence?

Elsie clasped her hands before her. "I should have been forthright with you," she acknowledged. "When I suggested we dine together, it was… a ploy, as you referred to it. It was not my right to trick you or force any meetings upon you." She drew in a breath. "Going forward, my intentions will be clear and forthright. I'll not use any ploys to gather information that I believe would be helpful for you to share." Elsie faltered in her avowal as he stopped a handbreadth from her, with only Bear between them. She swiftly regained her footing. "Rather, I will ask you any questions I have about your physical well-being and your past. You can of course send me to the devil, but you can rely upon honesty from me."

William rocked back on his heels.

He was unaccustomed to people who took ownership of their words and actions. Lords and ladies were trained from birth to believe they were wholly in the right and could never be wrong on any score. "Why the about-face?" he pressed, heavy skepticism layered within the question.

Elsie lifted her shoulders in a little shrug. "Because it is the right thing to do. I'm not so arrogant that I believe myself correct in all decisions, and I'm not unable to apologize for the times I am in the wrong."

William considered her with a deepening wariness. Everything within him said not to trust her. But an equal part of him was riveted by her directness. "Fine," he said crisply. "What do you want?"

People always wanted something. And with Elsie's gracious apology, he'd be mad not to mistrust that she possessed ulterior motives.

"To shave you."

An image whispered around his mind, enticing him. Of her fingers upon him, touching him—not in the mindless act of passion he'd allowed himself to surrender to, but instead with the delicate caress he'd known all too fleetingly in the breakfast room. Alas, his service to the Brethren had given him countless reasons to be dubious of all women's actions. Including seemingly innocent and well-meaning ones like Elsie Allenby.

He snapped his fingers twice, and Bear sprang to his feet and promptly moved into position behind him.

Elsie's eyes flared. "How did you…?"

"How did I what?" he asked. "Hmm?" he urged when she remained tight-lipped. William strolled a path around her. "Know the signals you use with your dog?" He didn't allow her a chance to answer. "I'm nothing if not *observant*, Elsie." All his facial muscles protested their overuse, and still he was compelled to engage her. "Why should I dare trust you with a blade in your hand and access to my throat?"

She blanched, leaving her a ghastly white. "I would not… I could not…" Hurt him?

The young woman wore her sincerity like a mark upon her stricken face. But God help him. His instincts had proven so bloody faulty. He'd made missteps, and the results had been catastrophic. He'd be a fool to not be skeptical of this curious woman before him. "I've reason enough to question everyone's motives."

"It is a sad way to be, isn't it?"

That brought him up short.

For she didn't seek to convince him, or spout words belonging to an innocent. Yet again, she spoke as one who had been burned by life. Her fingers shook, and he took in the telltale quake.

"It is a safer way to be," he said gruffly.

The young woman jammed her trembling digits back inside her pocket once more. The haunted glint he'd detected in her eyes glimmered bright, even in his dimly lit rooms. Again, an inexplicable hungering to drive that darkness away superseded logic.

"You wish to shave me, then."

She wet her lips. It was a statement more than anything, but she answered anyway. "So that I might freely inspect your jaw and facial muscles."

"There are no scars," he warned. It was a waste of time to search for surface wounds.

Her gaze slid past his shoulder, and he knew the moment she ceased to see him and lived within her own mind and memories. "The scars one carries are often deeper and more painful than anything on the surface," she whispered.

Gooseflesh rose on his arms.

Elsie blinked slowly and then glanced almost dazedly about the room before she settled her stare on William. Clearing her throat, she favored him with a small smile. "Shall we begin?"

CHAPTER 13

ELSIE'S FINGERS STILL SHOOK.

Before, they had trembled at unwanted memories raised by William's mistrust and ruthless reminder that men… and women were given to evil acts, but now they quaked for altogether different reasons.

A short while later, with the items she'd requested delivered by a small army of servants and laid out upon the boulle shaving stand and mirror, Elsie stood with her back presented to William.

Her nape burned from the intensity of the stare he directed on her. And she stole a quick peek at the mirror. Her gaze collided with his. A faintly mocking smile ghosted his lips—and hers burned with the remembered feel of his mouth upon hers. *Stop.* Elsie redirected all her focus on the task at hand. What accounted for that cynical, mirthless grin? Had he sensed her unease and reveled in it? Was it that she'd been so rubbish at her furtive observation of him?

Either way, the gentleman remained a mystery in every way.

Nay, not necessarily in *every way*.

He'd agreed to her request—yet again. When the cynical glint in his eyes had hinted of a man who wanted to order her gone, he'd capitulated. He'd also allowed Bear to enter his rooms. What did it all say about William Helling, Duke of Aubrey, and this state of isolation he'd imposed upon himself?

It indicates he wants to be free…

It proved he was a man who carried guilt and pain.

She picked up the scissors and tested their sharpness. All the while, she contemplated William. No doubt, based on her own experience with those within the Brethren, William flagellated himself for crimes that he could never atone for. Why, he'd brought misery upon her own household and did not even recall the man whose life he'd so upended.

The scissors slipped from her fingers and clattered noisily upon the wood.

"Are we ready?" His melodious murmur rumbled around the room.

Elsie stiffened. "Just a moment more." To steady herself, she hurriedly shifted the straight-edge razor, shaving scuttle and brush, and scissors so they lay in a neat row. When she'd finished, she stared at the items. "You may sit," she called, directing that to the scissors.

The floorboards offered not so much as a groan to indicate the stealthy gentleman had moved. Silent as night, William slid into the ridiculous Venetian Green Man carved and gilded wood throne befitting a king. But then, William was not very far from that exalted state. He would sit on such a hideous piece of furniture that would cost more than all her personal possessions combined and would have been more beneficial to her to burn the mahogany wood portions for warmth.

"You disapprove," he noted when she reached for a towel.

"Of?" Elsie dipped the fabric into the washbowl.

"The chair," he clarified.

Elsie squeezed out the cloth, splashing droplets within the bowl. "I don't like it," she said matter-of-factly. "There's a difference between disapproving and disliking." Good God, was there nothing he missed? She was in over her head with him. And in being here, in helping him, she was making the same naïve mistakes her father had. "It is hard to disapprove of an inanimate object."

A laugh exploded from William's lips. Coarse and ragged, it was a primitive half growl that originated in his chest and shocked her motionless, for there was also a sentiment she'd not witnessed from him—genuine mirth. Unlike the cynical half grins he'd flashed since her arrival. He cradled his jaw as he laughed.

William stopped abruptly. He opened and closed his mouth.

And then tried again. "I haven't laughed..." he whispered, letting his hand fall to his lap. "I..." Shock-filled eyes met her own, an almost-plea buried within their depths.

Her heart squeezed. This raw pain was something she knew something of. In this, the two unlikeliest of people paired together were kindred spirits. "I haven't either," she confessed into the quiet.

His body went still, the silence encouraging her to continue.

And yet, she couldn't. Elsie wrung the cloth out once more, squeezing out the remaining drops. She applied it to his thick beard and held it in place.

"It was a gift from my wife," he said quietly. The jolting admission came out slightly muffled by the damp cloth covering his mouth.

Elsie lifted the fabric and returned it to the bowl.

"I hated it," he confessed, another laugh escaping him, this one less raw and containing memories that only he saw but wished to confer. "I thought it garish and better fitting a place in the king's palace than in my chambers."

Her lips twitched. She and William were alike in that thought, too.

His laughter faded to a distant smile. "But it was a gift from her, and she was so very proud of the piece she'd had commissioned. And so, I told her thank you and that I loved it. It's been here ever since."

William gave his head a little shake, dislodging an errant drop of water that clung to his beard.

Propelled back into movement, Elsie gathered the towel once more, dunked it several times, wrung it out, and pressed it to his cheeks. "My father whittled me a dog."

She'd not shared the memory before because there had never been anyone to share it with.

Over the edge of the white cloth, William met her eyes. Mayhap this was why men such as he probed the secrets of strangers on behalf of the Home Office, for an unexplainable need to share that part of herself slipped forward.

"My father knew of my love of animals, and it was my birthday. I wager he could have talked circles around any scholar trained in medicine, but"—amusement bubbled in her chest—"a whittler he was not. The dog had five legs."

Another laugh exploded from him. "Five?"

She joined in, and their laughter melded and rolled together, his heavy and deep, hers lighter and lyrical. And it felt so very good to laugh again. And with him, the most unexpected of men to make her feel… anything outside of her own resentment. "It… it was to be a tail," she managed to squeeze out through her hilarity. She shook with the force of the healing amusement until tears streamed down her cheeks and William's visage blurred. "A-and because the additional leg was slightly larger than the two hind ones, he was perched upright, perpetually s-standing." Elsie doubled over and clutched at her sides, letting the lightness fill her chest and spread out to every corner of her being. How she missed this… carefreeness.

Their laughter dissolved together as the present intruded, along with the memory of her role here.

Elsie dusted the amusement from her eyes and, with a soft sigh, removed the damp cloth from William's face.

Collecting the scissors, she set to trimming the slightly coarse hair of his beard.

As she worked, she felt his stare on her. No further words passed between them.

Elsie paused periodically to assess the length of William's beard. She tugged lightly at the errant strands, cutting them. "There," she murmured, setting the scissors down. She traded them for the brush scuttle and stirred the warmed soap into a frothy lather. The quality brush knocked a calming staccato against the porcelain. Next, she applied the lather to his bearded cheeks.

His eyes slid closed, a tiny but infinite evidence of his trust. Did he even realize what he'd done?

"How does a young woman learn how to shave a gentleman?" The quiet murmur came so hushed, she thought for a minute she'd imagined it, until William opened his eyes and revealed the question there.

"You are bound to be disappointed, I fear, William," she explained, setting the shaving scuttle aside. "Alas, my experience has largely come from the animals who required their wounds tended."

Cursing, he jerked upright with an alacrity that pulled another laugh from her. "Bloody hell, Elsie," he hissed, ensnaring her wrist in his larger, firmer grip. Yet, there was a gentleness to that touch, and her pulse picked up its beat where William held her.

"Hush," she scolded. "I was teasing." Another moment of brevity had felt so cathartic.

He eyed her for a moment with his usual darkened gaze, and then the faintest glitter danced in his eyes.

All the air lodged in her chest as she caught a fleeting glimpse of the man he must have been… before his life had fallen apart. "You have shaved those of the human sort?"

"I have."

As he weighed that promise, there was a boylike suspicion in his gaze that transformed him from a ruthless, angry duke into someone endearing. Her heart flipped over in her chest.

"Minx." William slackened his grip and then seemed to think better of it. "How many?"

Ah, so he was taking no chances. "Enough that I've not nicked one's cheek in more years than I can remember." She'd not point out the reason for that had more to do with her lack of human companionship than any real improvement of her skill.

He roved his eyes over her face. "Have you ever been married?"

It was a deeply intimate question that had no bearing on her place here. However, in order for her to help him, they had to have a reciprocal relationship in which she sought information and answers from him and he was entitled to the same.

"No," she said quietly. "I told you my name is *Miss* Allenby, and I didn't lie to you. I've never been married." The dream of a husband was not one she allowed herself.

"And why not?" he asked, pulling another little laugh from her.

"I don't know if I should be insulted by your question—"

"No insult was intended," he rushed to reassure in crisp tones that spoke to the dual role he played for the world. Proper. Polite. A duke in every way. That was, in every way when he was not doing the work of the Home Office.

"It is fine." She waved off his apology. "I was teasing." For a second time that day.

William sat forward in the throne-chair, shifting his body closer to hers.

Elsie curled her toes into the soles of her serviceable boots to keep from squirming under the force of his scrutiny. "Has there been no kind village boy to earn your affections?"

"Given I'm nearly thirty-one, Your Grace, I'd hardly desire a match with a boy."

His jaw went slack.

"I'm short in stature, William," she said dryly. Lather slipped down his chin, and she caught it with her hand. "There's no correlation between a grown woman's height and years. Now, turn."

He complied, presenting his right cheek.

"So why no husband?"

He was… tenacious, and on the unlikeliest of topics. Nonetheless, if he wished to engage in discussion, she'd encourage those attempts. "I don't know, William," she murmured, wholly concentrating on her hand as she scraped the razor along his cheek. "Mayhap I was too busy. Mayhap there was no man who'd be a good match for me." She paused and stared at the bit of skin she'd exposed. "Mayhap time simply marched on, and I failed to note its passing." Until it was too late. And because of that, there would never be a family of her own, no babe to birth or child to hold, or husband to laugh with freely. Sadness swept through her.

Elsie dipped the foamy blade into the water, rinsing it off. She added lather to his right cheek and resumed her efforts.

"So it was not a father you shaved, nor a husband, nor a beau," he murmured, his lips barely moving as he spoke. "It begs the question, just who were these… clients?" Before she could replay, he ventured, "Patients?"

"Patients," she conceded, running the razor carefully along his chin. Those patients had also no doubt been the poor, wounded souls who'd answered to this very gentleman.

"Ah," he said, as if he could see. When, in fact, he saw not even the truth of who she was. Would it matter to him either way?

William flinched.

Elsie gasped and jerked the razor back. A single crimson drop pebbled on his flesh. "I am so sorry." Dropping the razor onto the table, she collected a damp cloth and applied faint pressure to the mark.

"I assure you I've suffered far greater injuries than a nick from a razor," he said from around the towel. His eyes sparkled again with amusement. "And I fear you've shattered your impressive run on uninjured clients."

"You are correct on that score," she said, returning his smile.

"In full, if belated, disclosure, I should have indicated that I've not shaved anyone in nearly five years." As soon as the statement left her mouth, she wanted to call it back, for it ushered in a heaviness, tossing darkness where there had just moments ago been light.

Swallowing painfully, Elsie picked up the razor and, pulling the skin taut at the right corner of his sharp cheekbone, glided the sharp edge of the blade over the growth. She continued scraping the razor downward to his neck. The faint scratch of the razor filled the quiet, punctuated only by William's measured breaths. Setting the metal blade down, she reached for the brush and reapplied lather to his face and neck. All the while, his gaze remained trained upon her.

"Your father has been gone five years, then," he said in somber tones, as if she'd only just now mentioned that passage of time. "You've been on your own… five years."

"Yes," she murmured. Five years going on forever. "Turn slightly," she instructed.

He complied, and Elsie's fingers tightened on the razor. She forced herself to lighten her grip and resumed shaving him. William was again drifting too close to topics she'd rather not talk about. And certainly not with him. The unlikely connection they shared marked a barrier between them. Focusing on that past, revisiting that resentment made it impossible for her to do the work she'd been brought here to do. Work her father would have wished her to oversee.

For the first time in the whole of her life, she hated how very much like her father she was, because when everything inside her implored her to run from this man with his piercing eyes and probing questions, her promise to help him kept her at his side.

WILLIAM HAD PROVEN LONG AGO he was a selfish bastard.

The greatest of that sin being that he'd married a woman he'd had no place marrying and had done so when a union to him only opened her to peril.

And now, plying each secret and story from Elsie Allenby's lips when she didn't wish to give them, and when he had no intention of sharing in return, was just another mark of his selfishness.

His reasons for wanting to know more about her, however, had nothing to do with the reasons she'd sought his information. Simply put, he wanted to know about her. He wanted to again witness her eyes sparkle and her expression light up with joy at those stories she carried. He wanted to know how she'd become this woman before him: composed and honorable enough that she could apologize when he himself had always been too proud to so easily muster those words.

Elsie alternated the razor for the brush and worked the soap into a finer lather before then applying it to his nearly shaven cheeks.

"You don't wish to speak of him," he surmised, his lips barely moving as she scraped the edge of the blade along his upper lip.

"Shhh." Her brow puckered in deep consideration of the task she attended. "I'll cut you."

"You worry you'll cut me? Or rather, you wish to distract me?"

Her full crimson lips pulled at the corners in the hint of a smile. The delicate expression of amusement pulled him deeper into her snare. "Both," she conceded.

"You don't wish to speak about your father, then?" Or more specifically, about his passing. The man who'd sired her, whom she spoke of with such fondness, was not one she carried rotten memories of.

"No," she agreed unashamedly. "I don't." Elsie dropped the razor and dusted her palms together. "But I will." She stared expectantly at him. Waiting. Waiting for any query he put to her, fully prepared to answer.

As the Sovereign, he'd all but written the code followed by the agents within the Brethren, detailing countless brutal ways to exact information one sought. Simply asking and receiving a direct answer had never been a possibility in the work he, or the men who worked for him, did. "Why would you do that?" he shot back, ignoring the dull ache that had begun to settle into his jawbone from overexertion. William eyed her through narrowed eyes. Surely there was a trap there. The men and women he'd dealt with in his line of work divulged nothing, even under the cruelest tortures.

Elsie resumed shaving him. "I've nothing to hide," she said with an innocence he'd not even been born with. "Secrets are dangerous," she murmured, scraping away more of his previously thick beard. "They destroy."

Ice coursed through his veins, freezing him from the inside out. Elsie Allenby might be innocent and unjaded, but she proved markedly accurate in that. His currency, by nature of his role with the Brethren, had been the secrets of those who sought to harm the Crown or country. Those who sought to bring down English men of power and influence. Why, his very identity among Polite Society had been false, crafted by the Home Office with the intent to deceive. "The people I deal with do not simply turn over intimate parts of themselves to strangers," he said gruffly, not so much as moving his lips as he spoke.

"Then those, sir," she murmured, her brow puckered from the depth of her concentration, "are not people I'd wish to keep company with."

Which begged the question… "Who are the people you do keep company with?"

Pain contorted her features, twisting them into a briefly ravaged mask of grief. "It was just my father and me." She paused. "And the men who required care. Patients. The occasional villagers who needed medical attention."

A niggling rooted around the back of his mind, an unpleasant one he didn't want to ask, because he didn't want to know that she lived alone, without a soul in the world for friendship or companionship. And yet, the question was pulled from him anyway. "When your father passed… did you continue your work with his patients?"

"Turn," she instructed, gently guiding his chin sideways so she might reach his opposite cheek. "The villagers in Bladon are hardly so progressive that they'd enlist the help of a woman."

His gut clenched. There it was. A confirmation he didn't want. She'd existed on the fringe of the world, with no one there. "Fools," he muttered.

She chuckled. "I've not helped you in any way," she pointed out.

Her observation was a matter-of-fact. There was nothing she'd provided in the way of medical treatment to alleviate the oft-times debilitating jaw pain that made a chore of meals and speech.

And yet, at the same time… Of its own volition, his gaze drifted over her endearingly focused face. She'd also, in her brief time here, pulled him from an abyss of despair and made him feel… something other than the dark emptiness that he'd descended into.

She'd infuriated him. Amazed him. Held him completely captivated. This, whatever it was, was a betrayal of Adeline's memory. Because this was not the emotionless sexual encounters he had with the whores and actresses who wanted nothing more than his coin and connections. This draw to Elsie Allenby came from a genuine fascination with who she was—as a person.

While his mind was in tumult, Elsie drew back and assessed her work. "Nearly finished." She again reached for the lather brush and swirled it in small, soothing circles over his face.

"What manner of man was your father?"

"Are you asking if he was kind?"

"No," he corrected. "A man who so knew his daughter's interests that he'd whittle her a dog is a man who was devoted."

"Loving," she whispered. Her heartbroken expression wrenched at a heart that proved itself not so very broken after all. "He was loving."

"What happened to him?" Again, her fingers slipped, and she cursed.

"I'm sorry," she said quickly and grabbed for the damp cloth. She made to press it to the slight nick in his flesh, but William relieved her of the fabric.

"It is nothing," he assured, applying pressure himself.

Elsie chewed at her lower lip and glanced over her shoulder at the door. She contemplated escape. That hungering for flight was clear from the tension in her slender frame and the tightness of her lips.

She wouldn't, though.

He'd come to recognize Elsie Allenby as a woman who'd never run from any challenge or threat. Even for self-preservation.

Moments, or minutes, might have passed, with time blurring before she returned her attention forward. Elsie brought her shoulders back and, with a skill and ease his former valet would be hard-pressed to learn, reapplied herself to William's grooming. "My father was a man who'd not reject any request or demand for help." As she spoke, her voice rang with both pride and regret. "It was a virtue but also a fault, and it would prove to be my father's downfall," Elsie explained, shaving the remaining hair from his neck, the blade scraping over his throat. One slight flick of her wrist, and she could end him if she wished. He'd not put himself in such a vulnerable place at the hands of any stranger. Until her. She made one more expert stroke with her impressively steady hand. "There." She set down the razor and assessed him. "We've finished," she said softly, her eyes lingering on his face before she returned her attention to cleaning up the work area she'd set up.

William followed her every methodical movement.

They'd finished. Which meant Elsie would leave, which he should vastly prefer. So why did a slight panic build in his chest at the thought of her departure?

"…I'll send servants for the dirtied waters," she was saying. Elsie bowed her head. Not a curtsy, as was customary, which made this unconventional woman all the more intriguing. "Until tomorrow, William."

Tomorrow? He shot to his feet. "What of your requests to take meals…?" His face went hot, and he yearned for the restoration of that hair to hide his flushed cheeks.

She gave him a reassuring smile. "Is this a test?"

A test? He puzzled his brow.

"I promised I'd not seek to trick you into spending additional time with me. I can gather all the information I need when you break your fast." She stared expectantly at him, prodding him into saying something.

"Tomorrow," he said gruffly, the realization leaving him oddly bereft. His eyes went over her narrow shoulders to the clock atop his mantel. Nearly two and twenty hours. What did she intend to do in that time?

Elsie offered another smile and then snapped her fingers twice. "William," she said in parting, and moments later, with Bear close at her heels, Elsie closed the door behind her and left William feeling more alone than he had in the whole of the year.

CHAPTER 14

"You are not chewing."

"Because I'm not accustomed to someone watching me chew," William muttered, glaring at the small piece of sausage he was *still* dicing.

After two days of the same lessons together, he was very well imagining that she was that poor, breakfast meat carved into impossibly minute pieces.

He speared a piece, but instead of forking it into his mouth, he held it over the side of his chair.

Bear immediately sprinted over.

"William," she chided.

"What manner of mistress do you have that she'd begrudge you a morning meal?" he asked Bear in gentler tones than he'd ever used with her.

Warmth wound its way through her. Not even her late father had engaged Bear in discourse. Elsie's lips pulled at the corners, and she repressed the smile. "Oh, come, you're a duke, William. I trust you're accustomed to people watching you."

"Not while I break my fast," he clarified, dropping another piece of sausage over the side of the table.

Bear snapped his head back and caught it in his mouth. He lingered a moment at William's side, and when it became apparent that no more offerings were coming, he returned to a more neutral place between Elsie and William.

William returned to mutilating that piece of meat. When he finished, he set his knife down but made no attempt to sample his breakfast. Instead, he glowered at the food on his porcelain plate.

And mayhap she had more of her father's goodness in her than she'd believed herself in possession of, for the evidence of the pain this man dealt with and the struggle he faced to complete a mundane task such as eating sent pangs to her heart.

As if he felt her gaze, William looked over, and she swiftly smoothed her features. He'd mistake her response for pity, and proud as he was, that sentiment would only send the walls he'd built about himself all the way back into place.

Elsie forced a smile. "Furthermore," she went on, sitting back in her chair, "I've been assessing you for two days now. Three, if one includes the first morning meal we took together." Though, in fairness, given the fact he'd stormed off without touching a bite, that day hardly counted.

"Watching me," he gritted and winced, swiftly stabilizing his jaw with his palm.

Elsie picked up her glass and took a slow, casual drink. Among the earliest lessons her father had passed down was never, ever reveal to one's patient a hint of sadness. Doing so left those men and women scared and oftentimes hesitant to reveal the true extent of their pain for fear of the respective diagnosis.

She'd had all number of patients whom she'd tended over the years, most of the nonhuman sort, but a good number of the two-legged ones. Some had been morose, others angry with their circumstances.

William Helling, Duke of Aubrey, however, was certainly the orneriest of all of them. He was proud, and hurt, and he hated that she, or anyone, would be privy to that. She'd known him only a short while and had ascertained as much about him.

With a thunderous expression, he grabbed his fork and stabbed one of the prongs into a minuscule bit of sausage.

She set her glass down with a firm *thunk*. "William?"

He froze with the silver utensil halfway to his mouth and stared questioningly at her.

"*How* have you eaten this past year?" How, when he should know such misery still nearly a year after his accident?

"Slowly. Small bites."

Again, Elsie examined the contents of his dish.

As he'd done yesterday when they'd first met for the agreed-upon morning meal, William set his fork down. "I did not begin with the child's bites."

"The child's bites?" she echoed.

"That is what one of the"—his lips curled in a sneer—"doctors," he said with an angry slash of his hand, "suggested would prevent me from overtaxing my damned mouth." Splotches of color splashed along the ridge of high cheekbones. His aquiline features that had once been hidden were now pronounced and on full display. And he was splendorous in that masculine beauty better reserved for chiseled statues.

She recognized this uncharacteristic volubility as a defensive mechanism. He was a man stretching out the moments before he had to commit an agonizing task. And she welcomed it for all he revealed in the rare exchanges.

"Has it helped you?" she put to him.

William reclined in his chair and rested his palms along the arms of his seat, settling in for their exchange just as he had yesterday. "It was a different strategy that was originally presented to me at a point when I would have tried anything."

"And what were some of the original plans of treatment?" She both needed to know and loathed the answers that he'd provide.

"Eat but once a day. Stabilize the bones with my hand as I chewed." He grimaced. "Chew larger pieces of food so that the muscles received greater use."

Elsie gasped. "No. That was incorrect." Absolutely wrong. It would have been torture.

"I discovered that early on, but not"—he lifted a single finger—"soon enough."

"Speech has been less difficult than eating," she noted.

"It has. I can control the movements of my lips enough in discourse, far more than I can while trying to eat or drink."

And yet, that had been a misconception on his part. "It is all connected," she said, sitting forward in her seat. "All of the muscles and bones impact the others." Elsie trailed her fingers along the edge of her jawbone, down to her chin and lips.

His gaze caught and held on her mouth.

Fire flashed in William's eyes. This was not the familiar sentiment of anger he cloaked himself so well in, but rather, the heat of desire that burned unexpectedly between them.

Warmth fanned low in her belly.

"You were saying?" he asked in a husky murmur that whispered of seduction and marked him as a rogue.

What was *I saying? Focus. You are not a young girl in the first blush of youth. You were ordered here and came for the sole purpose of helping him as you're able...*

Elsie swept to her feet. "I'll show you."

From his position between their seats, Bear picked his head up, eyed his mistress with lazy eyes, and then fell back into his usual morning slumber.

Positioning herself behind William, Elsie placed the tips of her forefingers and middle fingers along the opposite sides of his cleanly shaven face, framing him. "Try to take a bite," she gently encouraged.

The muscles of his face tightened under that request.

"Shh," she urged, lightly working her fingertips in soothing circles until some of the tension left him. "Tension in your body will cause strain and discomfort. Just take one bite for now, so that I might show you."

"Are you attempting to"—he angled his head, bringing their gazes into contact once more—"torture me?" he finished in hoarse tones. His eyes lingered on her mouth.

She swallowed hard. "Hush. Look forward as you chew," she ordered in shaky tones. *Coward... you go weak-kneed with nothing more than a glance from this man.* "Otherwise, it will distort your bite," she finished lamely. The fact that it was true mattered not. What mattered was that in this instance, his unwavering focus took precedence over her evaluation.

William hesitated a moment and then returned his stare forward.

Elsie waited, composing herself and collecting her thoughts until he picked up his fork and slid a piece of diced sausage into his mouth.

Instantly, all her energies shifted.

She lightened the grip she had upon his face. Closing her eyes, she felt the movement of his jaw and muscles. Uneven, with a slight slide of his jaw.

"Feel this," she murmured, gliding her fingertips up and down the tense muscles that moved. His head fell back slightly so that it rested against her chest. *Attend your task. Focus on what you said you'd be evaluating.* Even with those glaring reminders rolling accusatorily around her mind, Elsie slipped her gaze away from the source of his discomfort and to his closed eyes. That softening implied trust. She forced herself to speak. "Each movement elicits a like response." Elsie drifted her fingers closer to his lips.

And a memory blared to life of his mouth as it had covered hers, awakening a passion she'd never thought to know.

And that you desperately wish to know again… with this man.

Elsie abruptly released William. She tripped over herself in her haste to get away, stepping on Bear's long tail along the way.

Her dog let out a high-pitched cry.

William wheeled in his seat, a question in his stare.

Oh, blast.

Besieged by equal parts guilt and shame, Elsie fell to a knee alongside Bear and made soothing sounds.

What was happening to her? Surely she was not enamored of… William Helling, Duke of Aubrey. It would be folly and defied logic. And—

"Elsie?" he asked, narrowing his eyes upon her.

She shoved to her feet. "I'd like to conduct a complete evaluation." As she spoke, all the words rolled together, tumbling from her lips jumbled. "Later. Soon." His eyes narrowed even more.

Elsie curled her toes so tight, her arches ached. William's was a spy's stare, one that said he could surely see within a person's soul to every last secret they carried. "Or… or as soon as you've finished your morning meal," she finished lamely. *Leave now.* "We should adjourn to your chambers." The final syllable of that word hadn't even fully left her lips when a mortified blush blazed across her cheeks. The husky suggestion rang in her own ears.

William drew his shoulders back, and the rogue's grin was firmly in place once more, far more devastating and dangerous than the sneer he'd worn at their first meetings. "Very well, Elsie."

What?

At the protracted silence, he sent a black brow arcing up.

"I shall… see you then," she said, breathless. Bowing her head slightly, Elsie took her leave, with Bear following along.

When she reached the hall, she didn't break stride, continuing a brisk clip through the corridors until she reached the end.

Ducking around the corner, Elsie leaned against the wall and borrowed support.

William had simply *agreed*. And what was more, he'd done so without so much as a trace of hesitation or thread of condescension in his voice. When, for years, every patient who'd entered her cottage had balked when her father included her in their medical treatment. Those men had chafed at a woman having any role in their care.

And this mark of how William was so very different from those others, how it set him apart, was even more dangerous than the hungering he stirred within her.

She forced her eyes open and stared blankly at the gilded frame opposite her.

Since Lord Edward had invaded her cottage, and she'd allowed herself to be brought to London to oversee William's care, she'd believed the greatest peril she faced was from her dealings with the Brethren.

Only to find that there was something even more dangerous. Something even more terrifying that put her at even greater risk: this undeniable awareness of William.

For he wasn't the monster she'd made him in her mind, ruthless, cold, and wholly unfeeling.

He was a man who so deeply mourned his wife that he'd shuttered off the lady's gardens and preserved the rosebush he'd gifted her. He was also a man who'd spent the year buried in drink and other wicked pursuits to try to forget the pain. Because he'd still not gleaned what Elsie had long ago—nothing in the world could ever truly drive away the memories that haunted one.

Except, you've not been haunted by your past and that dark night when everything changed.

Since she'd entered William's household, she'd remembered how very wonderful it had been to tease and engage in a quick repartee.

"Enough," she mouthed into the quiet. *You're just enamored of a man who respects you and trusts your capabilities.* No, it was nothing more than that. Just because he'd kissed her, and she'd dreamed of it since, and had butterflies dancing in her belly whenever he was near, didn't mean anything. Not really.

Giving her head a shake, she pushed herself away from the wall and resumed a more sedate walk through the ducal residence.

Except, why, as she found her way to her temporary chambers, did it feel as though she had merely told herself a lie she so very badly needed to believe?

CHAPTER 15

SINCE THE INJURY HE'D SUSTAINED had resulted in doctors coming in to assess his condition, William had been humiliated.

He'd been outraged.

He'd been annoyed.

In fact, he'd thought he'd felt everything there was to feel about his injury.

Until this morning.

Until Elsie Allenby.

More precisely, until Elsie had placed her delicate fingertips upon his face and gently traced the contours. And this time, there had been no pain accompanying the human touch. Rather, *her* touch. She'd glided her hands over his face in a caress that had been fleeting.

Standing at the window overlooking the gardens below, William stared out at Elsie as she worked. Her hands flew quickly, tugging weeds free and tossing them into a sizable pile alongside the faithful dog who was never far from her side.

Those hands held him riveted.

Hers were capable and determined hands, and they were not like the satiny-soft ones of the late wife he'd buried or of the whores who'd filled his bed in the long, lonely year after her passing.

Elsie had callused palms and slightly rough fingertips that marked her real in ways that no other woman before had been.

She was one who reveled in all the work she carried out, and

God help him, there was a sensuality to that self-assuredness and strength that was far more entrancing than the overt sexuality of the women he'd bedded this past year.

Just then, Elsie sat back on her heels. The fabric of her faded violet dress stretched, highlighting the graceful expanse of her back.

William swallowed hard. His pulse kicked up a beat. What in hell had become of him? The women he desired were blonde, statuesque beauties, as his late wife had been. He wasn't a man enthralled by a small slip of a woman such as Elsie. Or he hadn't been.

But then, you've never known a woman such as her.

This fascination came not from what she looked like, or a mere physical hungering, but from something that ran far deeper.

His palms went moist, and he dusted them against the sides of his trousers.

It was madness. Madness that came from the state of isolation he'd embraced. For… he enjoyed her company. He enjoyed the banter he'd not known he'd missed. A banter that wasn't at all deferential and didn't take into consideration his title. She spoke to him as though… he was a man.

Not a duke.

Not the Sovereign.

But a man.

That was an unfamiliar state he'd never known, even as a child. The world saw in him his title, and that had resulted in a boundary going up between him and the rest of the world. As such, he'd never known what it was to be challenged, and at every turn, as Elsie did. There was a brutal honestly to every word that left her lips, and that only added to this dangerous fascination with the lady.

Don't be a bloody fool. She speaks to you as though you are nothing more than her patient.

William flexed his fingers at the taunting reminder at the back of his head. Insecurity in his own worth, once foreign but now all too familiar, dwelled within him, and this time, he thrust it aside.

He might have become a recluse. He might have forgotten how to be and function and exist among polite company… or any company, really, but he well knew the faintest inhalation of a woman's desire, the heated glimmer that lit her eyes.

Nay, theirs was a shared passion. That was a certainty. It was a sentiment that she fought. It had sent her racing from the breakfast room. And that flight… also set her apart.

Elsie shifted, and he leaned forward on the balls of his feet, as drawn to her as those blooms she'd recently allowed their desperately craved sunlight.

Except…

She jammed the hideous ancient bonnet back atop her head, grabbed her scissors, and set to work pruning the next bush.

The crystal pane reflected his scowling visage, and William fell back on his heels. Yanking out his watch fob, he checked the time.

It had been nearly two hours since she'd taken her leave and advised they should meet in his chambers, a delicious prospect made all the more enticing by her crimson blush and breathlessness as she'd fled his company. And when he'd sought out his chambers after his morning meal, it had not been an eagerness to be alone that had fueled his quickened strides, but rather, the prospect of again being alone with her, of listening to the singsong quality of her voice that was a balm upon his blackened soul as she spoke with skill and confidence of the human body and pain.

She was an enigma, this woman.

Nothing short of a siren who stirred a potent desire within him, not only because of the curve of her hips and the taste of her lips, but because of the words of wisdom she breathed at their every meeting.

Elsie shifted, and William's muscles went on alert once more as she stood. His heart knocked around in anticipation as she gathered up her things and carried them—

His brow dipped.

—over to a row of once expertly sculpted English boxwoods?

Dropping the items onto the thick grass, Elsie retained her hold on a gingham blanket. She snapped the fabric open, and a light gust of wind caught the edges, toying with them before they settled onto the earth. She spoke, her voice muffled by the distance and glass between them, but still light and entrancing.

Elsie snapped her fingers, calling Bear over.

Dutifully, that loyal creature came to his feet and joined her on the blanket. It was a pull William himself well understood, an inexplicable draw that she possessed. She favored the dog with a loving caress that William would gladly sell the rest of his dark soul for.

And with that, Elsie began clipping the tree closest to her.

Bloody hell.

Why, she was settling in once more. It was as though she'd forgotten their agreed-upon meeting. He gnashed his teeth before he realized what he was doing. An involuntary groan ripped from his chest, and he squinted, all his muscles tightening to ward off the pain.

Tension in your body will cause strain and discomfort... Each movement elicits a like response...

The sage advice she'd given, pinged around his memory.

Spinning on his heel, William stormed from his room and marched through the corridors. With every step that brought him closer to the minx, William fumed.

How dare she? They'd had an appointment, one that she'd requested and he'd agreed to.

And then she'd simply not shown? Instead, she'd remained in the gardens, with that wistful smile and the company of her dog?

A trio of chambermaids caught sight of his approach and went wide-eyed, hurriedly stepping out of his path. Whispers followed in his wake.

His neck went hot.

Of course, the world had grown accustomed to the man who'd shut himself away in his chambers and wandered the halls only when the world slept, who otherwise didn't leave this self-imposed prison.

It was just more evidence of the stranger he'd become, a man he didn't recognize, and he hated Elsie Allenby for opening his eyes to that truth.

He reached the door that led out to the gardens and stopped.

No, he didn't hate her. William swallowed hard. He despised what she'd made him see—that he hated himself. For that was a good deal worse. One could shut away strangers and staff and even family, but one could not alter the visage of the man reflected back in the mirror each day.

A man who'd so failed the world around him.

With jerky movements, William tossed the door open.

A bright blast of sunlight streamed inside.

Where days before his eyes had strained under that imposition, now he barely squinted. This time, William easily found her. Her hands flew quickly as she cut the overgrown tree. She did not, however, make any move to turn, to stand, or even acknowledge him.

Bear, however, sprang to his feet. With a happy yelp, the too-stupid-for-his-own-good mutt abandoned his mistress' side and sprinted over to William as fast as his old, graying legs would allow.

Elsie's complete absorption in her task only set his fury ratcheting up a notch.

"You," he barked, stalking forward.

The late spring wind gusted, filling his nostrils with the crisp scent of warm air that had shed its winter chill. The subtle hints of flowers and greenery wafted, the pure scents of his youth, back when he'd innocently raced through the grounds with his siblings.

Misery stole through him, as unexpected and debilitatingly acute as all the other losses he'd suffered this year, and he jerked to a halt.

William stood immobile, his hands curled at his sides, frozen under the weight of all he… missed.

He squeezed his eyes shut.

Uncle William, you may be fast, but you shan't catch me…

The echo of his nephew's laughter, forgotten until now, flooded his mind, as clear as when the boy had last visited William's country estate. Back when Adeline had been alive, and William blissfully untouched by the ugliness that had visited so many of the men and women under his command.

"Hullo, William."

His eyes shot open. That casual, lyrical greeting was a stark juxtaposition to the bleakness that gripped him.

He stalked forward. "Where were you?" he snapped. He was a bastard. Even as he knew it was the height of wrongness to take his frustrations and furies out on this woman, he could not suppress the irrational sentiments. William came to a stop over her, with Bear dropping onto his back legs alongside him.

Elsie paused in midclip of a branch and, with her spare hand, doffed her bonnet.

The sun's rays toyed with those dark strands. She wiped the back of her hand along her damp brow. "I trust it is clear what I'm doing." Elsie snapped another too-long branch, and it landed on a rapidly growing pile.

He growled. "You know what I meant, Elsie." How could she be so infuriatingly calm? So immune to him that she should not care whether or not they met, while he was consumed by the need to be with her? To see her. To talk with her.

My God, what is happening to me?

CHAPTER 16

ELSIE'S HEART RACED, JUST AS it had since he'd stormed the gardens.

Her reaction was not a product of any fear that he might wish her harm, but rather, her body's inexplicable awareness of him and his presence.

Just as she'd been aware of him watching her from the window while she'd worked.

How to explain it?

Setting her scissors inside her pocket, Elsie climbed to her feet and at last faced him.

"Why?" she asked simply.

He cocked his head.

"Why?"

Of his own volition, he'd come to her.

"Why have you sought me out?" she clarified.

"Is this some manner of game?" he snapped.

"No game."

He continued as though she hadn't spoken. "Do you wish to exert control over me in this?"

"I've no control over you, William, or anybody. The only person whose actions I am in full command of are my own. And I've given you my word I don't intend to trick you into complying."

"You did not come," he gritted out. His jaw throbbed in a telltale sign of the effort that reflexive movement cost him.

She opened and closed her mouth several times. He'd noted her absence. Which also implied that he'd wanted her there.

Color splotched his cheeks. Was he embarrassed by his own admission?

Elsie shook her head slowly. "I don't…"

William took a step toward her so that only a handbreadth of space divided them. Energy thrummed to life, crackling like the volatile air on the cusp of a lightning storm.

"We had agreed to meet in my chambers, and yet, you've been out here tending trees." There was a husked quality to his tone, which was stripped of the earlier indignation, gentler, warmer, revealing a man who'd come out here not to compel her, but who'd genuinely wished for her company.

Butterflies fluttered low in her belly. Over the years, she'd been treated as an oddity with whom the villagers would not even interact. Aside from her father, people had all sneered at her skills and knowledge. Until this man. "Shrub," she said softly, forcing herself to say something.

He angled his head. "What?" he whispered. A bemused glimmer sparked in his eyes.

The air stuck somewhere in her chest. This was who he would have been before his wife perished. He would have been a rogue with gentle tones and a lighthearted gaze.

Through her sadness for him and all he'd lost, Elsie forced herself to go on. "Trees are generally closer to twenty feet or taller," she explained. Shielding her eyes with her palm, she glanced to the flowering dogwood at the center of the gardens. "Trees are also in possession of trunks several inches in diameter. Whereas shrubs, on the other hand?" Elsie pointed to the neglected boxwoods, and William's gaze followed her gesture to the object in question. "They are smaller. Rounder. And…" Catching the amusement in his eyes, Elsie let her unintended lecture trail off.

A smile ghosted his lips, erasing the last vestiges of tension from his chiseled features. He brought a hand up between them and palmed her cheek. Searing heat spilled from his hand to her skin, and she leaned into that touch. "I cannot determine whether you are attempting to distract me," he said without inflection, "or whether you're making light of me."

Her lashes fluttered. "I-in this instance, I am not."

His smile deepened, setting off another round of wild fluttering in her belly. "But in other instances, you might?"

Elsie tipped her chin back so she might better meet his gaze. "It would depend upon the circumstances," she whispered. "One would be wise to avoid speaking in absolutes." Their breath blended in a union that urged each owner to press their mouths together.

All lightness fled William's eyes. The sapphire depths darkened. His throat moved. His gaze went to her mouth. "That is not altogether true."

What was not altogether true? Everything was becoming so very jumbled in her mind. Or it already had been. Even *that* detail was muddled. "Some things do hold true in all times and in all places, Elsie. Some evidence is empirical and holds that there are some truths because they are logically true."

Her lips parted. "Euclid," she breathed. William was versed in the great Greek philosophers. It was shocking. Unexpected. And contrary to everything she'd come to believe about noblemen and academic studies. And it also revealed him as a man learned in the books she'd pored over since girlhood.

He chuckled. "Do you take all nobles for indolent lords, unfamiliar with learning and scientific teachings?" he asked, his breath a blend of coffee and hazelnut.

"I didn't…I don't…" Quite simply, she'd never known. Her experience with the nobility had included the wounded gentlemen who'd come to her family's cottage. During their recovery, they had bypassed the books she'd offered them to read while they convalesced in favor of gossip pages and documents pertaining to their official Crown business. Not a single one of those men, in all those years, had ever demonstrated the slightest interest in any of the sciences.

William flicked the tip of her nose in an endearing gesture that forced her mind to the present. "By that damning silence, it seems *you* are speaking in absolutes, Elsie."

"You are correct," she said softly.

He gave his head a bemused shake. "I'm fairly certain you are the only woman… nay, person in the whole of the world that I know, or will ever know, who is unashamed to claim ownership of one's mistakes."

"I'm not too proud to own when I am wrong."

"And *that*," he murmured, working the pad of his thumb in small, soothing, counterclockwise circles that brought her lashes down, "is what marks you as different."

"Different," she repeated dumbly. That familiar word, an oft-hurled insult, shattered the splendorous pull. It was all she'd ever been. Elsie stepped away from him and, to give her fingers something to do, urged Bear over with two snaps. The recently disloyal dog remained planted behind William. Suddenly, she fought silly tears… over all of it. Elsie dropped to a knee, claiming a much-needed distance from his stare. Fishing the scissors from her pocket, she resumed cutting the bush.

"You took that as an insult." There was a frown in his voice.

"Isn't it?" she asked with a forced casualness she didn't feel. Her father had insisted the world's opinion didn't matter, and yet, what made her different had also isolated her. "It's hardly ever intended as a compliment." Her time on this earth had proven that to be an absolute.

"Who has insulted you?" This time, there was such affront in his voice that she paused midcut.

Aside from her father, who had *not*?

"Your father's patients," he muttered.

Patients who'd also happened to be gentlemen who answered to William. She sat back on her heels and shrugged. "My father's patients. The villagers in the town where I lived." Elsie resumed shaping the boxwood.

William dropped to a knee beside her, and she stiffened. "You are different."

She flinched, but did not stop trimming.

He brushed his knuckles along her chin, forcing her to stop, urging her gaze to his.

"I wanted to send you away the moment you set foot in my chambers," he murmured. "Until you spoke." A small grin dimpled his cheeks, shattering the hardened mask he'd worn these past days. "You debated my word selection and did so admirably."

"Because you had opted for the incorrect word," she whispered, her heart doing a little leap.

William chuckled, the expression of mirth still rough from lack of use, but no longer as jaded as it had been. "I didn't send you away *because* you are different. You've proved yourself unlike the stodgy doctors and healers to come before you, who alternately preened at their own *skill* and avoided my gaze. So do not let anyone shame you for being different. Wear it as a mark of your strength and take pride in what sets you apart."

A fragment of her heart slipped free from its proper place and into the hands of the unlikeliest holder. Elsie's grip slackened, and the scissors fell from her hand.

William cursed, and still dazed, Elsie glanced unblinkingly at the place where the tool had landed… on his lap.

She gasped. "Blast," she whispered. Running her fingers over his thigh, she searched for evidence of blood indicating a wound.

"I'm fine." His voice emerged as garbled.

Only… Elsie bit the inside of her cheek. "You do not sound fine." She probed the slightest tear in his trousers. "You sound hurt."

At his silence, she looked up and stilled.

Desire burned within his eyes, touching her like a physical caress.

Elsie yanked her hands back. "Forgive me." Heat exploded upon her cheeks. *What are you doing?* She'd been required to come here to try to help William, and now she lusted after him in his gardens like the tavern keeper's daughter in Bladon. And because it was far easier to focus on the task that had brought her to his household and her role here, Elsie stood and took a step away, composing her features… even as an inner tumult waged within her. "We should begin our treatment."

His brow creased, William glanced around.

"Here," Elsie confirmed, settling more easily into the role she'd been born to in her family's household. Snapping her fingers three times, she cleared Bear from the blanket. With a purposefulness to her every action, Elsie straightened the wrinkled blanket and then moved the gardening tools off to the edges.

When she finished, she paused to assess her makeshift workstation. She gave a pleased nod and then glanced up at William.

She might as well have sprung a second head and was in the process of sprouting a third, for all the horror stamped on his features. "Surely you are not expecting to treat me"—he dropped his voice to a hushed whisper—"here."

Elsie lifted her shoulders in a shrug. "There is no better place *to* treat you." That had just been one more vital lesson handed down by her father in what had become an unofficial schooling in healing and medicine.

William snorted and proceeded to tick off on his fingers. "My chambers. My offices. The library *Your* chambers. One of ten parlors."

"Ten parlors?"

"Mayhap thirteen," he corrected. "Something 'round there."

She laughed. "There is something cleansing about nature, though."

With a slightly bemused expression, he did a sweep of the grounds. "London is hardly the epitome of a bucolic landscape." There was something wistful and something sad, all together, in his tones. Once more, a yearning to know more about this enigmatic gentleman pulled at her.

"You've created a sanctuary amid the city," she said softly. "One that allows one the illusion of something else." A kestrel landed at the corner of a long-empty fountain and ducked his beak into the smallest of puddles left by a recent rainstorm. Elsie stared at the bird. "And sometimes, the eye and the soul can come to believe the trick that the mind sought to play." A life of peace and tranquility and calm… when the mind truly knew the harsh reality that was life.

Feeling William's stare on her, Elsie glanced over. They shared a look, an intimate meeting of two people who'd both suffered and struggled and who also kept those secrets close. And then they both looked out at the kestrel once more.

Until the bird took flight.

"Since I was born, there has been the expectation that I have no vulnerabilities," William said unexpectedly, a gruffness to his tone.

That admission, from a man who'd snapped and snarled with every attempt she'd made to learn more about him, was one that surely cost him.

Having tended wounded animals, she'd learned the importance of timing in all her exchanges. As such, she let his pronouncement sink around the gardens, not rushing to a response. "Everyone has vulnerabilities, William," she finally said.

He clasped his hands behind him and stared straight on at the brick wall, as though engaging not Elsie herself but the ivy that grew there in discourse. "Dukes do not. Dukes do have obligations. Dukes have responsibilities and strict expectations which they must adhere to. At no point must one reveal any hint of frailty."

Sadness tugged at her heart. His was the rote deliverance of one who repeated back a familiar phrase that had been ingrained into him early on. "Dukes are also just men," she said gently.

A laugh tinged with bitterness tore from him. "Men who are not permitted any weakness."

How very different his life must have been from her own joyous, carefree childhood. For him, having slid into the role of leader of the Brethren, where feelings were a detriment and emotion was stripped from all interactions, it would have been a natural marriage. "Admitting one is human and flawed is perhaps the greatest mark of one's strength, William." Elsie sank onto the blanket. "As I promised before, I'll not force you. I'd have you come to me when you are ready."

"And if I'm never ready?" he gritted, the color leeching from his cheeks as soon as he tensed his mouth.

"You will be," she said with a sureness that came only from truth.

He fell to a knee beside her. "You speak with such certainty, Elsie Allenby," he said, the statement steeped in his usual faintly mocking edge.

"By your brother's admission, as well as your own, you do not leave your chambers, which upon consideration, I believe was false anyway. You have not interacted with your staff, stepped foot in the breakfast room or"—she glanced about—"your late wife's gardens." Grief contorted his features, her insides wrenching at the agony she'd inadvertently caused him. "And yet, you've done all those things in a short while. No, William," she concluded, sitting back on her haunches, "those are not the actions of a man who truly wishes a life of self-exile."

"Even if I deserve it?"

His question was so threadbare that, for a moment, Elsie believed she'd imagined it. And then the enormity sank in. He was punishing himself. She'd taken him as an unfeeling bastard. A man who'd left Elsie and her father to their fates and disregarded all the work they'd done for the Crown. This new side of him—a man conflicted, tormented—added a level of humanity to him she'd convinced herself he was incapable of.

Elsie sat and wrapped her arms around her knees. "I do not know all of the past that you keep so carefully concealed, William. I do not know the guilt you carry or the memories that haunt you." *But I want to.* For reasons that terrified the everlasting wits out of her. "But the fact that you are riddled with regret means you are not the beast you"—*or I*—"make yourself out to be."

All the muscles in his arms jumped. That tautness caused a rippling in the black wool fabric. He passed his penetrating gaze over her face. "What is it about you, Elsie, that makes me want to do whatever you ask?"

Her heart tripped. Foolishly. "You crave human connection, and I'm the only one who has not allowed you to push me away," she said, for his benefit as much as for hers.

"Very well. I'll agree to your evaluation."

"Treatment," she murmured. This was altogether different. At his capitulation, she should have been flooded with the greatest sense of victory. Instead, she had this unexplainable urge to cry at his lack of protestations to her earlier claim—he believed himself deserving of his pain.

He stared expectantly at her, jerking her into movement.

"Remove your jacket," she said swiftly.

Without hesitation, his hands went to the gleaming buttons of that expensive article, and he slid them free. He shrugged out of the jacket, and the casual movement sent all the muscles of his chest rippling.

My God. Her mouth went dry. *Focus.* "I'll take it," she said, avoiding his eyes lest he see the wicked thoughts there that no lady ought to possess. She accepted the garment and then folded it until the fabric formed a makeshift pillow. Elsie placed it beside Bear. "If you would lay your head there?" she urged.

Wordlessly, William lowered himself onto the blanket and closed his eyes.

It was an act of absolute trust, when past patients had insisted that her father tend them and had fought him on her presence in their rooms. And yet, William, a duke with strict views of people's placement and what was proper, ceded his care over to her.

Shifting herself behind him, Elsie framed his cheeks between her hands. She closed her eyes and familiarized herself with the bones and muscles there.

"What are you doing?" he asked curiously.

"Shh," she urged. Then, using her thumb and forefinger, she applied a light pressure from the start of his brow and worked outward. "Open your mouth, slowly."

He complied.

There it was. The joint slid slightly, leaving his mouth uneven.

Elsie leaned down, inspecting the old wound. "You broke it badly."

"Yes. I was unconscious for two months following... following the accident," he finished, his voice ragged. "The only time I awakened was when the bone was reset."

Oh, my God. That would have been excruciating.

"Shh, relax your muscles." Elsie continued working her palms over him. She applied her fingertips to various points over his face. "It is called massage. Asclepiades believed that disease and death resulted when movement was obstructed or disrupted. You've just been disrupted."

A small groan left him.

"Is it too much?"

"It feels wonderful and miserable all at the same time."

Her lips twitched. "Now, don't talk. Just feel."

They remained that way, with Elsie discovering every contour and groove of his aquiline-sharp features. A short while later, she dusted her fingertips along his cheeks and then reluctantly drew back and pushed herself to standing. "You would benefit from a straw diet, William. More liquid-based meals. Fruits that are ground up. Puddings."

He opened his eyes and stared up at her. "A straw diet?"

"It's a device made of wheatgrass that allows you to sip a drink and reduces the amount of movement required of your mouth when you eat."

William shoved himself up onto his elbows and worked his gaze over her face. "I don't think I know anyone like you."

Her cheeks warming under that praise, she grabbed her bonnet and jammed it atop her head. "The sun will do you good, William. It will invigorate you and restore you in ways you believed you couldn't be." She glanced at Bear so comfortably curled up alongside a man who was just a stranger a short while ago. "I will leave you to your own company." She hesitated, wanting him to ask her to stay. Craving his company.

When no request was forthcoming, she gathered her things and left him and Bear staring after her.

CHAPTER 17

THE NIGHT MARKED ANOTHER SLEEPLESS night for William, not unlike so many others that had come before it.

At the same time, it was so completely, so wholly different.

After his recovery, William had stalked these same halls while the staff slept, allowing himself only that brief time to wander the corridors, a self-imposed prison he rightly deserved.

With each time he'd wandered, he'd been dogged by guilt and misery—and—rage at all he'd lost. Now, as he walked, the usual darkness didn't hold him in its grip, but there was an ease he'd never expected to again feel.

Just as, in the past few days, he'd experienced life in ways long forgotten. He'd laughed again. Teased. Hungered for the company of another person, for reasons that had nothing to do with sex.

William was many things: a stubborn bastard, a pompous nobleman, a heartless scoundrel. But he was not one who lied to himself.

It was all because of Elsie.

He felt… alive, when before he'd only been deadened inside, craving death and embracing the emptiness that his life had become. Because that was what he deserved. His mistakes had cost his wife her life, and as such, what right did he have to live… or know happiness?

He'd allowed himself to believe that to be truth. He'd accepted it as fact. After all, having survived the same accident that had killed Adeline, did he not owe a penance to his late wife? Only, he'd betrayed her memory with every woman he'd bedded. Those unions had been mindless and as empty as he'd been. That had been the emotionless life he'd thought he wanted. Nay, it was the only existence he thought he'd be able to know—the life of a scoundrel.

That was not the future he wanted, or needed. He wanted to get back to the gentleman he'd been—honorable, respectable, one whose life was worth living.

Admitting one is human and flawed is perhaps the greatest mark of one's strength, William.

You crave human connection, and I'm the only one who has not allowed you to push me away.

He'd let Elsie's statement stand, for that had been easier than breathing the truth into existence… that this need to have her near, the ability to speak so easily, came not just because she was *anyone*, but rather, because she was… *her.*

William stopped at the end of the hall, before the last portrait ever painted of his wife, just six months prior to the accident.

It was an expert rendering of the late duchess captured in time. The faintest hint of a smile hovered at the edges of her lips, though as restrained as the young lady herself had been.

She'd not freely laughed, and she'd certainly not teased or challenged him.

Like Elsie…

William braced his palm on the wall next to the gold frame and closed his eyes. "I'm sorry," he mouthed into the silence.

He did not want to continue the unfaithful comparison of those two very different women. Not because of what it meant to Adeline… or his feelings for this mysterious woman who'd stolen into his home and cracked barriers he'd thought so perfectly erected.

The faintest of staccato clicks filled the corridor, and William forced himself to release his hold upon the wall and straighten.

He turned toward the fast-approaching sound just as Bear trotted around the corner. The dog froze and then, with a small yelp, bounded over with an agility that did not match with all his graying and white fur.

With an eager anticipation that he did not even try to deny to himself in this instance, William looked past the dog—to an empty hall.

All the lightness went out of him.

Well… not *all* of it.

Bear nudged his large head against his side. "Forgive me, I've been rude," William murmured and stroked that favorite spot just behind the shaggy dog's ears. "You're alone, I see."

Closing his brown eyes, Bear leaned into William's touch, emitting little groaning whimpers.

William sighed. If anyone within the Brethren should see him now. Chatting freely with a dog. Before now, he would have derided anyone for that nonsensicality. And yet, Bear, and the tale his mistress had told, marked William not so very different from the dog who'd kept him company these past days.

Elsie's lyrical voice whispered around his recent memory.

They are not so very different from humans.

"No, they aren't," he murmured to himself. Casting a last glance up at Adeline's portrait, William tapped his leg in the manner Elsie had numerous times, propelling the dog into movement beside him. "What is it? Unable to sleep?"

Bear panted happily as they walked, confirming nothing with that canine response.

"Or did your mistress send you?" As she'd done before. An act that had previously infuriated him and now sent a peculiar warmth to his heart. They reached the end of the hall, and the loyal mutt stopped. "I'm to my chambers, Bear."

Elsie's dog cocked his head, his tongue lolling out the side of his mouth, before ambling off—in the opposite direction.

William stared after the graying mutt and, with a sigh, followed along after him. For reasons that had nothing to do with boredom.

He knew ultimately where Bear was off to, and he was as drawn to her as the dog himself. An eagerness that he'd not known or felt or thought himself able to feel energized his steps as Bear led him through the townhouse to—

William stopped at the narrower hall the dog had taken him to, the unlikeliest of places.

Though not for a dog.

He sighed.

The kitchens.

William pressed the door handle, letting Bear in. "I'll feed you," he said warningly, "but I'll not join you in ea—" His words trailed abruptly off as he homed in on the small figure seated at the long, rectangular table.

Elsie stared back with wide, startled eyes. And then sprang to her feet. "William," she greeted without a hint of fatigue in her voice, despite the late-night hour.

"Elsie," he murmured, drawing the panel shut behind the three of them.

She hovered, with the bench at her knees. "You were talking to Bear again," she noted softly.

William gave thanks for the dimmer lighting in the servants' space that concealed the color burning his cheeks. Blushing, now. Was there no end to the changes this imp had inspired? "He makes for good company," he conceded gruffly.

"He does at that." And yet, despite the darkness, he caught the faintest of grins that dimpled her cheeks. It rang clear in her voice.

He should leave. At another time in his life, he'd never have visited the kitchens, and he'd certainly not have been one to steal time alone with a young woman in his employ. Only... William frowned. There was something so very wrong in seeing Elsie Allenby in that light. For she wasn't simply a member of his household staff.

Nonetheless, a gentlemanly sense of honor had been ingrained in him early on and remained an indelible part of him. "I should leave."

"It is late," she conceded, reclaiming her seat and promptly resuming... whatever it was she was doing.

His frown deepened. That was... it? She simply bowed her head and... and... went on to the task that had occupied her before his arrival? It was a foreign position for him to be in, a man accustomed to the world's attention, though it had become a thing of annoyance, a fawning he'd resented. Only, he'd been proven a liar... by this woman, for he wanted her attention. Instead, she sifted through blades of... what appeared to be grass?

For the first time, he took in the clutter spread out before her.

Stalks of grass and greenery lay scattered around the table.

She sighed. The soft exhalation hinting at the young woman's frustration drew him back from his musings.

That sigh—a siren's song, for the pull it had over him—compelled him forward. "What are you doing?"

"Evaluating the various types of grass growing in your gardens in search of one similar to wheatgrass."

"Oh." That explanation answered everything… and nothing, all at the same time. William stopped directly across from her.

Elsie looked up. "Sit," she urged, and William found himself dragging out the bench and sliding onto the uncomfortable oak planks.

"How long have you been here?" he asked curiously.

She shrugged, organizing her stalks of grass and leaves into neat piles. "What time is it?"

"I don't know." At one time, he'd known the exact second of every hour and the events to come after it. How very much his life had changed.

Elsie paused in her task. "Nor do I," she said with a smile in her voice.

A smile that was infectious and drew his own lips up in a grin that no longer strained the muscles of his face.

"Several hours or so," she finally acknowledged.

"You've been sitting here?" he pressed, his amusement fading as he took in that miserable seating.

"Mm-hm." Tapping her fingertip contemplatively against her lip, she lifted a stalk with her other hand. Turning it back and forth, she studied it before setting it aside.

New benches. His staff deserved something far more comfortable for the work they did. *And yet, I never noticed or appreciated how others live. Not outside my own social sphere.* Shame slapped at his conscience—also not so very dead, after all.

They sat in a companionable silence. She, unlike societal ladies given to filling any void with endless prattle about the weather and *ton* events, exuded complete calm in the face of quiet.

Elsie drew a faded blade of grass close to her eyes and squinted, deeply entrenched in her task, endearing in her focus.

"What are you doing?" he asked, besieged by a genuine interest in whatever occupied her attention.

With another regretful sigh, she dropped that piece of greenery alongside the previously discarded one. "Here," she said, gathering a small leather book near her elbow. Elsie passed it over, and he automatically captured the book. Turning it over in his hands, he searched for a title. The faintest gold-leaf lettering had long since faded and cracked so that a bare imprint remained.

William opened the book no bigger than the size of his palm. "*The Sumerians: A study in culture, character, history, and literature.*" He flipped through the pages, wafting a slight breeze in the otherwise stagnant airflow. "In addition to medicine, you have an appreciation for history," he murmured.

"The book belonged to my father. He passed on to me an interest in certain histories," she clarified.

William scanned the book, heavily marked with notes in the margins and words and phrases underlined. And stopped. "The straw-drinking you mentioned earlier."

"Precisely." Sifting through her piles of greenery, Elsie gathered up another stalk. "There is nothing definitive on who first invented it, but the earliest rendering found is from the Sumerians. Of course, the image rendered"—without asking permission, she arched over the table and slipped the book from his hands—"reveals what appears to be gold tubing." With her voice animated and her eyes glowing, she was beguiling.

William fought to tear his gaze from her and attend those pages.

"Here." Elsie turned the cherished volume out for him to see. She touched her fingertip to the minute sketch of the item she spoke of. "But if you read on…" Fanning the pages, she stopped without so much as a glance on a slightly dog-eared page. "They were created for the commoners with wheatgrass."

"With wheatgrass," he repeated on a murmur. With a dawning understanding, he took in her makeshift workstation with new eyes. "You're making a straw," he said softly.

Had he ever been so awed by any person, man or woman, member of the Brethren, or even his own wife, the way he was by Elsie Allenby?

She chewed at her lower lip. "I am trying. Without success." Her shoulders immediately came back. "But I've only just started. I expect I can create something similar."

William roved his eyes over her heart-shaped face. "And I'd wager my left and right arms combined that you'll accomplish something far greater."

Her lips went slightly slack. "Oh," she whispered.

By the glitter in her eyes, he might as well have climbed into the heavens and plucked down a handful of stars intended solely for her.

Their gazes caught and held—for a minute, for a lifetime?—before Elsie whipped her head down, back to the work she'd undertaken.

"Who are you, Elsie Allenby?" he murmured.

She stiffened. "I already told you who I am."

"Yes, yes," he said impatiently, with a wave of his hand. "You've told me your name. You've indicated you live in the country, alone, with only your dog for company. Why?"

"Why?" she asked slowly.

"It is a waste of your abilities and talents." The world should know of a woman as skilled and knowledgeable and courageous as she.

"I've already told you," she said, carefully placing a stalk of grass on the table.

"What? That the villagers in your town will not allow you to care for them? That you were doubted and disdained by your father's patients?" Fools, the lot of them.

She pursed her lips. "You say it as though it is somehow my fault."

Behind William, Bear sat up, his nails scraping the wood floor. William stretched a hand out and scratched the dog the way he so favored. "On the contrary," he amended. "It is the fault of the small-minded people."

Some of the tension slipped from her small shoulders.

"As well as you, for remaining behind with an ungrateful lot who never utilize the skills you possess."

Her back immediately went back up. "You don't know anything about it," she said tightly, reaching for another blade of glass.

"I don't know what?" he shot back. "What it is to have one's worth questioned by others?" William shook his head. "No, I do not. I do, however, know what it is to question my own worth." He'd been doing it for a year now. He'd simply done so without question—until her.

CHAPTER 18

THE PURPOSE OF ELSIE BEING here in this household was to help William step out of the prison he'd made for himself and reenter the living. She was to help him learn to live with the injury he'd suffered and the damage it had done to him.

As such, his being here now was a mark of the progress he'd made.

But this… his questioning her and challenging her? This was not part of the role she'd undertaken. It was awkward and uncomfortable, and she didn't wish to talk about it with him or anyone.

Elsie made a show of gathering several blades of grass. All the while, her skin tingled with the heat of William's gaze upon her.

How dare he presume to know what her life had been and why she'd closeted herself away in her cottage in the corner of the Cotswolds? It was because of him and the Brethren.

Liar.

You lived a narrow existence, with your father driving your actions, long before the Brethren rejected your father's appeals for help.

He stretched a hand out, and she stiffened, but he merely reached for the cherished book that had belonged to her father.

"Have you heard of the *King List*?" he asked unexpectedly.

Elsie paused in her task, and blinking back confusion, she looked up from the grass. What was he talking about? "I've not," she said carefully. All the information she'd been fixed on through the years had pertained only to ancient medical practices and the techniques and treatments she and her father might have used to help whichever patient inevitably came to them.

"It is quite fascinating, really," he said, returning the ancient leather volume to its previous place. "We know much about what we do about the Mesopotamians because of a clay tablet kept. This tablet is known as the *King List* and contains the names of most of the ancient rulers of Sumer, as well as the lengths of their reigns." As he spoke, William barely moved his lips. The white lines at the corners of his mouth marked his misery, and yet, he sat here talking on anyway.

"I don't understand," she murmured, setting down the latest grass she'd been evaluating.

"This tablet memorialized all the greatest leaders. They had a special concept of kingship."

"In what way?" she asked when it appeared he intended to say nothing else and leave her as confounded as she'd been moments ago at the abrupt shift in discourse.

"A kingship was more than a title. Rather, it was something with a lifelike force that traveled. As such, it went from city to city, not following any one person. Sometimes, it would remain in a respective city for a hundred years. Sometimes longer." William patted the empty spot beside him on the bench. Bear scrambled eagerly up onto all fours and promptly rested his head alongside William's knee. William immediately found that sensitive place at the base of his head that Bear loved so much.

Her heart quickened in her breast. Such a man who took enjoyment in a dog's presence, and who had learned so very swiftly what brought the ancient dog pleasure, fit not at all with what she'd expected of him. Nothing where he was concerned did. She'd believed all the worst about William, the Duke of Aubrey, only to have all of those beliefs ripped up by the reality of him.

"Among the many 'kings' to rule, there was one female."

Elsie sat upright. "Indeed?" It was a wholly foreign concept. In a world ruled and dominated by males, women were left to claw every moment just to survive.

William favored Bear with one more affectionate pat before laying his palms upon the table. "Her name was Kubaba. The recordings indicate she was a 'tavern keeper' first, who went on to take the throne of the city-state Kish after being rewarded for the work she did for the previous king."

She narrowed her eyes. "Are you funning me?"

With an endearing boylike gesture, he crossed a solemn X over his chest. "No." He lifted a brow. "And why *should* it be so unbelievable?"

Elsie snorted. "Why should it *not*? Women"—she slashed a hand in the air—"aren't granted roles of leadership. They are…" She let her words trail off.

"They are what?" he quietly compelled in the melodious tones Satan could have used to seduce God's own secrets from Him.

Elsie met William's gaze directly. "They are relegated to the role of the forgotten, bent to the will of whichever man has a need of her." Just as she'd been by Lord Edward. Just as she'd been by this man before her, and every man to come before him. She bit her lip. *I said too much.*

"A tavern keeper," she said softly to herself.

"She was a woman of *influence*," he said, slightly emphasizing the last word.

"She was one woman among thousands upon thousands of years of leadership."

William glanced pointedly around at the items laid out between them. "It's not the number of women who have ruled, but rather, the mark of one's greatness and capabilities."

If he believed that, he was more naïve than she'd ever expect of a man of his status and station. Frustration spiraled through her, at herself for her lot as a female, at William for daring to hint that it could be different for her as a woman. Women were not allowed any role—no matter how vaunted—among Society. And there certainly weren't women of medicine hired to care for any patients.

Or, there hadn't been… until him.

With shaking fingers, Elsie gathered up the next batch of grass she'd retrieved in the gardens and tested the strands for their suitability. No more words passed between her and William. The quiet stretched out, tense and uncomfortable in ways that it hadn't been before. Elsie abandoned the stalks of greenery and glanced around at the remaining pieces.

"That is all?" William murmured.

She stiffened.

Of course he should break their stony impasse. William Helling, Duke of Aubrey, was the manner of man who could command any silence and force it to bend to his will.

"It did not work," she muttered. "They are all too narrow." Elsie reached for another. Wider than the others, it had potential. She proceeded to arrange the stalks in a neat line. "I've been unable to find reed grass like—" William covered her hand with his own, staying her.

His touch enveloped her in a soothing warmth, oddly juxtaposed with the unease raised by his earlier questioning.

"That isn't what I was talking about, Elsie," he murmured. "You know that."

She stared at their entangled palms. Of course she'd known that. But it was a good deal easier to speak on grass and greenery and straws than on her place in this world that had little use for a woman skilled in medicine.

"What do you want me to say?" she asked tiredly, her gaze transfixed by how very different their two hands were. His large, the midfingers dusted with the faintest hairs. Hers callused, with mud-stained fingertips that retained the stain of dirt no matter how hard she scrubbed.

"I'd have you acknowledge that you can do more for yourself and others if you didn't live in some remote, forgotten cottage, a stranger to the world."

Elsie gritted her teeth and drew her hand away, going cold at the loss of his touch. "And you of all people would lecture me on leaving?"

"I'd lecture you on leaving because I recognize someone who's imposed the same prison upon herself that I have. The difference being, Elsie? I know what I've done and why I've done it. I acknowledge it." He gave her a sad, pitying smile that sent heat rushing to her cheeks. "But you? You cannot be honest with even yourself."

She jerked, his charge stinging like the blow she'd taken to the cheek from one of the men who'd killed her father. Only, this burned far more than the mere physical pain of that assault. This was a challenge to her soul and spirit and whole way of life. "How dare you?" she whispered.

"I dare because you will not," he said calmly. "Because you *have* not." William stood, and placing his palms on the table, he leaned forward. "You've not because of some ungrateful village folk who don't appreciate your skill or what you're capable of."

"You know nothing," she rasped, exploding to her feet and matching his pose. Her chest rose and fell quickly. She scoffed. "What do you think?" she asked, proceeding to tidy up her workstation. "That I'm just a simple village girl afraid of the world?" She didn't allow him a word edgewise. "I wasn't afraid of the world until I saw what men were capable of. Honorable men who simply take from good men."

WILLIAM TOOK IN ELSIE'S UNUSUALLY jerky movements as she cleaned the remnants of her efforts this night. Head bent, shoulders slightly hunched, she gave the task all her attention, leaving him to stare on.

Since Elsie had entered his household and his life, William had been filled with questions about the mysterious woman who challenged him at every turn. He'd been besieged by a burning need to know all there was about her.

Until now.

My father was a man who'd not reject any request or demand for help. It was a virtue, but also a fault, and it would prove to be my father's downfall.

All the pieces she'd revealed now rolled around his memory.

My father was a healer. He did not end lives... He saved *them.*

A niggling premonition took root.

And, coward that he'd proven himself to be this past year—a failing Elsie had opened his eyes to—he proved himself to be an even greater one in this instance.

Because he preferred to think of her just as she said—as a simple village girl. He wanted to think of a world where Elsie lived in the English countryside, caring for animals and villagers alongside her father, before she'd been left alone in this world. He didn't want to know her life had been in fact complicated by evil and darkness and the seediest side of a man's soul.

His stomach muscles tightened as Elsie finished lowering her items into a lidded basket.

Let her go. You don't need to know. No good can come from knowing...

For, ultimately, he'd known all along the lie in imagining her as a country girl. Known it because his brother and Cedric Bennett wouldn't have known of a simple village girl. But he'd allowed his mind to shy away from the questions and realities there.

Elsie stepped out from behind the table and tapped her leg once, springing Bear into motion.

Unease threaded through him. "You said your father's goodness was a fault," he called after her. "How was it a fault?" he asked, not wanting the answers, not truly, but seeking them anyway.

She stopped suddenly, her narrow back presented to him, her reply directed at the kitchen door. "My father was a good man."

"And he became entangled with… bad men?" Wasn't that invariably the case? Was she in danger even now?

"That would certainly be the simplest explanation for what happened to him," she said, her voice distant, as if she contemplated her own response. "It's certainly the one I had before…" Before…

Before…?

Did the men who harmed her father seek revenge upon Elsie, who was so closely entangled in her father's work? And I unwittingly brought her to London and exposed her to the same peril I did Adeline…

Bile stung his throat. *I am going to be ill.*

"What happened?" William urged, his voice slightly hoarsened. This query came not as a directive from the leader of the Brethren, one he'd issued so many times as a duke, but rather, as a man who wished to know about this woman. To keep her safe when he'd proven unable to help the other woman who'd relied upon him.

Elsie turned slowly back around, facing him. "His talents were discovered, and he was put to work for the Crown."

A pressure weighed on his chest as warning bells that had been faintly ringing at the back of his head chimed all the louder. *No.*

Elsie sucked in a shuddery breath and held the basket closer to her side. "He gave them his service, and others learned of that and wanted the information he had about his patients." Elsie held his stare. "When our lives were threatened"—*our* lives, not *his*, for it was as he'd reasoned, she, by her association with her father, had been in danger, too—"my father sought help from those who should have given it," she said simply, an uncharacteristic bitterness ringing clear in her singsong voice. "In the end, they didn't help, and he was murdered for the work he'd done."

He rocked back on his heels. "The bastards." The air hissed

between his clenched teeth.

"Yes, well, I certainly have been of a like opinion," she said, her voice clogged with tears. A sheen glazed her eyes, and she blinked the crystalline drops back, restraining them when any other woman he'd ever known would have let them fall freely and copiously. "Now, if I may?" She snapped her fingers twice, and the slumbering dog clambered to his feet.

Let her go. You don't truly wish to know…

"Elsie," he called out before she left, halting her at the door, her fingers clasping the handle.

She turned back.

"Who?"

Silence rang around the room.

Bear nosed at her skirts, as if offering canine encouragement.

Elsie said nothing for a long while, and something in her eyes shot straight through William, sucking the breath from his lungs and trapping it somewhere in his chest. Oh, God.

He shook his head as a vile, loathsome possibility slipped around his mind, like venom.

"My father's name was Francis Allenby, and he worked as a doctor on behalf of the Brethren of the Lords."

A loud buzzing filled William's ears as he stood there, motionless, afraid to move. Afraid to breathe. Everything within him ached. Only this… this was not the vicious agony that had been his jaw, but rather, one that rocked his entire body and soul, from the inside out. "No."

She compressed her trembling lips into a line. "Yes. He was murdered for his efforts." And with that pronouncement that ripped a ragged hole in his heart, Elsie left.

Her father, and she, had worked on behalf of the Brethren.

And I did not even know their names.

All the life drained from his legs, and he slid numbly onto the bench. All along, the only explanation that made any sense in his upside-down world, was that she, Elsie, was somehow connected to the Brethren. It had been a thought there at the back, and sometimes front, of his mind with every encounter.

But she'd not borne the same ruthless traits of the men and women he'd dealt with, of the ones he'd commissioned to work on behalf of the Home Office.

His pulse pounded loudly in his ears, throbbing there, near deafening in its intensity, drumming a beat that only added to the cacophony of confusion in his mind.

Think, man. Think.

Allenby. Allenby. Francis. Daughter, Elsie.

He dragged his fingers through his hair, tugging the too-long strands. *Why don't I know them?*

It was his responsibility to know them. To know everyone who served.

But what was worse… she'd known him. She'd known of the Brethren and his role with the organization that, by her own words, had failed her family, and she'd come here anyway. Because of a threat made by Edward and Cedric Bennett?

With every question, sweat beaded his brow.

Groaning, William buried his face in his hands and struggled to bring her name into clarity.

Mayhap Elsie and her father had been assigned different names by one of the agents within the organization to protect their identities. Only, she hadn't been protected.

She'd lost her father and had been alone since his death. What dangers had she known, then and now?

A beastlike groan lodged in his throat, choking him. William surged to his feet, threw the door open, and sailed through. "Stone," he bellowed as he broke into a dead run for his offices.

The spy who'd spent this past year overseeing William's household stepped into his path when he reached the corridor where his offices were located.

William stumbled to a stop.

"You summoned?" Stone asked in his gravelly tones, as though it was the most common thing in the world for his employer to call for him in the dead of night.

"Lord Edward," he rasped. "I want him in my offices five minutes ago."

Nodding, Stone took off in the opposite direction.

William shoved the door closed behind him and stalked over to the mahogany desk at the center of the room. Removing his watch fob, he snapped the back of the lid open and slipped free the key hidden there.

He dropped to a knee, and despite being a year away from it, his fingers instantly found the minuscule row of locks down the back left side of the desk. Drawing open the panel, William pulled free the ten ledgers tucked away there.

Heart racing, he shoved the door shut and, with the burden in his arms, climbed to his feet.

He swept the cluttered desk and, for the first time in the course of a year, damned the mess he'd let his office become. Balancing his books in one arm, he used his spare hand to push the leather folios and ledgers over to the far left corner of his desk. And then, dropping the leather journals in the middle of the cleaned surface, he sat.

A frantic energy pumping through him, William grabbed the first book, opened it, and scanned the names written there. Searching. Searching. He flipped to the next page. And the next. And the next, making quick work of the first book.

Nothing.

William shoved it aside and reached for another.

If she and her father had done work on behalf of the Brethren, they would be here, in one of these books.

Where were they? Where were they?

The search for any hint of their names kept him focused. The methodical task kept him from the horror of what she'd endured. He paused, his gaze frozen on some other unfamiliar name written there in Stone's hand.

"Because of me," he whispered into the empty stillness of the room. If what she professed was in fact true—and there was no reason for her to put forward any such lie—then that would mean—

His stomach pitched.

Giving his head another shake, William pored over the rows upon rows of names and occupations and other distinguishing details marked there.

Rap-pause-rap-pause—rap-rap.

"Enter," he thundered, abandoning the second book and finding another. He flipped it open.

The measured, familiar fall of his brother's steps echoed in the room, followed by the click of the door as he shut the panel behind him.

"Now, this is certainly not what I expected to see," Edward said quietly, his words hoarse not with sleep but with relief and joy.

William turned the page and froze.

His heart, soul, and body turned to stone as he stared at the lone name written there in Stone's hand.

Francis Allenby. Medical Consultant for the Brethren. Tending injured agents and others on behalf of the Brethren.

Oh, God. His stomach roiled.

"I'm going to be ill."

"William?" Edward's concerned tone drifted through the haze, but William remained firmly absorbed in that name, uncaring that he'd spoken aloud.

"What is it?" his brother asked, rushing over to the desk.

Elsie's father.

And yet…

William searched. "Where is it?" he whispered. His fingers trembling, he grappled with the edge of the thick velum page, turning it. He scanned. Skimming… There was not even a mention of her. She'd worked alongside her father on behalf of the Crown, giving of her services, and she was not so much as a footnote upon those pages? William turned back to Francis Allenby's name. "It isn't here," he repeated dumbly. Her life had been upended, her services enlisted to help William, and no one had thought to record her name.

Resent Stone, or Edward, or whoever kept notes on the staff in the fields, but you were the one who authorized the hiring of these people… whose names you yourself did not even know.

Edward opened and closed his mouth several times. "I don't know what you are ta—"

"You brought her here." Fury ripped that from him. "Surely you know something about her," he charged ahead before his brother could speak.

Understanding lit his brother's eyes. "Miss Allenby." Just that, her name. Edward drew out the winged chair and slid into the leather folds. "What is this about?"

"How did you know of her?" he asked in deadened tones. *How did you know of her, when I knew… nothing?*

When it had been his responsibility. Before.

But now… now, he wanted to know because of who Elsie was.

"Ah," his brother said, as if he understood everything clearly, when William himself couldn't make sense of up or down, left or right. Edward looped his ankle across his opposite knee and rested his clasped hands there. "Our father recommended Francis Allenby's hire more than two decades ago."

"Our father," he repeated dumbly. *His* father had hired *Elsie's*. Their families had been linked by their service to the Crown, and she had been a stranger to him, until now.

His brother waved a hand, infuriatingly nonchalant. "A former agent was thrown from his mount when riding through Bladon and taken to convalesce at Dr. Allenby's cottage. Father learned about the man's capabilities, and he was… petitioned."

Petitioned. Which, under his own leadership and the leadership to come before, would have really meant *forced*.

My father was a healer. He did not end lives… He saved *them. And that generosity extended to animals.*

A man such as the one described by Elsie would have never rejected any request to help any man who was wounded or suffering.

Winded, William fell back in his seat. "How did I not know any of this?"

Edward shrugged. "It was a long time ago, and overseeing Francis Allenby was delegated to Bennett. It was an irrelevant matter that wouldn't have commanded your time or energies," his brother said gently. His words were meant to lift guilt, but they only compounded the shame that stung at his insides.

"What happened?"

Edward's expression darkened, and he shook his head slightly.

Snarling, William leaned forward. "I am not asking you a question as your brother. I'm issuing a directive."

"Of course." His brother instantly sat upright in his chair, and as he spoke, he doled out details the way any agent might when asked for a full report. "Francis Allenby betrayed the Brethren."

William jerked. "What?" he demanded. "Impossible." He knew the man not at all, but he knew the daughter, knew Elsie, and of what she spoke and her own goodness. Those people were incapable of deceit or treachery.

As soon as the thought slid in, he faltered. For the whole of his adult life, he'd been led to question everyone's culpability and motives. To be wary and mistrustful. And yet… he inherently trusted her.

"Quite true," Edward said, nodding. "He confirmed to enemies not only the existence of the Brethren, but his role within the organization."

"Bloody hell." William swiped a palm over his forehead. "Why?"

"I don't know those details. We severed ties, but the damage was done."

The clock ticked. The fire hissed and popped.

"That is it?" William asked when it became apparent his brother had nothing else to say.

Edward lifted his shoulders and continued with a methodical telling. "From my understanding of speaking to Bennett, the moment he revealed the information, he realized his mistake and sought help from the Brethren."

Help that would not have been forthcoming for one who'd betrayed the organization. Allenby would have been left to flounder, owning his mistakes and crimes, and ultimately paying the price that was invariably paid—with his life.

William curled his fingers so tight into his palms he left crescent imprints upon them. "The men he would have given that information to…"

"Came for him," Edward confirmed with a somber note of finality.

Them. Elsie would have been there, too. "What happened?" he asked, his tongue thick.

"From my understanding, he was called out for being a liar and pressed for the names of the men he'd treated. Whether he withheld them or shared them?" Again, Edward shrugged. "I've no confirmation. Miss Allenby was spared. Beyond that, I've little information."

It was the *beyond that* that William needed. It would be the stuff of nightmares, and they belonged to Elsie.

What do you think? That I'm just a simple village girl afraid of the world? I wasn't afraid of the world until I saw what men were capable of. Honorable men who simply take from good men.

His vision tunneled as horror lapped at every corner of his consciousness, battering him with visions he didn't want, and yet, they came anyway. William struggled to breathe, focusing on drawing in a steady, even cadence.

"William?" his brother asked, concern heavy in his question.

The world sharpened back into clarity with crystalline focus. "You brought her here," he seethed. "Knowing all *this*?"

Edward squirmed in his chair, the leather groaning in protest. "I evaluated the facts I was in possession of and made a choice based on that. And by your recent emergence from your rooms, and you're not having whores in your bed, or spirits on your breath, as well as your renewed interest in the organization, I say it proves my judgment correct." His brother straightened an already immaculate cravat.

"I want the file," he said in steely tones. "I want every goddamn bit of information we have about Els—" His brother's eyes sharpened on William. "Miss Allenby," he swiftly amended, "and her father at the Home Office and in Stone's possession, and anyone else within the organization."

His brother made a sound of protest. "Stone indicated it's been five, maybe six, years. The records will have been filed and locked away at the Home Office."

"I don't care where they are. I want them collected. Everything. Every last detail about the whole damned... situation. And when you have it? I want all of it here. Am I clear?"

Edward inclined his head. The faintest glitter filled his younger brother's eyes. "As you wish." He hesitated, and his throat moved up and down several times. "I'm glad you are..." His words trailed off, and color splotched his cheeks. "I'm glad you are... back."

Back from the dead, restored to the living... but not because of his work or his title. Not even because of his family. Rather, because of Elsie Allenby.

"Go, Edward," he urged.

His brother offered a deferential bow and started for the door.

"Send Stone in," William ordered after him.

As soon as his brother had gone, William scrubbed his hands over his face. Elsie would have been within her right to send him on to the devil before offering him any medical assistance, and yet, she'd not. For all the rightful resentment and animosity she undoubtedly carried, she'd evaluated his injury and issued more meaningful guidance than all the previous doctors or healers who'd come before her combined. He closed his eyes. He was in awe of her strength and spirit and purity of heart.

And I'm a blackhearted devil who has only ever taken. It had only ever been about his happiness, and his needs as a duke, and as the Sovereign. Even his marriage had been representative of that. He'd enjoyed the thrill of the unfamiliar innocence Adeline had represented, and he'd wanted to continue knowing that sentiment, even though doing so put her and those connected to her at risk.

He'd taken too much. From everyone. And now Elsie. Elsie, who deserved to be free of him and any requirements his brother and Bennett had placed upon her.

He slid his eyes closed.

Only… mayhap with this next decision, one that left him empty and aching before it was even carried out, proved he wasn't so very selfish, after all.

Rap-pause-rap-pause—rap-rap.

William swiftly opened his eyes. "Enter," he boomed. The final echo of his voice hadn't even faded before the door opened, and Stone appeared.

"Your Grace?"

"Summon Miss Allenby," he said before the other man fully stepped into the room. William got the command out while honor won out over his own desires. "I want to see her now."

Stone rushed off.

Alone once more, William fetched the book lying open damningly before him and reread words he'd already largely committed to memory.

Dr. Francis Allenby. Unconventional doctor, with skills superior to some of London's most notable names. Allenby's father and grandfather were both proficient doctors. Allenby removed himself from London for Bladon only after meeting his wife, a young village girl.

No name was mentioned for the woman who'd given birth to Elsie.

William lingered on the afterthought of Francis Allenby's wife, the young woman nothing more than a detail to explain how the doctor had come to leave London for a distant corner of England.

This was it.

This was all there was.

The Brethren had not recorded anything about Francis Allenby's capable daughter, who was versed in ancient massage and able to identify pain and alleviate it when every man before her had failed.

The pages revealed nothing of what her life had been like as an assistant to her father, or what had become of her with Dr. Allenby's passing. For all intents and purposes for the Crown's business, she'd ceased to exist that day, as well.

He dug his fingertips into his temples and rubbed. Was it a wonder she'd mocked him for his simplistic challenge of her decision to remain tucked away?

What a bloody fool he was. How self-important and ignorant, and—

Footfalls echoed outside his office, and a moment later, Stone reappeared—alone.

The spy coughed into his hand, and for the first time in all the years he'd served William, the other man avoided his gaze.

"What is it?" William demanded.

"I checked her rooms." William's stomach fell, and he knew with the same sick intuition that had met him when he'd awakened after two months and searched for his wife. "She's gone."

CHAPTER 19

ELSIE'S FATHER HAD SPOKEN OFTEN of his time in London.

Aside from the tale he'd told of meeting Elsie's mother, the extent of those stories had been about the university he'd attended, the medical lectures he'd given or observed, and the markets where a healer might find unconventional products that traditional doctors invariably scoffed at but in which her own sire had seen medicinal value.

That was why Elsie was just then riding through unfamiliar streets with a singular intent—to find reeds so she might properly construct a device through which William might drink and take partial meals.

Liar. You're running from William and from what you revealed to William… and the horror that all but rolled off his powerful frame in waves.

Closing her eyes, Elsie sank into the miserable folds of the hired hack.

She didn't hate him. She wanted to. Elsie wanted to carry the same abhorrence that had always been a part of her feelings for William and his organization and all the men who served its *noble* ranks.

But those gentlemen were not like… like… William. Or rather, he was so very different from all of them. William, who'd likened her to a Sumerian queen, and who'd lauded her for a strength that she did not feel, and who'd accused her rightly of hiding herself away. William, who'd seen, after only a short while of knowing her, what she'd not seen for the five years she'd been living on her own.

But that had been before she'd revealed her identity as the daughter of a supposedly traitorous fringe member of their organization.

It didn't matter what he, or anyone, thought about her sire. She'd told herself as much through the years. They could all go hang, for she knew precisely the manner of man Francis Allenby had been.

At her feet, Bear barked once.

She groaned. "Oh, fine. I'm a bloody liar." He yapped twice. "A blasted liar, then," she muttered.

Elsie *enjoyed* being with William. When they were together, he didn't treat her as the peculiar healer who dwelled on the side of civilization at Bladon. She wasn't jeered for her talents, or chided for speaking to her dog or her unconventional views on animals and their place in this world.

Her father had loved her unconditionally, but beyond that, society had been content without her in it.

Until William, who'd not mocked her, but praised her talents, and who'd also urged her to do more and be more. Elsie absently stroked the top of Bear's head. William was a man who spoke with her dog with great ease.

She stopped her distracted back-and-forth caress.

What would become of them now?

No, what becomes of you?

Elsie hugged her arms around her middle to ward off the sudden chill that stole through her. Likely, William would send her on her way and free himself of "the traitor's daughter," as she'd been called when an agent with the Brethren had taken his final leave of her and her father.

Which was precisely what she'd wanted after Lord Edward and Mr. Bennett had shown up and compelled her to return with them.

But everything had changed.

She enjoyed being with William, enjoyed speaking with him about her craft and his own unconventional knowledge. And when she was with him, for the first time in more than five years, the nightmares didn't come. They didn't haunt her at every turn. They'd been replaced by thoughts of him.

The carriage hit a large bump, jarring her back to the present. Grunting, Elsie spread her feet on the dirtied floor and hugged her arms about Bear, stabilizing them both.

At last, after an endless ride, the conveyance rolled to a stop.

Gathering her basket from the opposite bench, Elsie waited until the driver drew the door open. Bear jumped out first. With a word of thanks, she accepted help climbing down.

As soon as her feet landed upon the cobbles, she looked more closely at the young man. Young, with a scar intersecting half of his face, the stranger took pains to avert his marked visage from her gaze. "Miss," he said gruffly.

Her heart clenched. She'd seen too many like him. His had been a knife attack, and by the jagged, lingering white ridges to it, the wound had cut deep and been… deliberate. It had been stitched improperly, at that. "If you'll… wait?" she ventured. "I can offer a penny more." Even as she said it, she recognized the inherent silliness in him remaining behind for such a paltry amount.

He adjusted the brim of his cap. "It would be my pleasure, ma'am." His cultured tones were better reserved for one belonging to far grander stations. But then, all people, regardless of station or birthright, all found themselves falling at some point or another—she, William, her father, and all the other men she and her father had cared for were testament to that.

Elsie started toward the market square that was just being assembled. Vendors and merchants hefted carts of goods and busied themselves, readying for their day. She drew her cloak closer about herself to ward off the chill that lingered in the air and proceeded on through the wares and goods being put on display throughout the market. Bear hung close to her side, his presence comforting in these unfamiliar grounds. He nosed at the air as they walked. The thick scent of refuse that hung in the air was so very different from the crisp clarity of Bladon. Moving along the perimeter of the marketplace, Elsie searched her gaze over the raw meats hanging for the various cooks' inspection.

Of course, everything that her father had shared and journaled about would have changed through the years. Time marched on, and everything invariably did. It was foolish to expect that the items he'd found of value should still be sold at this very market.

Nonetheless, Elsie drifted deeper into the increasing fray of the morning activity. All around her, calls went up as vendors hawked their wares.

She stopped abruptly, and Bear collided with her legs.

"I believe I've found it," she whispered, with a loving stroke between Bear's ears.

The bright splash of green at the center of the other goods stood out, a stark, cheerful expression of the countryside in this desolate part of London. With a spring in her step, Elsie rushed over. The same thrill at finding a valuable herb in the countryside moved through her now as she examined the items on display.

Searching. Searching…

Elsie chewed at her lower lip.

"Need 'elp, dear?"

She glanced at the gap-toothed, graying woman, who smiled back. Arms filled with flowers, the rotund vendor held them out. "Blooms?"

Elsie returned the smile. "No flowers this day." The woman's face fell. "I'm looking for something different," she said, softening the rejection. She moved slowly around the cart filled with greenery and stalks. "Certain… blades of grass. Wheatgrass."

The woman made a *tsking* sound. "No wheatgrass here in this part of London."

Of course not. Elsie sighed. "Something like it, then."

"Feather reed grass?" The vendor held up several stalks.

Elsie briefly considered the dried plants. "No."

Tapping a muddied fingernail against her lips, the woman spoke quietly to herself. "Bur reed?"

"No… I…" Her words wandered off as she was drawn over.

"Ah, thatching reed?"

"Yes," she whispered. With reverent fingers, she lifted the cylindrical stalk, dried from the sun, hardened. Of course.

"Lovely, isn't it?"

She stiffened and glanced back.

A darkly clad stranger came over. He strode with idle steps, unthreatening in the languid pace, and yet, there was a jaded hardness to his eyes.

Reflexively, Elsie moved closer to Bear. And for the first time since she'd gone off on her own, even with her dog at her side, fear settled around her, for she and Bear had been alone together once before. The end result had been her father's death and her near murder. Her palms moistened, and she discreetly wiped them along the sides of her skirts. But she'd not been cowed before, and she'd not do it now for a stranger. "May I help you?"

The interloper tipped the edge of his bowler hat. "An odd purchase," he noted by way of greeting, nodding at the items in her hand.

Elsie thinned her eyes. What was he on about? "It is only odd if one does not have a proper use for it."

"Fair enough." The ghost of a smile grazed his lips, lending him an almost wolflike quality. "Please, do not allow me to keep you from making your purchase."

And yet, as Elsie completed her transaction, buying the remainders of the thatching reeds, the stranger remained at her side, taking in her every movement.

From the corner of her eye, she caught a flash of movement as he tugged free his fine leather gloves and—

Elsie's body jerked.

Bear growled, baring his teeth.

The metal signet ring glinted, unnaturally bright in the early dawn light.

It was *the ring*. The same one worn by so many patients who'd been brought to her father, a glittering scrap that marked their order.

Fear turned her mouth dry, choking off the ability to draw a breath, at the reminder of the perilous world William inhabited and the world in which her father had inadvertently embroiled her.

With fingers that shook, Elsie exchanged coin for the reeds, and then, unlatching her basket, she dropped her purchase inside, atop the precious books there. Snapping her fingers once, Elsie, Bear at her side, took a hurried step around the stranger.

"Do you think they'll help him?" he called after her.

A chill scraped along her spine. *Leave. Do not engage. He is one of them. Everything with these gentlemen is a game.* Bear nudged her, urging her to leave. "Beg pardon?" she asked, turning to face him. Nonetheless, she'd lived in fear too long because of them… and because of herself. William had helped her to see that.

"Come," he called out, almost cheerfully. "You're not very good at dissembling. Do you trust those reeds? Will they help His Grace?"

She huddled deeper within her cloak. "I don't know what you're speaking of. Now, if you'll excuse me."

Not even sparing a glance for the bearlike dog at her side, the stranger moved himself into her path. "I suspect the better question is *why* should you want to help him?"

So that was what this was about, then? Those within the hated organization still saw her as the traitor's daughter. They questioned her honor and motives. Elsie curled her fingers tight around her handle and faced the hard-eyed stranger once more. "Because that is what decent people do." She enunciated each syllable slowly. "They help."

"And the wronged ones seek revenge," he remarked, tucking his gloves inside his jacket. "Which one are you really, Miss Allenby?" he asked, almost conversationally. However, the steely edge to the query belied any hint of true friendliness. Something within his eyes indicated that whatever answer she gave mattered very much.

Elsie drifted closer, and the stranger's eyes flared with surprise. Good. Did he believe she'd back down from him? "The problem for those who live a life of treachery and lies is that they come to expect that is all *anyone* is capable of. But there is more to everyone and forgiveness to be found."

"Never tell me that you haven't had resentment over how someone treated you or yours, Miss Allenby? That you didn't hunger for revenge?"

Her breath lodged in her lungs, she shook her head. "I'd be lying if I told you that." Elsie looked over her shoulder to an old vendor struggling to shove her cart along the uneven cobbles. "But I find that my anger didn't bring me solace, and the only thing that can bring me peace"—and contentment—"is letting go of the darkness and finding the light." There was something so very cathartic and freeing in that. A healing buoyancy suffused her chest and lifted her. She and William had both been haunted. They weren't different in that regard. He'd helped her to see that.

The man gave her a long look. "That is… not the answer I was expecting, Miss Allenby." The agent gave her a long, pitying look. "You're naïve if you believe that."

"I'm hopeful for believing it," she countered softly.

With that, he touched the brim of his hat and started off through the throng of carts and tables.

Elsie's heart kicked up a panicky beat, and she followed his retreating form with her gaze until he'd gone. This stranger knew who she was. He knew and sought to gauge the depth of her loyalty. Well, he and the rest of the Brethren could go to hell with their ill opinion of her, and the world on the whole.

Somewhere, a rooster crowed, the country sound at odds with the bustle of London activity.

Springing into movement, Elsie held her basket close and, with long strides, found her way to the hack. The driver sat atop the perch and immediately jumped down when he spied her.

Too many missteps in the past had proven how rot she was at identifying the perils around her until it was too late.

"Miss?" the driver called impatiently.

Steadying her basket, Elsie accepted his proffered hand and climbed inside. Bear jumped in behind her. As the carriage started its slow roll down the unfamiliar cobblestones of London, Elsie peeled the curtain back a smidge and peered out.

The stranger's words lingered in her mind.

And the wronged ones seek revenge. Which one are you really, Miss Allenby?

Before she'd come to London, she would have said she was just that… consumed by her own hatred that she could not separate it from the fabric of her soul. Living alone in the Cotswolds, removed from the villagers and the rest of the world, it had become all too easy to believe that about herself.

William, and the other men within the Brethren, had existed in her mind as entities and not people. It had been far too easy to see him as a caricature of a person, one who was maniacally evil and who destroyed lives without a thought and who was wholly incapable of love.

But he wasn't. She bit the inside of her cheek. He was a man who'd so desperately loved another that he'd become a shell of a person, dwelling in a prison of guilt he'd constructed for himself.

For everything his wife had lost, how very lucky she'd been to have that gift.

It was certainly a mark upon Elsie's own soul that she sat here envying the late duchess for the love she'd known with William.

Elsie's mind balked, shying away from the path her thoughts were dangerously traversing.

The carriage rolled to a halt, and reaching inside her basket, Elsie fished out the fare.

Opening the door, her driver took the basket from her hands and, with his spare hand, helped her down. With a word of thanks, Elsie collected her things and started down the narrow alley between William's Mayfair townhouse and the next. Using the servants' entrance, she let herself into the kitchens already bustling with men, women, and children at work for the day.

The same kitchens where she and William had sat hours ago—a lifetime ago?—when he'd at last gathered who she was, and the truth had been laid bare between them.

Climbing the narrow stairwell at the back of the household, Elsie found her way to her chambers. She shifted her basket to her hip and reached around it to open the door.

Bear ambled into the room and, with an excited yap, bound over to—

Elsie gasped. Stepping inside the room, she set her basket down.

"William," she breathed as the fear left her. He stood at the side of her bed, the slight wrinkle to the coverlet hinting that he'd sat there. His face was a somber mask, and Elsie searched for a hint of what he was thinking. What did he want?

SHE IS HERE.

As Elsie closed the door behind her, juggling the basket she was never without, William stood there, afraid to so much as breathe lest she vanish. As all good things and people invariably did.

Except, she didn't. She glided forward with long, sweeping strides, fiddling with the wood clasp at her neck, divesting herself of the coarse wool cloak, and setting it along the back of a desk chair.

"You're here," he said hoarsely, the observation nonsensical.

Elsie stopped with several paces between them. Watching him with guarded eyes, she retrieved her basket and moved deeper into the room. "I am," she said in veiled tones.

That was it.

I am.

Nothing more than the simplest of confirmations that revealed nothing in terms of her intentions.

He took a step toward her. "Where did you go?" he gritted out, his jaw immediately radiating agony.

Fire flashed in her eyes, and Elsie dropped her basket to the floor. "Is that what this is about, William?" He opened his mouth, but she continued over him on a rush. "Did you wonder if the 'traitor's daughter' would deceive you and you set your team of spies after me?"

That was what she thought of him. "Of course not," he sputtered, heat suffusing his cheeks. "It wasn't about your father. It was…" All his senses went on alert as he homed in on the latter part of the accusation she'd tossed. "Who approached you when you were out?" he demanded, his voice coming out sharper than he'd intended.

Ignoring his query, she settled her hands angrily on her hips, breathtaking in her fury. "My father was not a traitor." Ice dripped from each word she clipped out.

Her upset pierced the panic knocking around his chest. She was hurting… because of crimes her father had been accused of. Charges that mattered more than the peril she'd unwittingly found in London. Tabling the questions demanding to be asked, he modulated his tones. "I didn't know who or what your father was until now," he said quietly, having learned long ago to diffuse most conflicts before they escalated into a heated row.

Alas, she proved unlike every person, in every way, he'd ever dealt with. Elsie took an angry step toward him, sending her skirts whipping about her ankles, displaying a flash of that trim flesh. "No, that is correct. You didn't know him. Or about his service. Or anything about his life, and yet"—Elsie turned her hands up almost pleadingly—"you have condemned him as dishonorable to king and country."

He swiped a hand through his hair. Theirs was a debate that had been due since she'd stormed off with the truth of their connection at last breathed aloud. "I did not condemn him."

Elsie shook her head sadly. "No. But 'not knowing' about the lives of those who worked for you on behalf of the country does not pardon you from guilt over their fate."

William winced. Her ill opinion struck like a well-placed kick to the gut. *My God*. What was worse was that Elsie deserved to have that opinion. In failing to know anything about her or her father, he'd failed the both of them. *And how many other men and women who served on behalf of the Brethren did he also wrong?* "You are correct," he said hoarsely.

She rocked back. "What?" He might as well have stated the earth was in fact flat and they were all about to sail over the edge of it.

William glanced down at the signet ring upon his finger, the metal scrap that marked his connection to an organization, a marriage that he'd been more loyal to than even his own.

You are never wrong, William. You are always and only... correct.

His father's booming command, issued as he'd passed the role as leader of the Brethren on to William, echoed around his mind. Admitting failure in any way went against every lesson ingrained in him. He weighed his words. "You are correct. I don't recall your father's name. I don't know the circumstances surrounding whatever decision he made or did not make." In the past, the Brethren's final ruling would have determined guilt and the assignment closed. How... flawed. And how had he failed to see that until now? "But I have reopened the case and have ordered anything relating to his file gathered and brought for my review."

Elsie hugged her arms around her middle, searching her eyes over his face. "Why would you do that?"

"Because it is the right thing to do," he said simply.

She took a hesitant step toward him. Then another. And another. Until they were separated by only a handbreadth. "You'd simply take my word against that of... the Home Office."

"I would." Before her, he'd have doubted God himself before questioning the Brethren.

"Thank you," Elsie said softly.

Discomfited by the undeserved gratitude, William held a palm up. "You mentioned earlier that you believe I sent a team of spies after you..."

"You did not?" she asked, unease creeping into her tone.

Christ. It was a prayer and a curse together. *Not again. Not again.* "I did not. I would not have you followed. I'd simply ask any questions I have for you myself."

"Oh." She worried at her lower lip. For the first time since she'd launched the defense of her father, worry darkened her eyes.

Because of me. I've brought peril into this woman's life. Just like Adeline. Just like...

No! He'd not allow it. "Can you tell me everything about him… and this meeting?"

Elsie twisted her hands together and proceeded to offer an accounting of the encounter. When she finished, William stored each detail. He'd need to speak to his brother. They'd require additional men stationed.

"Do I… have reason to worry?"

"Yes," he said, offering that truth because the lie of omission had left another woman in peril.

Elsie brought her shoulders back and nodded. "I see."

Any other woman would have dissolved in a weepy mess. Any other woman, except this brave creature before him. William started to leave and then stopped at the front of the room. "I'd have you know… my response a short while ago was not because I do not trust you." His fingers curled tight around the door handle. He forced himself to glance back. "I thought you'd left."

She cocked her head. "I don't… understand."

Closing the space that divided them in three long strides, he gripped her by the shoulders and squeezed, assuring himself she was real, that the first flash of light in his otherwise dark existence had not been extinguished. "I thought you'd left," he repeated, his fingers clenching reflexively upon her. As she should have. As she needed to. Soon. Pain lanced at his gut.

Her lips formed a soft moue. "Why?"

With a broken laugh, he closed his eyes. "Why did I think that?" he repeated incredulously. She was the only woman who'd dare ask that. The only one who'd not have hurled in his face her birthright and connection to a man who'd served the Brethren and send him on to the devil. "Why should you not have gone when I did not even know the name of a man who served…" Shame killed the remainder of that admission. At one time, he'd have been so cynical that he'd not have seen beyond Edward's and Stone's revelations that the doctor had been a "traitor."

Elsie's heart-shaped face softened. She stretched a hand up and caressed his cheek. "And it… mattered to you? That I'd gone?"

It would gut him all over again when she left. Squeezing his eyes briefly shut, William leaned into her touch, accepting that warmth that had been missing in his life. How could she not know? How could she not know how much she'd come to mean to him? She'd restored light to an otherwise dark world. He managed a shaky nod. "The moment I first saw you, I wanted to send you away." Just as he'd wished to do to every other doctor and healer who'd arrived.

Filled with a restiveness, he took several steps away from her. At sea. Lost, but at the same time found in the unlikeliest of ways. William stared blankly out. "Every other person to come before you was nothing more than a charlatan, pretending at something they couldn't do. But, Elsie?" His throat convulsed. "You were real." She'd teased him and challenged him and bewitched him at every turn. "And…" *I want you to remain here.* But she couldn't. Today was proof enough of that.

"And?" Elsie gently prodded. She leaned forward, almost expectantly.

"I…" He struggled to wrap his mouth around what his soul craved.

And…

Elsie fluttered a hand about her breast. "What is it, William?"

He held her gaze, his words emerging gravelly to his own ears. "I did not realize how very much I'd missed 'real' until you." William dragged a shaky hand through his hair. "I want you to remain here for…" *Ever.* Elsie's eyes went wide. He had to let her go. Now. Soon. Eventually. Just not now. "…our agreed-upon term." He settled for the lie, his voice flat.

"Oh," she said, her reply nothing more than a faint exhalation. Did he imagine the crestfallen note there? The one in her eyes and stamped in her delicate features? Or did he seek out only that which he wished to see?

She briefly studied her toes. "I… see." Pray she didn't. Because if she did, she'd sense the lie there.

"I have no right to ask anything of you," he said on a rush. "And certainly have no right asking you to remain." William grimaced. "My brother no doubt coerced you into coming."

And just like that, William restored them to the familiar relationship they'd established more than a week ago: patient and healer, two people who'd begun at odds, but whose lives had become more naturally and meaningfully intertwined.

Elsie clasped her hands before her, attending those interlocked digits. "I came of my own volition, William," she said softly, falling to a knee beside her basket. He stared down at her bent head as she ruffled through her basket and drew out a cylindrical stalk of grass.

He puzzled his brow.

"This is where I went," she said by way of explanation, coming to her feet. Elsie held it out. "I wasn't leaving. I was searching for... this." Chewing at her lower lip, she considered the stalk. "I believe it will work as a straw, but won't know until you try using it with liquid."

Wordlessly, he accepted the piece of grass and turned it over in his hands. "*This* is where you went? Searching for something for me?"

"Of course. I said I'd help as I'm able, and that's what I'll do."

"There is no other woman like you," he said softly, lowering the blade to his side.

A pretty blush exploded on her cheeks as she plucked the thatch reed from his grip. "Do not make me out to be a martyr, or something different from what I am. It was my decision to come here." She paused. "Just as it was my father's decision to aid the Home Office. Not your brother's. Not yours. Not anyone else's."

Those who dealt with the Brethren never truly had a choice, or that had been the case before her. Now, she called into doubt every last ruthless practice or decision he'd carried out when he'd not thought about the people affected by the Brethren's influence.

Something shifted in his chest, emotions he'd believed dead and himself incapable of feeling anymore. William brushed his fingertips along her jawline, gently bringing her gaze up to his and cracking once more the fragile barrier that needed to be erected between them. "Anyone would resent me. *Anyone*," he repeated, running his gaze over her sun-kissed cheeks.

"I have hated you before I even knew you." The admission found a direct blow to his chest, because of both its truthfulness and rightfulness. Elsie drew in a breath. "I blamed them"—*I am them*—"for his murder, but I vowed to help you." Because her soul was pure in ways that his was blackened. "And that is what I'll do, William. I promised you three weeks, and I'll not renege upon my pledge." She'd already given him one week.

"A fortnight," he murmured, though her meeting with the mysterious man proved he needed to send her away sooner rather than later.

"A fortnight," she vowed.

Before he did something irrational, like ask her to stay beyond that with the ancient dog who'd slipped inside his household, William quit her rooms.

As she closed the door behind him, he lengthened his strides, seeking out his offices once more.

Fourteen days. Just fourteen more days with her in his life and in his household.

It was enough.

It would have to be.

CHAPTER 20

WITH HER HEAD BENT OVER a patch of earth and the sun beating down upon her neck, Elsie could almost believe she was back at Bladon.

Bladon, which seemed a world away, that remote, tucked-away place on the corner of existence. She'd not truly noted how lonely it was until these past weeks here in London. For in Bladon, there was no one to speak with about her craft and obscure bits of history she'd never before known. No one to laugh with. Or dine with.

She paused, her gaze fixed on a fat earthworm winding its way through a moist patch of black earth.

There was no… *him*.

"You've finished," William murmured from just over her shoulder, forcing her mind away from the melancholy musing.

After more than a fortnight living in William's household and daily work carried out in the gardens, she'd converted this space into something no longer strangled by too much life. It was perfectly ordered for when she soon left. A pang struck in her chest. "I have," she said as she assessed the grounds. Neatly trimmed boxwoods, the orderly beds, the tamed rosebushes—she rested her gaze upon the one wildly grown tree—well, with the exception of one.

Together, her gaze and William's went to that bush.

And a sentiment increasingly familiar and wicked and all things wrong wound through her—envy for the woman who'd had a precious gift with and in William that Elsie would never know.

To give her fingers something to do, she toyed with the strands of her bonnet, and stared wistfully out. "Though it is not ever truly done, you know." She forced the response out. "Caring for the gardens, that is," she clarified when she finally looked at him.

He was seated on a rusted white wrought-iron bench. The bucolic tableau had come to represent their time together: he at work with a stack of leather ledgers on the bench beside him, while she tended his gardens. "Weeds always return. Leaves always grow. You'll need to have someone attend them when I'm..." *Gone.*

He stiffened.

And she braced for him to condemn these grounds as he had more than two weeks ago. But the display did not come.

Not wanting to shatter the moment, she patted the ground beside her. "I'd show you something." *Before I go.* Another blasted pang struck, and she fought it back, not wanting to shatter the peace that had sprung between them.

Without hesitation, he abandoned his books and joined her on the mud-stained blanket she'd spread out, kneeling upon it when any other lord would have recoiled at the idea of lowering himself to the damp earth.

Doffing her bonnet, Elsie sat back on her haunches and tossed it aside, so she had an unfettered view of the plants before her. She reached down and clipped a yellow bloom free. Elsie gathered William's hand and placed the flower in his grip.

He eyed it. "What is this?"

"What do you think it is?" she returned.

"I'm a novice to the work you do out here, but I know enough to say it is a flower." His lips twitched, and where there'd once been a sneer, now there was only a smile. One that wrought a dangerous havoc upon her heart.

"That is precisely what it is," she said, her voice faintly breathless. "It has a fragrant scent." She guided it up to his nose, and the slight aromatic smell wafted between them. Did she imagine that his hand trembled? "And satiny-soft pedals." He caressed the pad of his thumb experimentally over one of them. "On the surface, that is all most will see." Elsie collected the stalk from him and laid the yellow bloom upon her palm. With four fingers, she crushed the petals and compressed them against her hand for several moments. She felt William's eyes taking in her every movement. "And if that is all one sees, one will miss all the wonders it is capable of." When she lifted her fingers, a distinct pine-sage odor danced around the air. Elsie applied the watery ointment upon his jaw, coating a portion of his right cheek.

"What are you—?"

"It is called arnica. I've read records that indicate it's been used as far back as the 1500s," she explained, crushing another handful of pedals so that this time her fingers were slicked with the natural ointment. "It soothes aches," she explained as she applied it to his opposite cheek. "Reduces swelling. Heals wounds."

"And you've used it before... with such results?" Heavy skepticism hung in his tone, along with something else—hope... and awe.

"I've used it countless times with such outcomes," she confirmed. "Has your jaw ached with the same intensity this past week?"

She knew the answer before he even shook his head.

Elsie winked.

His eyebrows shot up, and he looked between the bloom in her hand and then back to her face. "Why... why... this is what you've applied to my jaw each morn?"

Dropping the crumpled remnants of the flower, she let them fall beside her. "Ointments are invariably looked upon more favorably when they come in proper containers."

William stared wistfully at the vibrant plant. "And all along it has been here."

"Oh, yes. Along with basil"—she pointed across the gardens—"and cloves." Elsie leaned closer. "Cloves, William," she added excitedly. "They've the ability to numb your gums, which would have aided with your recovery. It can still help you," she rushed to assure him. "Nature is surrounded by gifts that have the ability to help us. But we have to be respectful of those gifts, honoring them." And she'd left his late wife's gardens in a state where they'd been restored to their former glory, and he'd... Elsie glanced up. A soft smile played about William's lips. Heat washed over her face. "You're laughing at me." She stood and stepped around him.

"Never." He leaped up with an agility he'd not shown weeks

earlier and moved into her path. His gaze moved over her face, warmer than the sun, like a physical caress. "How could I take you… or any part of this"—he motioned to the gardens—"as silly?"

"Because everyone, except my father, invariably does," she said guardedly.

"We've already established they were fools," he reminded.

Her heart swelled.

"You have no idea," he breathed, continuing forward until they were but three steps apart.

Her eyes fixed on his, riveted. "What?" she whispered.

William brushed his palm down her cheek in a fleeting caress that brought her eyes briefly closed. "How very special you are, Elsie Allenby."

Special.

In the whole of her life, she'd been called odd, peculiar, strange. In some cases, villagers had whispered the word *witch* as she'd passed. Never had anyone spoken with a reverent awe about her or what she did, wholly trusting her work. Not even the patients she'd tended for the Brethren had been willing to accept her treatments unless her father had been present. Warmth stole through her.

As he slid his gaze over her face, lingering upon her like a touch, his Adam's apple jumped.

The air crackled between them.

"What is it?" she asked softly.

"I want to kiss you," he said, an aching quality to that admission.

He wanted to kiss her. Since their embrace more than a week ago, he'd revealed no hint of desire for her. She wetted her lips, and an agonized groan filtered from him and filled the air between them. "Y-you did," she reminded him. Nine days, ten hours, and some handful of minutes ago. The single most erotic, passionate moment of her life.

"Again," he said hoarsely. "I want to kiss you again."

And yet, he did not. It was a contradiction of passion and restraint that made no sense in the scheme that was desire.

"That was different," he explained, his response moving with a synchronic harmony to her unvoiced thoughts.

"In what way?" she asked and then cringed. How very easy that question could be confused for an entreaty.

Because isn't it? Isn't his embrace what you want?

"I was horrid before, and I'm... trying now because I wasn't always dishonorable." With a sound of disgust, William began to pace. "I was a gentleman once, you know." He stalked an angry rhythm back and forth, and as he spoke, Elsie made herself go as still and silent as possible, afraid to move lest he stop the healing diatribe he so desperately needed. "I was polite to ladies and staff, and I was certainly never the lord who drank too much." He dragged a hand through the tangle of his unfashionably long black tresses. "And I was certainly never one to kiss a woman on my staff."

Me. He is speaking of me.

A servant in his employ and nothing more.

Why did that leave her so forlorn inside?

He stopped abruptly so that he faced her.

Elsie schooled her features lest he spy the inexplicable misery that his statement had stirred.

"After all, you are here at my..." He flashed a strained grin. "Behest."

A laugh exploded from her, and she caught it behind her hand.

"Minx," he muttered, looping a hand around her waist and tugging her close in a gesture that was so very natural that they both stilled. All laughter died between them. William closed his eyes. "Tell me to release you."

"But what if I don't want you to?" she whispered. If she were a proper lady, she would never admit to that wickedness. But she was no lady. She was a woman born to an altogether different station, one who yearned for another taste of this man's kiss. "What if I tell you I want to kiss you as much as you want to kiss me?"

Passion glinted in his eyes. Passion, along with something else contrary to that emotion—regret. "I can't offer you more."

He could not or would not? There was a fine distinction, with the same end result—them parting. And then she did something that she never did. She lied. "I don't want more than this, William."

"Elsie." Her name was a prayer and a benediction all at once. With a groan, he slammed his mouth over hers, and this kiss was different from the one they'd shared before. Heat, white-hot, warmer than the sun that now beat down upon them, set her ablaze.

Elsie climbed her hands about his neck and, going up on tiptoes, leaned into him and all that he offered.

He slanted his lips over hers, and then she parted her mouth, allowing him entry. William swept his tongue inside, and they tangled in a beautiful dance, both primitive and tender all at once.

"Elsie," he groaned against her lips, the reverberation of her name tickling and pulling a breathy laugh from her. He swallowed that sound, claiming it as his own.

Cupping her under the buttocks, William drew her to the vee between his legs.

His length throbbed against her belly, and she pressed herself closer to the feel of him.

A sharp ache settled at her core.

Guiding her back down upon the blanket, William never broke contact with her lips. He continued to slant his lips over hers, and then he shifted his mouth.

She cried out in an incoherent protest, tangling her fingers in his hair to claim more of that kiss, but William continued his search, trailing his lips down her cheek. Every swath of flesh he caressed with them burned and sent that heat spiraling further within her.

"You have bewitched me, Elsie," he rasped against her ear. He flicked his tongue out, teasing her lobe and then suckling that flesh.

"I have been c-called a witch before," she said between frantic little spurts of indrawn breaths.

"Damned villagers?" he muttered, moving his exploration lower until he found the place where her pulse frantically beat with her hungering for him.

Elsie bit her lower lip to stifle a moan, and her head tipped reflexively, affording him open access to that skin. "Th-the very same. S-some of my father's patients, t-too." Her speech dissolved into a partial whimper, partial plea.

He reached a hand between them and, through the thin fabric of her wool day dress, palmed her breasts, bringing them together, and she cried out softly. "Siren, then. Enchantress."

Her lashes fluttered, and she dropped her head back, allowing him access to her. "A-an enchantress is really much the same as a w-witch, you know."

William's mouth again found hers for a hard kiss. "Goddess, then."

As he continued to tease her through the gown, the restlessness built at her core, a throbbing ache that grew with his every caress.

The fabric of her dress, a thin barrier, only added a heightened level of eroticism to his touch. Nothing more than a scrap of cloth divided them, and all one needed to do was peel it back, and his skin would be upon hers.

Of their own volition, her hips undulated, seeking more of him. "I-I know so much about the human body, you know, and yet, I've never known I could feel like this."

Masculine pride glinted in his eyes. "Let me show you everything your body is capable of feeling, Elsie."

He already had. He'd opened her heart in ways that she hadn't known existed. And he would give her this most primitive of gifts.

When I want more. I want so much more with him, and from him.

Elsie fought back the wave of melancholy. She nodded slowly and turned herself back over to simply having William in this way. "I want that," she said quietly.

With another groan, he caught her to him.

His fingers made quick work of the buttons down the back of her gown, a vague reminder that before she'd come here, he'd been a scoundrel bedding beauties, and that for him, this was surely just an extension of that act.

But God help her, mayhap she was not so very honorable after all, because she didn't care if this made her no different than the whores or actresses to come before. She wanted to know pleasure in William's arms. She wanted to know the offer he'd made and lose herself in his embrace.

William worked her dress down past her shoulders, guiding it lower, taking her chemise along with it, gradually exposing her skin to the warm early summer sun—and then he stopped.

Elsie remained there, her breasts bared to him, exposed, as reality slipped in.

She looked up, and all the air was squeezed from her lungs.

Heat. It blazed from William's eyes. A look that was a tangible touch, that radiated a hungering—for her. It was for her.

You're a fool. It would be for any woman. He's offered you nothing more. You are no different.

"You are so beautiful," he whispered, and slowly lowering his head, he caressed his lips around one of those pink tips.

She gasped and curled her fingertips in his hair, anchoring him close. William worshiped that peak, suckling it, laving it, until he pulled keening little moans from deep within her throat.

And then he shifted his attention to the previously neglected breast.

"William." His name emerged as a moan, desperate and entreating.

His only response was to guide her back down upon the blanket until she lay beneath him. His hands were everywhere upon her, sliding her gown lower over her hips, along with her undergarments, until she was naked.

His breath coming hard and fast like one who'd run a great race, he drew back. A groan rumbled in his chest and lodged somewhere in his throat. "So beautiful," he whispered and slipped a hand between her legs.

Elsie's entire body stiffened. The air hissed between her teeth as she tightened her thighs about his palm.

"Relax, love," he urged. "Lie back and let me love you."

Panting, she slowly splayed her legs open.

William palmed the thatch of dark curls there, applying an exquisite pressure with his fingers in a touch that simultaneously tormented and eased that ache. Even as pressure built within her. A yearning to know… precisely the gift he'd offered.

He slipped a finger inside her wet channel.

"William," she gasped his name, her hips shooting off the blanket.

He drew it out slowly and then continued a rhythmic stroke, until she was incapable of nothing more than feeling.

The pressure built within her like water behind a dam. Biting her lower lip, she lifted into his touch. Desperately seeking. Wanting. Needing.

She was so close. So—

Elsie cried out as he drew his hand back, and she was left with an empty void of unsated desire.

Passion darkened his gaze as he sat back on his haunches. Never taking his eyes from her, William shrugged out of his jacket and tossed it aside. His lawn shirt followed suit.

Riveted by the broad display of rippled muscles and coiled strength, Elsie shoved herself upright. "You are magnificent," she breathed, stroking her fingertips through the light matting of dark, coiled hair upon his chest. She ran her palms down the silken fur.

He groaned, clenching his hands into tight fists at his sides.

Emboldened, Elsie circled the flat discs of his nipples, so different from her own. "Elsie," he pleaded, reaching for her.

She went into his arms and lifted to reach his kiss. Her skin burned hot against his, her nipples pebbled against his chest. William palmed her breasts once more, lifting each to his mouth for one last, lingering kiss that stole the breath from her lungs.

William drew back. He yanked first one boot free and tossed it atop the slowly growing pile of their garments. His next boot followed, landing with a thump too close to Bear.

The dog lifted his head in affront, before lowering onto the ground once more. He emitted a loud snore.

Breathless laughs escaped Elsie and William, but instantly faded as he reached for the waistband of his breeches. Slowly, he pushed them down his hips, lower, and then he kicked them aside until he stood before her in all his masculine splendor.

Elsie went absolutely motionless. His manhood jutted long and thick from a thatch of black curls. It pressed against his flat stomach. "I've seen many men in a state of undress. Naked," she corrected. She shook her head, unable to look away from that length. "Never like this."

William chuckled, the expression more pained than amused as he reached for her. Drawing her into his arms, he claimed her mouth and brought them both back upon the blanket.

He slid his palm between her legs once again and stroked the nub hidden within her curls until she thrashed her head back and forth upon the blanket, garbled whimpers spilling from her.

Sweat beaded William's brow as he slipped a knee between hers, urging them apart and then between her thighs. "Elsie," he whispered against her brow. "I wish—"

"I know it hurts," she breathed, moving her hips in little circles in a bid to alleviate the throbbing there. William continued to tease that nub of flesh. "I've read s-several journals about it and—" She bit her lip and arched into his touch. "What was… I… I can't…" She closed her eyes. "Just make love to me," she ordered.

With her name on his lips, William thrust inside.

He swallowed her sharp gasp with his mouth and went absolutely still.

Elsie's pulse pounded in her ears as she considered the feel of him buried within her. His length throbbed and pulsed.

"I'm so sorry," he said against the corner of her mouth.

"It did not hurt nearly as bad as I'd believed," she said. "I'd expected more..." Elsie's breath caught as he slowly moved.

"What was it you expected?" William's lips teased at the tip of her right breast.

"I..." *Oh, goodness.* Elsie closed her eyes. "I..." *Cannot remember. Cannot think.* She was incapable of anything but feeling. She lifted her hips slowly, tentatively at first, meeting each measured thrust of his until the faint throbbing pain there receded and only pleasure remained.

She panted. Nay, it was not only pleasure. It was an unsated yearning more agonizing than when that barrier of flesh had given way.

Wrapping her arms about him, Elsie lifted her hips. Seeking. Searching.

"That is it," he urged, a like desperation in his own gruff voice matching that which dwelled within her. Her body climbed higher toward some unknown precipice. "Come for me, love."

Love.

That was it.

Elsie hurtled over that edge and exploded into a schism of color, screaming her release to the London sky. Pleasure washed through her in waves. Lapping at reason and leaving raw nerve endings of feeling vibrantly alive.

William's shout blended with the echo of her cries as he withdrew and spilled himself onto her belly.

A moment later, he collapsed atop her, catching his weight at his elbows.

Her heart hammered wildly in a cadence that could surely, after this, never return to normal. He... nay, they two together had been... "Magic," she mouthed to the cloud-filled blue sky. She stroked his back, a sated smile upon her lips.

"Elsie," he whispered against her ear.

Elsie stilled, wanting that which he'd already claimed he could not give.

Waiting for it anyway.

And as they lay there, with no words forthcoming, her smile faded.

She'd lied to him and to herself.

This was not enough.

She wanted more from him.

Elsie closed her eyes.

God help me—I love him.

CHAPTER 21

Three days later

THE WORLD AS WILLIAM KNEW it had resumed its natural course.

His desk had been tidied, with each file and ledger in its proper place. His hair had been trimmed and proper garments donned. The misery that had held him in an unrelenting snare had since lessened, leaving him to feel again. William once again… lived.

At that given moment, he sat, scanning the folder in his hands.

"This isn't the most recent," he said, flipping to the next page.

"No, Your Grace," Stone murmured.

When no additional information was forthcoming, William paused in his examination and glanced up. The spy who'd served in the role of assistant and butler—and whatever else William had needed him to be—shifted on his feet.

William arched a single brow.

Stone coughed into his fist. "It is my understanding that Lord Edward has been conducting interviews with those familiar with the case."

The case.

William gripped the corners of the leather folio. Yes, not very long ago, that was all the Allenby family would have ever been. He'd have required no additional information outside the barest that had decreed Francis Allenby a traitor, and that would have been the end of it. He'd been blinded to humanity and ceased to see the people who were impacted by the Brethren. How narrow his world had been. How calculated his views of life and people and everything. *I just failed to see it until Elsie.*

Closing the folder, William rested it atop the stack before him. "And where is Lord Edward?"

Stone opened his mouth.

Rap-pause-rap-pause—rap-rap.

Of course, still punctual all these years later.

"Enter," he boomed.

His brother and Cedric Bennett stepped inside. Still attired in their cloaks and hats, they strode forward.

Despite himself, and the familiarity of having spies report with whatever information they'd uncovered, William's heart slowed and then knocked hard against his chest. For this information… was different. For it was about her. "You're dismissed for now, Stone," he said in carefully measured tones. Motioning to the leather winged chairs, William urged the pair to sit. He made his way over to the sideboard. "You are late," he called, after the two men had taken their seats.

Edward scoffed. "By a handful of moments," he pointed out, still very much the younger brother who delighted in tormenting his older brother, stuck in the ducal classrooms, while he himself had been running the countryside, reveling in the freedoms permitted the spare.

William reached for a decanter and froze with his fingers on the stopper.

I do expect you to give up liquor until you learn proper restraint over it… and yourself.

And he had. He'd found his way when, after Adeline's passing, he'd believed himself eternally lost.

Once more, because of Elsie.

William splashed several fingers of spirits into a glass and turned to face his brother and Bennett. "What have you found?"

"I conducted interviews with every patient treated by Allenby," Edward said as he withdrew a palm-sized leather diary from his jacket. "In his tenure, he provided some form of care or another to more than twenty-five of our men."

"Thirty-five, if one counts the family members of those men,"

Bennett interjected.

Edward nodded. "Some of those who were served by the doctor bore injuries related to their service. Some unrelated. Some took place during travels. Others, years after they'd served. Some illnesses."

"And?" William stared intently over the rim of his untouched drink.

"And the opinions of him and his service"—Edward and Bennett exchanged a look—"were high. No one reported anything of less-than-stellar service. No man died while under his care."

There was more.

It hung in the air, as real as if it had been spoken. He forced himself to take a small sip, collecting himself, fighting for restraint.

Bennett fished a small folded sheet of velum from his cloak.

Standing, he crossed over and held it out.

William made himself take another drink, and only after he'd swallowed did he accept that officious-looking scrap.

"He was a traitor," Bennett said bluntly.

William struggled to keep from choking on his brandy. After all, Bennett's was the expected statement, even as it didn't fit with the optimistic accounting reported by his brother on the late doctor's work and patients. It did not matter how many acts and actions one had done justly and honorably. The one that mattered most was the one in which one chose treachery.

"You are dismissed," William managed to say, his voice steady, as if Bennett had delivered that pronouncement about any other subject of an investigation.

The spy let himself out, leaving the two brothers briefly alone.

Bennett was a cynic. The most jaded, field-hardened member of the Brethren. He'd have found the Lord himself guilty for having forged a relationship with the once-sin-free Lucifer. "Well?" he asked when the door had closed.

Edward pressed his gloved fingertips together and rested them under his chin. "Does it matter so much if he was?"

It did, but not for the reasons his brother surely thought or wondered after.

It mattered because Francis Allenby had been a saint in his daughter's eyes and because she deserved more of a sire… and God help him, William didn't wish to be the one to contradict her.

Abandoning all pretense of drinking, he set down his glass and swiped a hand over his face. "That wasn't an answer, Edward," he said impatiently. It was the deliberately vague shite one fed another whose response or reaction one feared.

"No." Edward came to his feet. "I'd advise you read it yourself, but… yes, as Stone indicated, you'll find the records in order, the interviews thorough, and a statement of guilt."

That was what he'd been handed.

William glanced down at the faintly yellowing sheet.

It was a letter of guilt from the doctor himself. It was a note William could give to the man's devoted daughter… and it would break her heart.

A dull ache throbbed in his chest, and he resisted the urge to rub at that misery. "That will be all," he said quietly.

"Of course." Edward dropped a bow and left.

After he'd gone, William stared at the page in his fingers. Not wanting to read the words there. Wanting to return to the way life had been these nearly three weeks with Elsie.

But there could be no *them* joined in any way. Not in the way he yearned for.

And so, with dread slithering around his gut, William unfolded the note… and began to read.

THE SMALL HEELS OF ELSIE'S boots clicked rhythmically upon the hardwood floors, and as she walked the corridors of William's home, the *butler* cast sharp glances back her way.

As if her every action was to be watched.

As if he feared she'd bolt.

As if…

You are the daughter of a traitor.

Bitterness stung like vinegar upon her tongue. For, to the men who served the Brethren, that was all she was… or would ever be.

Only William hadn't treated her thus. In the greatest irony, he, the leader of that noble organization, had never looked upon her with disdain or mistrust. She and William had forged a bond that had somehow defied even her father's supposed sins.

And yet, even with that connection, she now strode these halls as more servant than anything. In fact, this moment might as well have been the first day of her arrival and not that of a woman who'd lived nearly three weeks with the head of this very household. That man had taught her to laugh again and find pride in the work she was capable of and had urged her to be more. And had made love to her.

Elsie fisted her hands in the fabric of her skirts. For William hadn't given any hint that he felt anything for her. Not truly. Nothing beyond the stolen exchange in his gardens where they'd made love under the summer sun.

Sex he'd given to whores and actresses… and now her.

His heart? That gift had been buried with the wife who'd died.

Stone brought her to a stop outside William's office. He knocked once.

This wasn't the rap of the Brethren, but rather, the polite scratch of a servant's knuckles announcing a guest—or in this case, another servant.

"Enter," William called out.

The butler pressed the handle and let her inside.

Elsie entered, taking several steps, and then stopped.

William sat before her, but not as he'd been almost three weeks earlier. Less gaunt. Less pale. His skin reflected an olive hue from the hours he'd spent in the gardens alongside her. That magnificent tangle of black curls had since been neatly trimmed and was drawn back at the nape of his neck.

This was a man in full command of himself and the empire he ruled.

As such… she didn't know how to be around this newer version of William. Selfishly, she preferred him as he'd been in their intimate exchanges prior to this one: relaxed, no work or rank between them, and only a friendship existing there.

Friendship.

Is that truly what you want with him?

No. She wanted more. She wanted to be his partner in life, laughing with him and teasing him. Alas, that was not to be. Elsie stared at Bear resting at the foot of William's desk, as content as one who'd found his rightful place and had no intention of relinquishing it. All the while, the gentleman who'd become Bear's master attended whatever important reports lay open before him.

And I'm not even an afterthought. Elsie clenched and unclenched her hands. She would not, however, curtsy or announce herself.

William finally closed that book and glanced up. "Elsie," he greeted.

He spoke with a somberness that conveyed formality and belied the use of her Christian name.

To hide the tremble in her hands, Elsie clasped them behind her. "You've been avoiding me," she said by way of greeting.

William's features immediately gave way to a smooth, unreadable mask. "I've been working."

"Yes, but also avoiding me." He'd given her only truths before this. She'd not accept his lies now.

Sitting back in his seat with a small chuckle, William rested his hands on the flat of his belly. "Has there ever been a woman more direct and forthright than you?" There was a wistful quality to that murmur that sent warning bells clamoring at the back of her brain. "Will you please sit?" he asked, finally standing.

No. Every muscle within her body strained in protest. She didn't want to cross over to that blasted desk and sit and engage in a discussion… that had traces of "goodbye" hovering within the room.

They still had four more days before the terms of their agreement were met. Four more days. Elsie drifted over and claimed one of the leather seats.

"I received the entire file on your father."

She jerked.

Of everything she'd been expecting, that had certainly not been what she'd thought he might say. He'd vowed to find out. He'd pledged to learn everything there was to learn. But never had she truly believed he would share that privileged and confidential information… with *her.* An outsider. She wet her lips. "And what have you learned?"

William sat back, and yet, his corded biceps strained the fabric of his black wool jacket, making a mockery of that hint at calm. "I learned your father was a skilled doctor committed to his patients," he said quietly.

Her lower lip trembled, and she bit at that flesh to steady it. "He was," she managed to at last say. But the unspoken regret and remorse hung heavy in his tone. "But?"

Gathering up the file he'd been reading, William stood and came 'round the desk.

Bear sprang to his feet and accompanied a man who'd become his new loyalest of friends and joined him at Elsie's side.

Or mayhap it was just that Bear sensed she needed him more in this instance than William did. She wove her fingers through the dog's coarse fur, seeking comfort—and this time, finding none.

William held out the leather folio etched with a golden seal. "What is this?" she asked, making no move to take it.

"These are the men you and your father treated. You're not mentioned."

She glanced at the seal. "No," she said softly. "I wouldn't be." Women weren't included in the marks upon pages that mattered.

William dropped to a knee beside her, and she ached to feel his touch again, that most meaningful of connections, a tender caress, a show of support. "But you should be. You should be, Elsie."

With a sound of frustration, she sailed to her feet. "It was never about that," she cried, whipping away from him. "It was about—"

"Helping," he supplied for her, and there was no judgment there. He proffered the folder again. "And that is precisely what your father did."

Elsie recoiled, jerking her hands close, refusing to take the records still. For when she did, everything would be established as fact, and coward that she was, Elsie didn't know if she wanted all of it. Coward that she was, she was content with the image of her father and what they'd done and wanted nothing that called any of that into question, in any way. "Just say it," she whispered. "Be done with it already."

William unfurled to his full height, towering over her. "I will not." He drew forth an aged yellow paper from his jacket.

Her heart jumped at the scrawl across the front, barely distinguishable, dashed in the hand of one whose mind had been far too busy attending his craft to worry about the quality of his penmanship.

She shook her head and, holding her hands up protectively, backed up a step.

"You should read it, Elsie."

No.

"You are no coward, love. It is what makes you so wholly different from me and any other man or woman," William said with a tenderness that brought tears to her eyes.

Blinking back those bothersome drops, she made herself take the note, and before her courage deserted her, Elsie unfolded it and read.

I will preface the contents of this note by taking ownership of my grave mistake and expressing my sincerest of apologies.

Her stomach lurched. *Don't read anymore. It doesn't matter. You know who and what your father was.* Only, why did that now ring with a good deal less conviction in her mind? Why did it seem like it had only been a lie she'd fed herself? The page shook wildly in her grip, and she forced herself to steady those digits and kept reading.

I am guilty of the crimes which you will soon learn of. I revealed the existence of the Brethren. I confirmed my role within it. I offered the name of but two patients—

Bile climbed her throat. Her father had revealed the identities of young men who'd served the Home Office. Her piteous moan filled the office. "I was so sure," she whispered into the quiet.

All the while she read, William stood close. Hurled epithets and accusations would have been easier than… this, his quiet support.

Needing to have the rest of those damning words finished, she hurried through the remainder of the letter.

Should I have failed to confirm and provide some evidential proof, my daughter's existence was threatened. I pledged my loyalty to the Brethren, king, Crown, and country… but not at the expense of her. I ask that you please send supports for mine and my family, so that—

Elsie quickly read through the rest and then folded the page along its original crease.

It had been a confession… and an appeal for help—help that he'd not deserved. Unable to speak through the emotion clogging her throat, Elsie held the letter out.

William took it and tucked it back inside his jacket.

"Just say it," she said tiredly.

He shook his head. "I will not."

Because he was far more honorable and trustworthy and good than she'd ever credited. "Just say it," she cried, and this time, the tears flowed freely, and she let them. "Say it." Elsie slammed a fist against his chest, over and over.

He caught her wrist in a delicate hold, halting the next blow. With reverent gentleness, he raised her fingers to his mouth and pressed a kiss atop them. "Your father was a traitor. Is that what you wish to hear?"

There it was. Words she'd believed didn't matter ran through her like a blade, slashing at every myth she'd believed and proving the greatest lie she'd managed to convince herself of. She did care. She didn't want to know that her father had betrayed king and country. Before, she would have snarled and hissed at that, calling William all kinds of liar. But now she could not. The intensity of his gaze upon her pierced her, and unable to meet that regretful stare, she yanked the folder from his hands.

Stepping around him, she wandered over to the drawn curtains and stared out.

"The thing about… the truth, Elsie," William said from over her shoulder. "We tend to take it as white or black. Something definitive. Something clear. One is either a liar, or not. Good or bad. Truthful or dishonest." The floorboards groaned, indicating he'd drifted closer, and she studied his towering frame in the crystal windowpane. "It is an understanding that exists among most. That belief in absolutes once drove my own life and every decision I made." He rested his palms upon her shoulders and leaned down. "Until you, Elsie."

She stiffened, refusing herself that warmth and reassurance, and then she weakened, collapsing against him.

William placed a fleeting kiss against her temple. "You taught me that the world exists in varying shades of gray, and people and circumstances cannot exist in absolutes. We're all a product of life and loss and… love." Her heart lifted and then, with his next words, fluttered back to its usual place. "Your father loved you and did what he did to protect you. I cannot… will not fault him for that, Elsie." He gave her shoulders a light squeeze and stepped away.

Those words moved through her, light and freeing and healing in every way. She'd been so fixed on resenting those who'd wronged her father and seeing him as a martyr who'd been failed… when the truth was as William had said. He, just like William and every man who'd come to their cottage, had been merely human. A man who sought to be the best he could be, but who inevitably faltered and failed.

Elsie hugged her arms around her middle and faced him. "Thank you." How very inadequate those words were.

William gave her another sad smile. "You'd thank me. You never owed me your gratitude. It was wrong of my brother to bring you here."

And there it was.

Elsie drifted closer to him. "I want to be here."

"I wanted you to be here," he said softly.

Wanted. His use of a past tense spoke of a parting, an end. A pressure was weighting her chest, squeezing at her airflow, making it impossible to breathe.

"I didn't do anything, William."

"No. You did *everything*." He cupped her cheek. "If it hadn't been for you, I'd still be drinking and whoring and locking myself away indoors when there are people who need me. You showed me how I'd shut everyone out. My brother. My nephew…" His Adam's apple moved. "My late sister's young son, Leo."

Leo. A child related to this man, and she knew nothing of him. Would never know anything about him. He'd remain a stranger.

Elsie bit at the inside of her cheek, focusing on the pain of that. "You're sending me away."

"I'm setting you free," he corrected.

How was she going to pick up her life and go on without him in it? All the teasing and joy she'd had in simply being with him and speaking to him would fade into memories. "You are sending me away," she repeated, forcing him to own that, even though he'd never pledged anything more than his body in the gardens three days ago.

He drew in a slow breath through his lips. "You have helped me recover in ways I believed I never would or could… but you are not safe here, Elsie," he said, faintly entreating. "You would never be safe with me."

Elsie wandered back to the window and stared at the fancy conveyances and fine horseflesh traversing the fashionable streets of Mayfair.

William's words were the closest he'd ever come to hinting at wanting her here. This time, Elsie did fold her arms close in a solitary embrace. Even so, his words weren't of love but of keeping her safe. The sad smile on her lips reflected back in the window.

All the while, did he not see that she was no "safer" alone in her corner of the Cotswolds?

Elsie gave her head a slight shake and let her arms fall to her sides. Either way, she didn't want him that way. She loved him, wanted a life with him, but would not guilt or worry him into keeping her close. Returning to his side, she stretched a hand out.

He stared at it in befuddlement before folding his fingers into hers.

She shook his hand. "I have enjoyed my time here"—*with you*—"more than I'd thought possible," she said softly. *Oh, God. How am I so steady when I'm splintering apart inside?* "I will miss"—his grip convulsed around hers—"it," she settled for lamely.

"That is almost a compliment," he said, retaining hold of her hand, and she clung to him, stealing those last vestiges of warmth.

"Almost," she agreed with a teasing grin. Reluctantly, Elsie drew her hand back and smoothed her palms down the sides of her skirts.

"I've had your belongings packed," William went on in peculiarly flat tones that effectively killed her smile. "Stone will accompany you back. You'll be safe with him."

What was safe anymore? Her heart was crumpling into dust within her chest because of this man's rote accounting of her travel plans.

"Given you and your father's service, I'll see you afforded the same protections as any other member of the… Home Office," he was saying. "Someone who will… remain in Bladon and…"

She shook her head. What was he saying? "And… look after me?" she ventured.

He frowned. "See that you're *safe*."

The guilt he carried over his late wife would be forever with him. She'd not allow it to cloud the remainder of her existence. "I don't want that, William."

"Elsie," he pleaded.

"I do not want anyone assigned to me, William. I'm a grown woman. I've lived for nearly five years on my own without incident, and I'll continue…" *alone*. Oh, God. Elsie averted her gaze slightly to hide the next wave of tears. He'd offered her his body. But so had he done with countless other women—and many more who'd come after she was gone.

He reached for her hands, and she hid them behind her back

until his own fell uselessly to his sides. His features spasmed. Was it grief? Good. Let him share the weight of misery now crushing her. "I wish you the best, William. I wish you peace and happiness."

With that, Elsie dropped a curtsy. *Do not cry. Do not cry. Do not cry.* It was a mantra that beat in her head in time to her footfalls. *Just go, before you dissolve into a pathetic, blubbering mess.* Only, she could not. She stopped at the door, facing him again. "William? What happened to your wife, the fault does not lie with you. It lies with soulless men who carry out that evil. Your guilt… nearly destroyed you, and it will once more, if you let it."

Two hours later, her meager belongings packed and stored within his carriage… she left.

CHAPTER 22

WILLIAM AWAITED A MEETING THAT was long overdue.

To be precise, nearly a year overdue.

He should be thinking solely of the exchange to come, and yet, William's gaze went to the slumbering dog on the Aubusson carpet at the center of his library.

She'd left her dog.

Nearly a week after she'd gone, Elsie haunted his memory and thoughts still… and her dog served as an eternal reminder.

That beloved *pup* had been part of her life and household for nearly fourteen years. And just as important, the dog had provided her, a woman on her own, some degree of protection and companionship.

He slid his eyes closed as a familiar cold swept through him.

Images flitted forward of Elsie alone in a cottage that Stone, upon his return, had reported was modest. Beyond that, he'd said little more.

She's returned, safely, and was polite at our parting.

That had been it. The first and only report he'd ever sought on Elsie Allenby, and it had offered none of what he'd truly sought from Stone.

Had she been happy to return? Sad at her departure? Fearful? What had she been? What?

I'm going mad.

Only, this—he swallowed hard—this jagged hole that had been

ripped open wide came not from mere worry, but because he missed her. He missed her clever wit and her unabashed challenges at every turn. And the gardens. He missed their time spent there, too.

And what was worse? This misery? This emptiness? No, the fact it was all a product of his own making. He'd sent her away. He'd made the decision for her to leave, when everything within her eyes had indicated she'd wanted to stay.

Or had she? Had he merely seen what he wished in a woman he'd come to love—

His body jerked ramrod straight, much the way it had when he'd been run through with a blade in his earliest training for the Brethren.

He couldn't… It wasn't possible… He missed Elsie. He enjoyed her company. But love? He'd vowed to never again give in to that dangerous emotion.

"I love her," he whispered. He'd thought there was nothing left in his heart to give or receive and that he was destined to a fate of deserved misery. Only to be proven so very wrong. He loved her. He loved her for her wit and talent and ability to talk on topics that no woman or man of any station in his whole existence ever had.

Bear rolled onto his back and wiggled on the carpet, emitting a forlorn whine that cut across William's panicky musings.

With a sigh, William joined the dog on the carpet. "I miss her, too," he confided, running his fingertips through the gray fur.

Bear stared back with wide, accusatory brown eyes.

"Yes, yes. I know. It's quite my fault. But I'll have you know… it is in her best interest."

It was.

Or, that was what he'd told himself with her departure. No matter what became of William's role with the Brethren, the threat of danger would remain for all those who were in his life. There would always be enemies lurking and peril for the work he'd done on behalf of the Home Office.

And he'd been selfish enough before that he'd taken what he wanted and put those desires first before another's well-being—his late wife's.

William sucked in a shuddery breath. Knowing all that didn't do anything to ease the ache that had come with Elsie's leaving.

Bear nudged at his hand, and he resumed stroking the dog in the way he so favored.

Rap-pause-rap-pause—rap-rap.

William found the ormolu clock atop the fireplace mantel and shoved to his feet. *He is here.*

Clasping his hands behind him, he called out for the expected pair to enter.

His brother came in first, a boy following after him. Somber, with too-serious-for-his-age eyes, his nephew who was never without a book cautiously came to a stop.

Another swell of emotion crested and threatened to pull William under.

Leo.

Only somehow more serious. More guarded.

Unable or unwilling to meet his gaze, the gangly boy shifted on his feet. "Uncle…" Then Leo's eyes formed round circles. "You have a dog!" he exclaimed, rushing over. Several curls tumbled over Leo's brow, giving him the look of one so much younger than his fourteen years.

From over the boy's head, William and Edward shared a smile before his brother backed out of the room. "I do. He's a loyal fellow." And Elsie had left that cherished gift for him. Emotion balled in his throat.

"When did you get him?" With an uncharacteristic excitement, Leo wrapped the surprisingly compliant dog in a tight embrace and continued before William could answer. "What is his name?"

"Just three weeks ago." Had it really been just twenty-one days in which Elsie Allenby had entered his life and upended his world in the most splendorous way? *And I sent her away*? William briefly closed his eyes. "His name is Bear."

"That is a good name," Leo was saying. "He *looks* like a Bear. Is that why you named him such?"

"Is that why…?" he echoed. *I don't know why she chose that name.* He knew the creature's history and how beloved he was, but he knew nothing more. *I want those pieces. I want every last detail about Elsie and her life and…*

"Uncle William?"

"He was named before he came to me," he offered.

Leo stared blankly at the dog. "They die, you know. Best not get yourself attached. Especially to an old one like this fellow." With that, his godson stood and backed away from Bear.

The last dog he'd had the boy's devil father had wrapped in a sack and tossed out into a lake on one of his many properties. William had beat the marquess senseless for the cruelty to the dog… and child.

The heart that Elsie had put back together splintered all over again under this display of cynicism from a child who'd been almost like his own. *And I failed him. I failed him. I failed him.*

The same guilt that had controlled him this past year reared its head once more, and he fought back the overwhelming sense of failure that gripped him.

Elsie's singsong voice drowned out the litany in his mind.

What happened to your wife, the fault does not lie with you. It lies with soulless men who carry out that evil. Your guilt… nearly destroyed you, and it will once more, if you let it.

William drew in a steadying breath. *I am here now.* He urged Leo to the leather sofa at the center of the room. "You've no books tucked under your arms," he noted once they'd sat. "Or in your ha…" As one, their gazes went to Leo's fingers. Oh, God. It was a prayer and an entreaty. "Hands," he forced himself to finish as rage spiraled through him. Vivid purple and blue bruises stood out upon the boy's pale skin.

Belatedly hiding his hands behind his back, Leo stared intently at the floor. His bent head and hunched shoulders, along with the fingerprint bruises, marked the child as one who still bore the abuse of his hateful father, the Marquess of Tennyson.

"He did not heed my warning," William murmured in quiet tones he used for the most skittish of men and women he interacted with through the Brethren.

Leo lifted his spindly shoulders in a little shrug. "He did… for a while." Until William had disappeared. His godson shot his head up. "It is not your fault. No matter what you'd have told him, it would not matter."

He seeks to reassure me. The boy was remarkable, and he'd deserved more in a father, and in an uncle.

"Not really," Leo went on. "It never did. Just for a bit, but he never stopped. Not truly." Despair clouded the boy's eyes. "And he never will. So... yes... that is the way it is, and I'd really rather we not speak any further on it."

They would. In time. But William wouldn't spend their reunion forcing his godson to relive all the horrors he'd endured. "I have something for you."

Leo sat up a little straighter. "Oh?" For, despite the horror that was his life, he was still a boy.

Reaching for the small leather volume on the rose-inlaid side table, William handed it over to the child.

"The Poetical Works of the Late Mrs. Mary Robinson," Leo murmured, turning the pale green leather tome over in his hands.

"It contains pieces that have never been published before."

Leo glanced up. "Have *you* read it?"

"I have." Bear trotted over and rested his giant head alongside William's thigh. He absently patted the dog. "I believe it bears the knowledge base of civilization as we know it."

"My father says women are empty-headed twaddles who should open their legs and not their mouths."

Hatred descended like a black curtain over William's vision, and he forced himself to speak calmly. "I know a good many women who are cleverer and more skilled than most men."

Leo puzzled his brow. "Indeed?"

"Your mother was one of them." His heart spasmed with that loss.

"Hmph," Leo said noncommittally.

"She could speak Latin and French faster than even her tutors and would debate them with such skill they often fled their placement."

A rare smile ghosted his nephew's lips. "You're just partial because she was my mother."

"Perhaps a bit," William conceded. "But she was clever."

"Was Aunt Adeline?"

Leo's question gave him pause. She'd been gentle and polite and proper and skilled at ladylike pursuits. But she'd despised reading and scholarly topics. "There are different kinds of knowledge," he settled for. "Your late aunt had different skills."

"You know *one* scholarly woman, then. My mother." His godson gave him a pointed look. "Who was also your sister."

The boy had a tenacity with debating suited for a barrister. William dropped his hands atop his knees. "Do you know why I've not"—he grimaced—"left the house in a year?"

"Because you were hurt in the carriage accident?"

He nodded. "Because I was hurt here." He touched his jawbone. "And here." William pressed his fingertips against his heart. "My soul was hurt, and I was lost. Your uncle Edward, he did not accept that as my fate. He brought doctor after doctor. Some of the most skilled men and minds in London. And do you know who healed me?"

Wide-eyed, Leo shook his head.

"A young woman," William said, his voice hoarse. "A woman who possesses more skills than could ever be taught in a classroom, but who also has an understanding of ancient texts, and she is more remarkable than anyone I've ever known."

"You love her," Leo said with a dawning understanding.

Of course, even a child should see.

"It is hard not to admire such a woman." *Nay, I do not just admire Elsie Allenby. I* love *her.*

"She's the woman you sent away?"

William opened and closed his mouth several times. "How…?"

"I hear more than people credit," Leo said dryly. "Uncle Edward was speaking briefly to Stone about it when I arrived."

God, with Leo's wit and skill, the Brethren would one day likely call him a member of their ranks.

His nephew persisted. "If you love her, why isn't she here?"

William shifted awkwardly on his seat. In sharing what he had with the boy, he'd not intended for this to be the direction of the conversation. "Life is complicated."

"You worry she'll die like Aunt Adeline?" the child correctly surmised.

William rubbed a hand over his mouth. "Yes. There is that."

His nephew scoffed. "Fear seems like a silly reason to send away the person you love. I'd never do that."

The air left him on a whoosh. The boy was… correct. He had sent Elsie away in fear, with her safety and well-being the motives for doing so. He'd never allowed her a choice. Just as he'd not shared with Adeline the threat that marriage to him represented. In the end, he'd chosen… for both of them. Reeling, he squeezed his nephew's shoulder. "You're right."

Leo smirked. "Of course I am."

There was a quick rap at the door.

Edward ducked his head in. "The marquess wanted him returned by the top of the hour."

His fingers curled around the boy's shoulder in a light squeeze. Bloody controlling bastard.

Leo's expression fell, but then he quickly composed himself in a way that no child ought and stood.

William came to his feet beside him. "Just a moment more," he commanded, waiting until Edward backed out of the room. "Leopold?" he urged in grave tones.

"What?" the boy mumbled, avoiding William's eyes.

"Look at me." He waited until his sister's child slowly lifted his gaze. "I'm going to do better to be the uncle you deserve. I won't leave you again. From now on, I'll always be there. Do you hear me?" Leaving a person… did not sever the bond or eliminate the danger or peril presented by life. It only left a different kind of hole in one's heart.

"Yes," Leo said, his voice threadbare. He started for the door with long, loping strides and paused in the doorway. "You're going to her, aren't you?"

For the first time in the whole of a year, the chains of guilt he'd donned were finally cut free.

William smiled. "I am."

CHAPTER 23

SNAP.

Elsie's heart pounded at the unexpected crack of brush. From where she stood at the multipurpose table, she stared through the dusty window that overlooked the gardens and woods beyond. Or… she attempted to. Squinting, Elsie struggled to see clearly through the cracked lead pane.

Remaining absolutely still, she lifted her palm and rubbed the window until she'd cleared a neat circle that afforded her a greater view of the grounds outside.

Elsie did a quick sweep.

A fawn lifted its head from the brush it had been chewing. The magnificent creature's ears went up as it went motionless. After several long moments, it ambled off.

All the tension lifted from Elsie's frame, and she sighed. "What in blazes has become of you?" she muttered.

She had lived alone for almost five years.

And yet, it had taken just three, nearly four, weeks for her to forget how very heavy the silence of living without another soul in the world in fact was.

Gathering the baskets set out on the small, scarred wood dining table, Elsie paused to stare at the hooked wool rooster rug her late mother had made by hand. The faded floor cloth had served as Bear's favorite place, so much that she could still see him there now.

Her dog had been such a part of her life for more than thirteen years, like a friend and sibling, in what had become an increasingly lonely world. Bear, however, was needed elsewhere, by a man who'd not known he needed him, but who'd taken every offering the dog held out.

Only for Elsie to find, even as the void of Bear's loss hurt like a physical ache, it was the loss of another who'd left her heart forever ravaged.

Unbidden, her gaze went to the small velvet sack Stone had carried into her cottage, along with her belongings, before he'd taken his leave a week earlier. That bag had remained atop her mantel, where it had taken on a life-like force. One she'd resisted. Until now.

Of their own volition, Elsie's legs carried her across the small quarters of her cottage. Dragging the sack from the mantel, she fiddled with the tie and then reached inside, fishing out—

"Money?" she whispered in disbelief. He'd given her—her eyes widened—a fortune. He'd given her a not-so-small fortune. Resentment stung her throat, making it a struggle to swallow. This was what he'd given her? She cringed. Like a whore. Elsie jammed the monies back inside and froze as her fingers collided with an altogether different texture. A note.

Wetting her lips, she drew it out.

My Dearest, Elsie—

Butterflies fluttered in her chest. Elsie brushed her fingertips along the bold, slashing letters inked there, lingering upon a single mark of punctuation that transformed William's greeting. The letter went on without introduction.

You're insulted by the contents of this package.

For the first time since she'd taken her leave of London… of him, a smile played on her lips. How very well he knew her.

The money isn't any form of… payment, but rather, a deserved gift so you can begin again. Not in some forgotten corner of Bladon, a stranger to the world, but as a woman whose works should be known and celebrated by people appreciative of you. There are funds enough to set you up in whatever new life you wish for yourself. But please know… when… and whatever you do, I shall remember you… with the greatest fondness and affection.

Ever Yours…

"William," she whispered. She caught a sob in her fist, crinkling the page.

That was all. A letter that was… everything. His words a testament to her strength and his belief in her and her place in this world.

"And I still want more." Tears blurred her eyes. "You are a fool," she whispered into the quiet, just to hear her voice. To hear something in an otherwise silent world, when so very recently there had been laughter and discourse and a reminder of what life truly was—

Elsie jammed the note back into the sack and returned it to the mantel. A single tear trickled down her cheek. "Fool," she repeated, swatting at it angrily. She hurriedly retrieved her baskets and snapped her fingers twice… before remembering.

There was no loyal dog. Bear was off enjoying the one person's company Elsie so desperately craved for herself.

With four jerky strides, she let herself out of the cottage. The early afternoon sunlight streamed through the doorway, once invigorating and healing, and she drew the Bladon air into her lungs, letting it fill her, forcing the tension from her shoulders.

Elsie took in the gardens that had begun to reflect their neglect at her absence.

This was to be celebrated, too. She'd never have William or a life with him, or children of her own, but she'd have peace in this lush, green sanctuary in the corner of the world… forgotten by all. She didn't need more. What he'd spoken of in his missive? Of her beginning again? It was not something she wanted to do. She was perfectly content.

Except, why, as she strode down the moss-covered stones lining the walkway, did it feel like she fed herself a pathetically weak lie? Setting her baskets down, Elsie knelt alongside her herb garden.

Over the next hours, Elsie poured her energies into cutting deadened leaves away from the wild plants and snipping off a collection of the vast array of herbs and spices to be preserved, returning them to the basket.

She worked until she developed an ache in her neck that eventually faded to a distracted throb. The sun climbed higher and higher into the sky. Pausing, Elsie brushed back the perspiration along her brow.

Just then, her nape prickled.

Yanking off her bonnet, she glanced around as something all too familiar to this place traipsed through her—fear. It held her immobilized as the darkest memories that had haunted her for nearly five years paraded through her mind. The rapid, too-loud intake of her own ragged breaths as she'd crashed through the brush. The sick anticipation as her would-be assailants followed in swift pursuit. A little moan spilled from her lips. *Do not think of it… Do not think of it…*

The memories had come far less and then nearly not at all while she'd been with William.

William.

Elsie clung to his visage in her mind: of William when he'd been teasing, his chiseled features softened, his laughter.

The nightmare of her past snapped.

Breathing deep, she patted her cheeks. "I am safe," she reminded herself. Picking up her half-filled basket, she carried it on to the next portion of overgrown space and set it down.

Snap.

She whipped around quickly, shooting her arms out to steady herself.

And her heart caught.

Elsie shook her head.

She'd merely conjured him from her own dreams.

His hair drawn back in a neat cue, his black garments immaculate, his Hessian boots shining, William stood before her, too perfect to be real and just five paces away. When he should be in London. She'd left him in London.

"William?" she whispered, afraid to move or breathe or blink.

Doffing his hat, William tapped it against his side and surveyed her gardens. "Do you know nature is surrounded by gifts that have the ability to help us? But we have to be respectful to those gifts, honoring them." His deep baritone washed over her. "Your gardens are in need of care, Elsie."

Dumbly, she followed his stare. When she was a girl, she'd journeyed but once from Bladon to London with her papa. While there, he'd taken her to a Drury Lane production, and one of the characters on the stage had needed to be whispered his every line. In this instance, Elsie felt very much like that at-sea actor. "Yes.

They are… in need." Was this real? Were she and William truly conversing… about her gardens?

He took a step forward, and every muscle and nerve in her body thrummed to alertness, but he stopped alongside a yellow flowering plant. With his spare hand, William trailed reverent fingers along one bloom. "It is called arnica. A healer once told me it's been used as far back as the 1500s," he murmured, echoing the words she'd spoken to him not so long ago.

"Did she?" she whispered, her voice trembling with emotion.

"Oh, yes. A very wise, skilled healer." William lifted his gaze from the flower to hold Elsie's eyes. Those deep sapphire pools glinted. "It soothes aches. Reduces swelling. Heals wounds." He released his gentle grip upon the bud. "They were neglected," he gently noted.

"Yes. They have been." What game did he play? "Is this why you've come, to speak about my gardens?" she asked, fluttering a hand about her breast.

"No." He drifted closer, and then stopped as he reached Elsie. The warmth reflected in his eyes robbed her briefly of breath. "I came to tell you that I'm an utter arse."

Elsie wet her lips. "You came all this way to tell me that?"

"Yes. No." William dragged a hand through his hair, freeing the strands from the…

She gasped, catching sight of the familiar scrap holding the remaining tresses in place. Her ribbon. Upon her return, she'd searched for the small velvet piece, and all the while, William had retained it. Her heart knocked an unsteady beat against her chest. What did it mean? Any of this?

"I am an arse," he said, and she jerked her attention back to his words. "I spoke to you about not hiding here in this forgotten corner of England. I encouraged you to begin again and all but called you a coward for not making more of your life." He lowered his voice, and his next words emerged hoarsely. "And all along, Elsie, I was the coward. I was the one afraid to begin again when I wanted that so desperately." William closed the handful of steps that still separated them and took her trembling palms into his own. Slowly, he raised first one and then the other to his mouth, bestowing a tender kiss upon each. "When what I so desperately wanted was… you."

Tears flooded her eyes, distorting his beloved visage. She shook her head.

"Yes."

Elsie gave her head another shake. It could not be.

"Yes. It is you," he whispered. "It was *always* you." William caressed his palm over her cheek. "From the moment I met you, I was hopelessly and helplessly lost, and sending you away"—the long column of his throat convulsed—"left me broken all over again, Elsie." He dropped his brow atop hers. "I cannot promise you safety. I cannot promise your life will not be a struggle because of who… of what I was—"

"Shh." Elsie pressed her fingertips against his lips, silencing him. "I'm not looking for assurances that no day can promise. I just want you. I love you."

He groaned and claimed her lips in a searing kiss that touched her soul.

Through the fiery magic of that embrace, something blared at the back of her mind. Laying her palms upon his chest, Elsie abruptly drew back and searched his face. "Was. You said… 'of what I was.'"

"I ceded my role, Elsie. You're what I want. You are who I love. My heart cannot fully be with the Brethren when it is so completely yours."

She sobbed and, wrapping her arms about his waist, clung to him for all she was.

"Now, this is precisely the response I'd hoped for." The slightly taunting announcement slashed across the clearing, jerking Elsie and William apart.

That voice… familiar. Her mind raced as the gentleman wound his way down the graveled path at the rear of the cottage, a gun trained on Elsie. Where did she know him from? Where…? And then remembrance dawned.

William cursed and moved to place himself in front of Elsie.

"Tsk, tsk, not another move, Your Grace," the gentleman ordered, pointing the barrel of his pistol at William's head. "Or I'll kill you first and then end her next."

CHAPTER 24

WILLIAM HAD BEEN CONSIGNED TO hell.

There was no other accounting for this moment, when he'd finally reached out to claim a life with Elsie, that his work should haunt him once more. Panic pulled at the edge of his consciousness. Unwittingly, he'd ushered her into this world.

Clear head. Calm mind.

Clear head. Calm mind.

Drawing on that mantra ingrained in every member of the Brethren, William forced a cool ducal grin. "I've a greater appreciation for those direct in their dealings," he drawled, the lazy effect ruined by the layer of steel he added to the statement. "And I have even more appreciation for those who do not draw innocent women into their"—he flicked a derisive sneer over the gun in the stranger's hand—"dealings." All the while, he searched his memory for how he knew this man. It was there, dancing at the back of his mind.

Fury burned brighter in the gentleman's eyes. "Come, Aubrey, I'm not the one who's drawn any woman into our business." *Our business.* "You're the one who has." A hoarse laugh burst from him. "But then, that is what you do, isn't it, Your Grace? You place your own desires and wants and needs before all else. Your wife. Miss Allenby."

The charged accusation found its proper mark like a blade thrust into his chest. A fresh wave of the never vanquished guilt washed over him. He was a fool for believing he could begin again and as selfish as this madman chided. And then through that… something this man had said rooted at his brain. "You killed her," he said, his voice blank. This was the man who'd destroyed his life. And every lesson he'd learned at the Home Office failed him.

William sprang forward.

The stranger leaned back and, with the agility of a panther, ducked behind William and brought his pistol crashing into the side of his head.

William stumbled and fought the stars that danced behind his eyes.

"Tsk, tsk. You shouldn't have done that. If you do so again, Miss Allenby dies."

Oh, God. His stomach roiled, and he held his palms up in supplication. Keeping his eyes upon his tormenter, William retreated, stopping only when he was at Elsie's side.

"I'll also have you know that I didn't wish to kill your wife. That wasn't my intention. Your misery from it, however, was an unexpected… pleasure."

It was… an odd statement that revealed a hint of humanity at odds with the person now threatening his and Elsie's lives.

Elsie slid her fingers into his and gave a light squeeze. The steadiness to her hand and the warmth there brought him back from the precipice.

"Who are you?" Elsie asked quietly.

William glared at her, urging her to silence. Of course, at every turn, from the beginning to now, she made up her own mind and acted as she thought best.

"Ah, forgive me," he greeted. "Formal introductions and all that." Bowing his blond head, the gentleman sneered. "Lord Brandon Barnes." Lord Brandon stared expectantly at William.

William frantically searched his mind.

The gentleman sucked in a slow hiss of air through his teeth. "You've no idea who I am," he breathed, shock and hatred filling his tone.

"I…" *Keep him talking. Keep him talking. Avoid angering him.* For, when the remainder of the gentleman's sanity snapped, he and Elsie would pay the price with their lives. William's palms moistened.

"You're a member of the Brethren," Elsie said quietly.

William whipped his focus to the stranger.

Lord Brandon stiffened. Shock paraded over his scarred features, and then he quickly masked it. Retaining his hold on his pistol, the gentleman clapped several fingertips against the base of his palm. "You are clever, Miss Allenby. But your goodness is also a poison. It's rotted you and allowed you to help a man who destroyed your father."

"Mm-mm." Elsie stepped out from behind William, and he made a sound of protest, reaching for her wrist, but she drew it close to her chest.

Every part of him roared to take command, to protect her.

Only…

He'd been doing that the whole of his life. He'd not allowed Adeline any control of her… and their… existence.

Elsie continued walking toward the threat.

Awe and frustration commingled at the bravery… or madness. *Elsie*, he silently pleaded, urging her back. With Lord Brandon's attention momentarily fixed on the spitfire before him, William scoured the dense forest.

At last, she stopped before the gentleman.

"Elsie," William hissed.

She held up a silencing hand. "You felt betrayed by the Brethren. It is why you approached me at the market. You were not spying on me on behalf of His Grace." Elsie shot a brief glance over her shoulder at William before redirecting all her focus on Lord Brandon. "You sought to determine if I would turn on him."

Oh, God. William's body recoiled. This was the man she'd faced on her own when she'd gone off to the market. And all the while, he'd thought sending her away would be safer. Shame swallowed him.

"I was betrayed by the Brethren," Lord Brandon said in deadened tones. "As were you. Only, I remember it." His fingers convulsed around the gun in his grip.

William's stomach pitched, and he took a slow, measured step toward the pair.

"What happened?" Elsie urged in dulcet tones that could have called forth secrets held by Satan himself.

"What didn't happen?" Lord Brandon countered. "I gave my

service, I was wounded. Nearly killed for my efforts, and how did this man repay that service?" he whispered. "He turned me out. I was used and discarded. Just as your father was."

A distant recollection flickered to life. A young gentleman put forward to replace the former spy, Adam Markham, who'd been captured, freed, and then retired. The Brethren had sought a new spy to replace him.

We cannot have another Markham. We can't afford weakness. If he falters, cut him loose…

Oh, God. As his own voice whispered forward, his legs wavered, and he fought to steady himself.

"I see you remember me… now," Lord Brandon spat.

"Brandon," he began. "It was in your best interest."

"Quiet!" the young man thundered. His voice, slightly pitched, sent birds in nearby trees into a panicky flight. "Just… quiet," he repeated more evenly. A half-mad laugh spilled from Lord Brandon's lips. "Do not pretend you were ever acting in my interest."

William briefly closed his eyes. How ruthless he'd been. How blind to all but rank and order and the Brethren. Elsie had helped him to see—too late—all those failings. "No. You are right. I was solely focused on the Brethren." He'd failed to see people, and in so doing, he had lost his humanity. Until Elsie. Until she'd helped him to rediscover it within himself.

"And now you shall die," Lord Brandon said conversationally, shifting the gun to point at William's chest, but making no attempt to fire.

"You said my goodness rotted me," Elsie said quietly, freezing the broken spy before them. "You cannot understand why I forgave William and all the Brethren for my father's fate." Lord Brandon offered no words, and yet, he angled his head ever so slightly, the mark of how intently he attended her. "I'm not so very good. I hated William and the Brethren for five years, and then do you know what I realized?" Elsie did not wait for him to reply. "It was not their fault. My father knew what he was undertaking when he agreed to do the Crown's work. Just as you did."

"I didn't know," William said quietly. "But I should have. You worked on behalf of me and the Crown, and I had an obligation to see to your well-being. I failed you, and Miss Allenby, and I cannot undo those sins or mistakes, but I can try moving forward to be better."

Lord Brandon's arm shook. "Stop it," he whispered. "Stop. I'll not accept your excuses. That is not enough. I have to do this." *Had to.* Which implied he did not wish to.

Hope flared to life.

Elsie touched Lord Brandon's arm, and the gentleman jerked. "Your anger holds you as a prisoner," Elsie said softly. "Just as it did me." Leaning up on tiptoe, she whispered close to his ear, and William strained to pick up a hint of the words that were ultimately lost to him.

"He ruined me," Lord Brandon moaned.

"You can put yourself and your life together again. But not if you do this," Elsie said with an air of finality. She stretched a hand out.

Lord Brandon's eyes filled with tears. "I can't."

Elsie smiled, a delicate upturn of her lips that had ensnared William from the start. She nodded slightly.

The young man dropped the weapon into her hand, and his body immediately sagged.

"Do not move."

At last. Stone came charging, with Bear hot at his heels. He knocked Lord Brandon to the ground and immediately searched the young man for a weapon.

William surged forward and grabbed Elsie to him. "Why did you do that? Promise me you'll never do that again. My God, you are magnificent," he panted, dropping kisses upon her cheek. "What did you say to him?"

All his questions rolled together, incoherent and illogical in their ordering.

Elsie wrapped her arms about him and clung. The faint tremble to her lean body stood as a contradiction to her earlier steadiness, and he loved her all the more for her show of bravery.

"I love you," he rasped, cupping her cheeks. "There is no life without you in it." No, she'd shown him there were many reasons to live. He swallowed rhythmically. "You showed me the life I want to live is with you in it. Marry me. As I said, and as you… see…" Elsie followed his stare to the young man now being hauled to his feet, his hands tied behind his back. William waited, not saying anything else until Lord Brandon had been escorted off. When he and Elsie were at last alone, he faced her. "As long as you are in my life, you are at risk. But I am selfish enough—"

Elsie pressed her lips to his, kissing him into silence, ending those words. When she sank back on her heels, she brushed his hair behind his ear. "You asked what I said to Lord Brandon," she said softly. "I told him love is not selfish. Love is more powerful than any threat or danger. It is healing… if one allows it." Elsie pressed her palms against the place his heart hammered in his chest. "I love you and want a life with you, William."

"I love you, Elsie," he said hoarsely.

And with that profession, his love for this woman, and the joy he knew with her and because of her, chased off the last vestige of darkness. William kissed her once more, and with their giant, loyal dog barking excitedly beside them, William released the fears that had held him and embraced the future that would come with Elsie.

I am free.

THE END

OTHER BOOKS BY CHRISTI CALDWELL

TO ENCHANT A WICKED DUKE

Book 13 in the "Heart of a Duke" Series by Christi Caldwell

A Devil in Disguise

Years ago, when Nick Tallings, the recent Duke of Huntly, watched his family destroyed at the hands of a merciless nobleman, he vowed revenge. But his efforts had been futile, as his enemy, Lord Rutland is without weakness.

Until now…

With his rival finally happily married, Nick is able to set his ruthless scheme into motion. His plot hinges upon Lord Rutland's innocent, empty-headed sister-in-law, Justina Barrett. Nick will ruin her, marry her, and then leave her brokenhearted.

A Lady Dreaming of Love

From the moment Justina Barrett makes her Come Out, she is labeled a Diamond. Even with her ruthless father determined to sell her off to the highest bidder, Justina never gives up on her hope for a good, honorable gentleman who values her wit more than her looks.

A Not-So-Chance Meeting

Nick's ploy to ensnare Justina falls neatly into place in the streets of London. With each carefully orchestrated encounter, he slips further and further inside the lady's heart, never anticipating that Justina, with her quick wit and strength, will break down his own defenses. As Nick's plans begins to unravel, he's left to determine which is more important—Justina's love or his vow for vengeance. But can Justina ever forgive the duke who deceived her?

One Winter with a Baron

Book 12 in the "Heart of a Duke" Series by Christi Caldwell

A clever spinster:

Content with her spinster lifestyle, Miss Sybil Cunning wants to prove that a future as an unmarried woman is the only life for her. As a bluestocking who values hard, empirical data, Sybil needs help with her research. Nolan Pratt, Baron Webb, one of society's most scandalous rakes, is the perfect gentleman to help her. After all, he inspires fear in proper mothers and desire within their daughters.

A notorious rake:

Society may be aware of Nolan Pratt, Baron's Webb's wicked ways, but what he has carefully hidden is his miserable handling of his family's finances. When Sybil presents him the opportunity to earn much-needed funds, he can't refuse.

A winter to remember:

However, what begins as a business arrangement becomes something more and with every meeting, Sybil slips inside his heart. Can this clever woman look beneath the veneer of a coldhearted rake to see the man Nolan truly is?

To Redeem a Rake

Book 11 in the "Heart of a Duke" Series by Christi Caldwell

He's spent years scandalizing society.
Now, this rake must change his ways.

Society's most infamous scoundrel, Daniel Winterbourne, the Earl of Montfort, has been promised a small fortune if he can relinquish his wayward, carousing lifestyle. And behaving means he must also help find a respectable companion for his youngest sister—someone who will guide her and whom she can emulate. However, Daniel knows no such woman. But when he encounters a childhood friend, Daniel believes she may just be the answer to all of his problems.

Having been secretly humiliated by an unscrupulous blackguard years earlier, Miss Daphne Smith dreams of finding work at Ladies of Hope, an institution that provides an education for disabled women. With her sordid past and a disfigured leg, few opportunities arise for a woman such as she. Knowing Daniel's history, she wishes to avoid him, but working for his sister is exactly the stepping stone she needs.

Their attraction intensifies as Daniel and Daphne grow closer, preparing his sister for the London Season. But Daniel must resist his desire for a woman tarnished by scandal while Daphne is reminded of the boy she once knew. Can society's most notorious rake redeem his reputation and become the man Daphne deserves?

To Woo a Widow

Book 10 in the "Heart of a Duke" Series by Christi Caldwell

They see a brokenhearted widow.

She's far from shattered.

Lady Philippa Winston is never marrying again. After her late husband's cruelty that she kept so well hidden, she has no desire to search for love.

Years ago, Miles Brookfield, the Marquess of Guilford, made a frivolous vow he never thought would come to fruition—he promised to marry his mother's goddaughter if he was unwed by the age of thirty. Now, to his dismay, he's faced with honoring that pledge. But when he encounters the beautiful and intriguing Lady Philippa, Miles knows his true path in life. It's up to him to break down every belief Philippa carries about gentlemen, proving that not only is love real, but that he is the man deserving of her sheltered heart.

Will Philippa let down her guard and allow Miles to woo a widow in desperate need of his love?

The Lure of a Rake

Book 9 in the "Heart of a Duke" Series by Christi Caldwell

A Lady Dreaming of Love

Lady Genevieve Farendale has a scandalous past. Jilted at the altar years earlier and exiled by her family, she's now returned to London to prove she can be a proper lady. Even though she's not given up on the hope of marrying for love, she's wary of trusting again. Then she meets Cedric Falcot, the Marquess of St. Albans whose seductive ways set her heart aflutter. But with her sordid history, Genevieve knows a rake can also easily destroy her.

An Unlikely Pairing

What begins as a chance encounter between Cedric and Genevieve becomes something more. As they continue to meet, passions stir. But with Genevieve's hope for true love, she fears Cedric will be unable to give up his wayward lifestyle. After all, Cedric has spent years protecting his heart, and keeping everyone out. Slowly, she chips away at all the walls he's built, but when he falters, Genevieve can't offer him redemption. Now, it's up to Cedric to prove to Genevieve that the love of a man is far more powerful than the lure of a rake.

To Trust a Rogue

Book 8 in the "Heart of a Duke" Series by Christi Caldwell

A rogue

Marcus, the Viscount Wessex has carefully crafted the image of rogue and charmer for Polite Society. Under that façade, however, dwells a man whose dreams were shattered almost eight years earlier by a young lady who captured his heart, pledged her love, and then left him, with nothing more than a curt note.

A widow

Eight years earlier, faced with no other choice, Mrs. Eleanor Collins, fled London and the only man she ever loved, Marcus, Viscount Wessex. She has now returned to serve as a companion for her elderly aunt with a daughter in tow. Even though they're next door neighbors, there is little reason for her to move in the same circles as Marcus, just in case, she vows to avoid him, for he reminds her of all she lost when she left.

Reunited

As their paths continue to cross, Marcus finds his desire for Eleanor just as strong, but he learned long ago she's not to be trusted. He will offer her a place in his bed, but not anything more. Only, Eleanor has no interest in this new, roguish man. The more time they spend together, the protective wall they've constructed to keep the other out, begin to break. With all the betrayals and secrets between them, Marcus has to open his heart again. And Eleanor must decide if it's ever safe to trust a rogue.

To Wed His Christmas Lady

Book 7 in the "Heart of a Duke" Series by Christi Caldwell

She's longing to be loved:

Lady Cara Falcot has only served one purpose to her loathsome father—to increase his power through a marriage to the future Duke of Billingsley. As such, she's built protective walls about her heart, and presents an icy facade to the world around her. Journeying home from her finishing school for the Christmas holidays, Cara's carriage is stranded during a winter storm. She's forced to tarry at a ramshackle inn, where she immediately antagonizes another patron—William.

He's avoiding his duty in favor of one last adventure:

William Hargrove, the Marquess of Grafton has wanted only one thing in life—to avoid the future match his parents would have him make to a cold, duke's daughter. He's returning home from a blissful eight years of traveling the world to see to his responsibilities. But when a winter storm interrupts his trip and lands him at a falling-down inn, he's forced to share company with a commanding Lady Cara who initially reminds him exactly of the woman he so desperately wants to avoid.

A Christmas snowstorm ushers in the spirit of the season:

At the holiday time, these two people who despise each other due to first perceptions are offered renewed beginnings and fresh starts. As this gruff stranger breaks down the walls she's built about herself, Cara has to determine whether she can truly open her heart to trusting that any man is capable of good and that she herself is capable of love. And William has to set aside all previous thoughts he's carried of the polished ladies like Cara, to be the man to show her that love.

The Heart of a Scoundrel

Book 6 in the "Heart of a Duke" Series by Christi Caldwell

Ruthless, wicked, and dark, the Marquess of Rutland rouses terror in the breast of ladies and nobleman alike. All Edmund wants in life is power. After he was publically humiliated by his one love Lady Margaret, he vowed vengeance, using Margaret's niece, as his pawn. Except, he's thwarted by another, more enticing target—Miss Phoebe Barrett.

Miss Phoebe Barrett knows precisely the shame she's been born to. Because her father is a shocking letch she's learned to form her own opinions on a person's worth. After a chance meeting with the Marquess of Rutland, she is captivated by the mysterious man. He, too, is a victim of society's scorn, but the more encounters she has with Edmund, the more she knows there is powerful depth and emotion to the jaded marquess.

The lady wreaks havoc on Edmund's plans for revenge and he finds he wants Phoebe, at all costs. As she's drawn into the darkness of his world, Phoebe risks being destroyed by Edmund's ruthlessness. And Phoebe who desires love at all costs, has to determine if she can ever truly trust the heart of a scoundrel.

To Love a Lord

Book 5 in the "Heart of a Duke" Series by Christi Caldwell

All she wants is security:

The last place finishing school instructor Mrs. Jane Munroe belongs, is in polite Society. Vowing to never wed, she's been scuttled around from post to post. Now she finds herself in the Marquess of Waverly's household. She's never met a nobleman she liked, and when she meets the pompous, arrogant marquess, she remembers why. But soon, she discovers Gabriel is unlike any gentleman she's ever known.

All he wants is a companion for his sister:

What Gabriel finds himself with instead, is a fiery spirited, bespectacled woman who entices him at every corner and challenges his age-old vow to never trust his heart to a woman. But... there is something suspicious about his sister's companion. And he is determined to find out just what it is.

All they need is each other:

As Gabriel and Jane confront the truth of their feelings, the lies and secrets between them begin to unravel. And Jane is left to decide whether or not it is ever truly safe to love a lord.

Loved By a Duke

Book 4 in the "Heart of a Duke" Series by Christi Caldwell

For ten years, Lady Daisy Meadows has been in love with Auric, the Duke of Crawford. Ever since his gallant rescue years earlier, Daisy knew she was destined to be his Duchess. Unfortunately, Auric sees her as his best friend's sister and nothing more. But perhaps, if she can manage to find the fabled heart of a duke pendant, she will win over the heart of her duke.

Auric, the Duke of Crawford enjoys Daisy's company. The last thing he is interested in however, is pursuing a romance with a woman he's known since she was in leading strings. This season, Daisy is turning up in the oddest places and he cannot help but notice that she is no longer a girl. But Auric wouldn't do something as foolhardy as to fall in love with Daisy. He couldn't. Not with the guilt he carries over his past sins… Not when he has no right to her heart…But perhaps, just perhaps, she can forgive the past and trust that he'd forever cherish her heart—but will she let him?

THE LOVE OF A ROGUE

Book 3 in the "Heart of a Duke" Series by Christi Caldwell

Lady Imogen Moore hasn't had an easy time of it since she made her Come Out. With her betrothed, a powerful duke breaking it off to wed her sister, she's become the *tons* favorite piece of gossip. Never again wanting to experience the pain of a broken heart, she's resolved to make a match with a polite, respectable gentleman. The last thing she wants is another reckless rogue.

Lord Alex Edgerton has a problem. His brother, tired of Alex's carousing has charged him with chaperoning their remaining, unwed sister about *ton* events. Shopping? No, thank you. Attending the theatre? He'd rather be at Forbidden Pleasures with a scantily clad beauty upon his lap. The task of *chaperone* becomes even more of a bother when his sister drags along her dearest friend, Lady Imogen to social functions. The last thing he wants in his life is a young, innocent English miss.

Except, as Alex and Imogen are thrown together, passions flare and Alex comes to find he not only wants Imogen in his bed, but also in his heart. Yet now he must convince Imogen to risk all, on the heart of a rogue.

More Than a Duke

Book 2 in the "Heart of a Duke" Series by Christi Caldwell

Polite Society doesn't take Lady Anne Adamson seriously. However, Anne isn't just another pretty young miss. When she discovers her father betrayed her mother's love and her family descended into poverty, Anne comes up with a plan to marry a respectable, powerful, and honorable gentleman—a man nothing like her philandering father.

Armed with the heart of a duke pendant, fabled to land the wearer a duke's heart, she decides to enlist the aid of the notorious Harry, 6th Earl of Stanhope. A scoundrel with a scandalous past, he is the last gentleman she'd ever wed…however, his reputation marks him the perfect man to school her in the art of seduction so she might ensnare the illustrious Duke of Crawford.

Harry, the Earl of Stanhope is a jaded, cynical rogue who lives for his own pleasures. Having been thrown over by the only woman he ever loved so she could wed a duke, he's not at all surprised when Lady Anne approaches him with her scheme to capture another duke's affection. He's come to appreciate that all women are in fact greedy, title-grasping, self-indulgent creatures. And with Anne's history of grating on his every last nerve, she is the last woman he'd ever agree to school in the art of seduction. Only his friendship with the lady's sister compels him to help.

What begins as a pretend courtship, born of lessons on seduction, becomes something more leaving Anne to decide if she can give her heart to a reckless rogue, and Harry must decide if he's willing to again trust in a lady's love.

For Love of the Duke

First Full-Length Book in the "Heart of a Duke" Series
by Christi Caldwell

After the tragic death of his wife, Jasper, the 8th Duke of Bainbridge buried himself away in the dark cold walls of his home, Castle Blackwood. When he's coaxed out of his self-imposed exile to attend the amusements of the Frost Fair, his life is irrevocably changed by his fateful meeting with Lady Katherine Adamson.

With her tight brown ringlets and silly white-ruffled gowns, Lady Katherine Adamson has found her dance card empty for two Seasons. After her father's passing, Katherine learned the unreliability of men, and is determined to depend on no one, except herself. Until she meets Jasper…

In a desperate bid to avoid a match arranged by her family, Katherine makes the Duke of Bainbridge a shocking proposition—one that he accepts.

Only, as Katherine begins to love Jasper, she finds the arrangement agreed upon is not enough. And Jasper is left to decide if protecting his heart is more important than fighting for Katherine's love.

In Need of a Duke

A Prequel Novella to "The Heart of a Duke" Series
by Christi Caldwell

In Need of a Duke: (Author's Note: This is a prequel novella to "The Heart of a Duke" series by Christi Caldwell. It was originally available in "The Heart of a Duke" Collection and is now being published as an individual novella.

~★~

It features a new prologue and epilogue.

Years earlier, a gypsy woman passed to Lady Aldora Adamson and her friends a heart pendant that promised them each the heart of a duke.

Now, a young lady, with her family facing ruin and scandal, Lady Aldora doesn't have time for mythical stories about cheap baubles. She needs to save her sisters and brother by marrying a titled gentleman with wealth and power to his name. She sets her bespectacled sights upon the Marquess of St. James.

Turned out by his father after a tragic scandal, Lord Michael Knightly has grown into a powerful, but self-made man. With the whispers and stares that still follow him, he would rather be anywhere but London...

Until he meets Lady Aldora, a young woman who mistakes him for his brother, the Marquess of St. James. The connection between Aldora and Michael is immediate and as they come to know one another, Aldora's feelings for Michael war with her sisterly responsibilities. With her family's dire situation, a man of Michael's scandalous past will never do.

Ultimately, Aldora must choose between her responsibilities as a sister and her love for Michael.

Once a Wallflower, At Last His Love

Book 6 in the Scandalous Seasons Series

Responsible, practical Miss Hermione Rogers, has been crafting stories as the notorious Mr. Michael Michaelmas and selling them for a meager wage to support her siblings. The only real way to ensure her family's ruinous debts are paid, however, is to marry. Tall, thin, and plain, she has no expectation of success. In London for her first Season she seizes the chance to write the tale of a brooding duke. In her research, she finds Sebastian Fitzhugh, the 5th Duke of Mallen, who unfortunately is perfectly affable, charming, and so nicely... configured... he takes her breath away. He lacks all the character traits she needs for her story, but alas, any duke will have to do.

Sebastian Fitzhugh, the 5th Duke of Mallen has been deceived so many times during the high-stakes game of courtship, he's lost faith in Society women. Yet, after a chance encounter with Hermione, he finds himself intrigued. Not a woman he'd normally consider beautiful, the young lady's practical bent, her forthright nature and her tendency to turn up in the oddest places has his interests… roused. He'd like to trust her, he'd like to do a whole lot more with her too, but should he?

A Marquess For Christmas

Book 5 in the Scandalous Seasons Series

Lady Patrina Tidemore gave up on the ridiculous notion of true love after having her heart shattered and her trust destroyed by a black-hearted cad. Used as a pawn in a game of revenge against her brother, Patrina returns to London from a failed elopement with a tattered reputation and little hope for a respectable match. The only peace she finds is in her solitude on the cold winter days at Hyde Park. And even that is yanked from her by two little hellions who just happen to have a devastatingly handsome, but coldly aloof father, the Marquess of Beaufort. Something about the lord stirs the dreams she'd once carried for an honorable gentleman's love.

Weston Aldridge, the 4th Marquess of Beaufort was deceived and betrayed by his late wife. In her faithlessness, he's come to view women as self-serving, indulgent creatures. Except, after a series of chance encounters with Patrina, he comes to appreciate how uniquely different she is than all women he's ever known.

At the Christmastide season, a time of hope and new beginnings, Patrina and Weston, unexpectedly learn true love in one another. However, as Patrina's scandalous past threatens their future and the happiness of his children, they are both left to determine if love is enough.

Always a Rogue, Forever Her Love

Book 4 in the Scandalous Seasons Series

Miss Juliet Marshville is spitting mad. With one guardian missing, and the other singularly uninterested in her fate, she is at the mercy of her wastrel brother who loses her beloved childhood home to a man known as Sin. Determined to reclaim control of Rosecliff Cottage and her own fate, Juliet arranges a meeting with the notorious rogue and demands the return of her property.

Jonathan Tidemore, 5th Earl of Sinclair, known to the *ton* as Sin, is exceptionally lucky in life and at the gaming tables. He has just one problem. Well…four, really. His incorrigible sisters have driven off yet another governess. This time, however, his mother demands he find an appropriate replacement.

When Miss Juliet Marshville boldly demands the return of her precious cottage, he takes advantage of his sudden good fortune and puts an offer to her; turn his sisters into proper English ladies, and he'll return Rosecliff Cottage to Juliet's possession.

Jonathan comes to appreciate Juliet's spirit, courage, and clever wit, and decides to claim the fiery beauty as his mistress. Juliet, however, will be mistress for no man. Nor could she ever love a man who callously stole her home in a game of cards. As Jonathan begins to see Juliet as more than a spirited beauty to warm his bed, he realizes she could be a lady he could love the rest of his life, if only he can convince the proud Juliet that he's worthy of her hand and heart.

Always Proper, Suddenly Scandalous

Book 3 in the Scandalous Seasons Series

Geoffrey Winters, Viscount Redbrooke was not always the hard, unrelenting lord driven by propriety. After a tragic mistake, he resolved to honor his responsibility to the Redbrooke line and live a life, free of scandal. Knowing his duty is to wed a proper, respectable English miss, he selects Lady Beatrice Dennington, daughter of the Duke of Somerset, the perfect woman for him. Until he meets Miss Abigail Stone…

To distance herself from a personal scandal, Abigail Stone flees America to visit her uncle, the Duke of Somerset. Determined to never trust a man again, she is helplessly intrigued by the hard, too-proper Geoffrey. With his strict appreciation for decorum and order, he is nothing like the man' she's always dreamed of.

Abigail is everything Geoffrey does not need. She upends his carefully ordered world at every encounter. As they begin to care for one another, Abigail carefully guards the secret that resulted in her journey to England.

Only, if Geoffrey learns the truth about Abigail, he must decide which he holds most dear: his place in Society or Abigail's place in his heart.

Never Courted, Suddenly Wed

Book 2 in the Scandalous Seasons Series

Christopher Ansley, Earl of Waxham, has constructed a perfect image for the *ton*–the ladies love him and his company is desired by all. Only two people know the truth about Waxham's secret. Unfortunately, one of them is Miss Sophie Winters.

Sophie Winters has known Christopher since she was in leading strings. As children, they delighted in tormenting each other. Now at two and twenty, she still has a tendency to find herself in scrapes, and her marital prospects are slim.

When his father threatens to expose his shame to the *ton*, unless he weds Sophie for her dowry, Christopher concocts a plan to remain a bachelor. What he didn't plan on was falling in love with the lively, impetuous Sophie. As secrets are exposed, will Christopher's love be enough when she discovers his role in his father's scheme?

Forever Betrothed, Never the Bride

Book 1 in the Scandalous Seasons Series

Hopeless romantic Lady Emmaline Fitzhugh is tired of sitting with the wallflowers, waiting for her betrothed to come to his senses and marry her. When Emmaline reads one too many reports of his scandalous liaisons in the gossip rags, she takes matters into her own hands.

War-torn veteran Lord Drake devotes himself to forgetting his days on the Peninsula through an endless round of meaningless associations. He no longer wants to feel anything, but Lady Emmaline is making it hard to maintain a state of numbness. With her zest for life, she awakens his passion and desire for love.

The one woman Drake has spent the better part of his life avoiding is now the only woman he needs, but he is no longer a man worthy of his Emmaline. It is up to her to show him the healing power of love.

A Season of Hope

A Danby Novella

Five years ago when her love, Marcus Wheatley, failed to return from fighting Napoleon's forces, Lady Olivia Foster buried her heart. Unable to betray Marcus's memory, Olivia has gone out of her way to run off prospective suitors. At three and twenty she considers herself firmly on the shelf. Her father, however, disagrees and accepts an offer for Olivia's hand in marriage. Yet it's Christmas, when anything can happen…

Olivia receives a well-timed summons from her grandfather, the Duke of Danby, and eagerly embraces the reprieve from her betrothal.

Only, when Olivia arrives at Danby Castle she realizes the Christmas season represents hope, second chances, and even miracles.

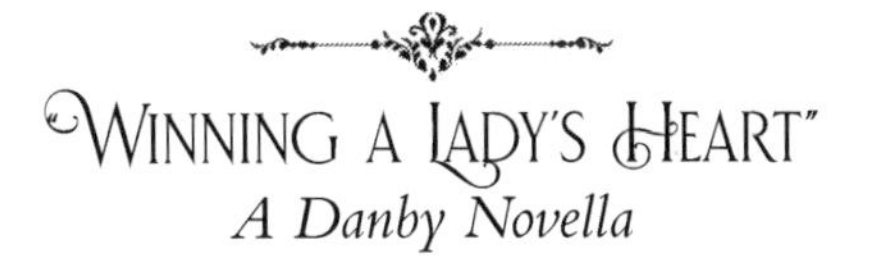

"Winning a Lady's Heart"

A Danby Novella

Author's Note: This is a novella that was originally available in A Summons From The Castle (The Regency Christmas Summons Collection). It is being published as an individual novella.

~★~

For Lady Alexandra, being the source of a cold, calculated wager is bad enough…but when it is waged by Nathaniel Michael Winters, 5th Earl of Pembroke, the man she's in love with, it results in a broken heart, the scandal of the season, and a summons from her grandfather – the Duke of Danby.

To escape Society's gossip, she hurries to her meeting with the duke, determined to put memories of the earl far behind. Except the duke has other plans for Alexandra…plans which include the 5th Earl of Pembroke!

Tempted by a Lady's Smile

Book 4 in the "Lords of Honor" Series

Richard Jonas has loved but one woman—a woman who belongs to his brother. Refusing to suffer any longer, he evades his family in order to barricade his heart from unrequited love. While attending a friend's summer party, Richard's approach to love is changed after sharing a passionate and life-altering kiss with a vibrant and mysterious woman. Believing he was incapable of loving again, Richard finds himself tempted by a young lady determined to marry his best friend.

Gemma Reed has not been treated kindly by the *ton*. Often disregarded for her appearance and interests unlike those of a proper lady, Gemma heads to house party to win the heart of Lord Westfield, the man she's loved for years. But her plan is set off course by the tempting and intriguing, Richard Jonas.

A chance meeting creates a new path for Richard and Gemma to forage—but can two people, scorned and shunned by those they've loved from afar, let down their guards to find true happiness?

"Rescued By a Lady's Love"

Book 3 in the "Lords of Honor" Series

Destitute and determined to finally be free of any man's shackles, Lily Benedict sets out to salvage her honor. With no choice but to commit a crime that will save her from her past, she enters the home of the recluse, Derek Winters, the new Duke of Blackthorne. But entering the "Beast of Blackthorne's" lair proves more threatening than she ever imagined.

With half a face and a mangled leg, Derek—once rugged and charming—only exists within the confines of his home. Shunned by society, Derek is leery of the hauntingly beautiful Lily Benedict. As time passes, she slips past his defenses, reminding him how to live again. But when Lily's sordid past comes back, threatening her life, it's up to Derek to find the strength to become the hero he once was. Can they overcome the darkness of their sins to find a life of love and redemption?

Captivated by a Lady's Charm

Book 2 in the "Lords of Honor" Series

In need of a wife…

Christian Villiers, the Marquess of St. Cyr, despises the role he's been cast into as fortune hunter but requires the funds to keep his marquisate solvent. Yet, the sins of his past cloud his future, preventing him from seeing beyond his fateful actions at the Battle of Toulouse. For he knows inevitably it will catch up with him, and everyone will remember his actions on the battlefield that cost so many so much—particularly his best friend.

In want of a husband…

Lady Prudence Tidemore's life is plagued by familial scandals, which makes her own marital prospects rather grim. Surely there is one gentleman of the ton who can look past her family and see just her and all she has to offer?

When Prudence runs into Christian on a London street, the charming, roguish gentleman immediately captures her attention. But then a chance meeting becomes a waltz, and now…

A Perfect Match…

All she must do is convince Christian to forget the cold requirements he has for his future marchioness. But the demons in his past prevent him from turning himself over to love. One thing is certain—Prudence wants the marquess and is determined to have him in her life, now and forever. It's just a matter of convincing Christian he wants the same.

Seduced By a Lady's Heart

Book 1 in the "Lords of Honor" Series

You met Lieutenant Lucien Jones in "Forever Betrothed, Never the Bride" when he was a broken soldier returned from fighting Boney's forces. This is his story of triumph and happily-ever-after!

~★~

Lieutenant Lucien Jones, son of a viscount, returned from war, to find his wife and child dead. Blaming his father for the commission that sent him off to fight Boney's forces, he was content to languish at London Hospital… until offered employment on the Marquess of Drake's staff. Through his position, Lucien found purpose in life and is content to keep his past buried.

Lady Eloise Yardley has loved Lucien since they were children. Having long ago given up on the dream of him, she married another. Years later, she is a young, lonely widow who does not fit in with the ton. When Lucien's family enlists her aid to reunite father and son, she leaps at the opportunity to not only aid her former friend, but to also escape London.

Lucien doesn't know what scheme Eloise has concocted, but

knowing her as he does, when she pays a visit to his employer, he knows she's up to something. The last thing he wants is the temptation that this new, older, mature Eloise presents; a tantalizing reminder of happier times and peace.

Yet Eloise is determined to win Lucien's love once and for all… if only Lucien can set aside the pain of his past and risk all on a lady's heart.

Only For Their Love

Book 3 in the "The Theodosia Sword" Series

Miss Carol Cresswall bore witness to her parents' loveless union and is determined to avoid that same miserable fate. Her mother has altogether different plans—plans that include a match between Carol and Lord Gregory Renshaw. Despite his wealth and power, Carol has no interest in marrying a pompous man who goes out of his way to ignore her. Now, with their families coming together for the Christmastide season it's her mother's last-ditch effort to get them together. And Carol plans to avoid Gregory at all costs.

Lord Gregory Renshaw has no intentions of falling prey to his mother's schemes to marry him off to a proper debutante she's picked out. Over the years, he has carefully sidestepped all endeavors to be matched with any of the grasping ladies.

But a sudden Christmastide Scandal has the potential show Carol and Gregory that they've spent years running from the one thing they've always needed.

Book 2 in the "The Theodosia Sword" Series

A wounded soldier:

When Captain Lucas Rayne returned from fighting Boney's forces, he was a shell of a man. A recluse who doesn't leave his family's estate, he's content to shut himself away. Until he meets Eve…

A woman alone in the world:

Eve Ormond spent most of her life following the drum alongside her late father. When his shameful actions bring death and pain to English soldiers, Eve is forced back to England, an outcast. With no family or marital prospects she needs employment and finds it in Captain Lucas Rayne's home. A man whose life was ruined by her father, Eve has no place inside his household. With few options available, however, Eve takes the post. What she never anticipates is how with their every meeting, this honorable, hurting soldier slips inside her heart.

The Secrets Between Them:

The more time Lucas spends with Eve, he remembers what it is to be alive and he lets the walls protecting his heart down. When the secrets between them come to light will their love be enough? Or are they two destined for heartbreak?

Book 1 in the "The Theodosia Sword" Series

A curse. A sword. And the thief who stole her heart.

The Rayne family is trapped in a rut of bad luck. And now, it's up to Lady Theodosia Rayne to steal back the Theodosia sword, a gladius that was pilfered by the rival, loathed Renshaw family. Hopefully, recovering the stolen sword will break the cycle and reverse her family's fate.

Damian Renshaw, the Duke of Devlin, is feared by all—all, that is, except Lady Theodosia, the brazen spitfire who enters his home and wrestles an ancient relic from his wall. Intrigued by the vivacious woman, Devlin has no intentions of relinquishing the sword to her.

As Theodosia and Damian battle for ownership, passion ignites. Now, they are torn between their age-old feud and the fire that burns between them. Can two forbidden lovers find a way to make amends before their families' war tears them apart?

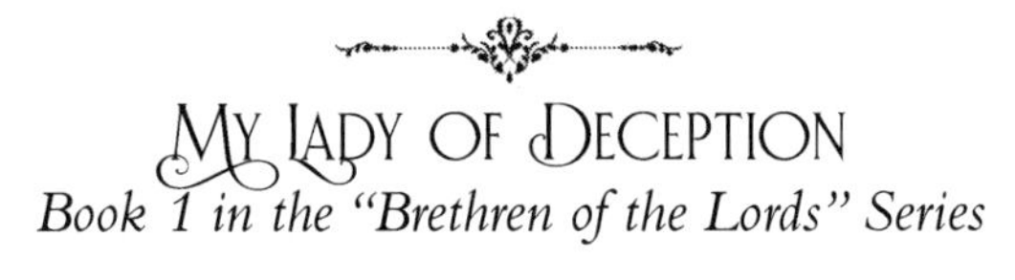

My Lady of Deception

Book 1 in the "Brethren of the Lords" Series

This dark, sweeping Regency novel was previously only offered as part of the limited edition box sets: "From the Ballroom and Beyond", "Romancing the Rogue", and "Dark Deceptions". Now, available for the first time on its own, exclusively through Amazon is "My Lady of Deception".

~★~

Everybody has a secret. Some are more dangerous than others.

For Georgina Wilcox, only child of the notorious traitor known as "The Fox", there are too many secrets to count. However, after her interference results in great tragedy, she resolves to never help another… until she meets Adam Markham.

Lord Adam Markham is captured by The Fox. Imprisoned, Adam loses everything he holds dear. As his days in captivity grow, he finds himself fascinated by the young maid, Georgina, who cares for him.

When the carefully crafted lies she's built between them begin to crumble, Georgina realizes she will do anything to prove her love and loyalty to Adam—even it means at the expense of her own life.

NON-FICTION WORKS BY CHRISTI CALDWELL

Uninterrupted Joy: Memoir: My Journey through Infertility, Pregnancy, and Special Needs

The following journey was never intended for publication. It was written from a mother, to her unborn child. The words detailed her struggle through infertility and the joy of finally being pregnant. A stunning revelation at her son's birth opened a world of both fear and discovery. This is the story of one mother's love and hope and...her quest for uninterrupted joy.

BIOGRAPHY

Christi Caldwell is the bestselling author of historical romance novels set in the Regency era. Christi blames Judith McNaught's "Whitney, My Love," for luring her into the world of historical romance. While sitting in her graduate school apartment at the University of Connecticut, Christi decided to set aside her notes and try her hand at writing romance. She believes the most perfect heroes and heroines have imperfections and rather enjoys tormenting them before crafing a well-deserved happily ever after!

When Christi isn't writing the stories of flawed heroes and heroines, she can be found in her Southern Connecticut home chasing around her eight-year-old son, and caring for twin princesses-in-training!

Visit *www.christicaldwellauthor.com* to learn more about what Christi is working on, or join her on Facebook at Christi Caldwell Author, and Twitter *@ChristiCaldwell*

Printed in Great Britain
by Amazon